He liked the way she felt in his arms.

She didn't know the steps to the tango, but she subtly swayed against him, like a woman who had secrets to tell. He deliberately pulled her closer, then, inserting one leg between hers, he dipped her. He suspected that in real life, the woman didn't like being kept off-balance, literally or figuratively, yet she allowed him to hold her that way for a few beats, her dark eyes flashing challengingly as she looked up at him. As he slowly straightened back up, he slid his hand from her neck down to her upper back, taking away her support and thus not allowing her to get out of position.

Because it was a dancer's move, he had expected Lily to grab him out of instinct. Instead, she took the leg that he had trapped between his and curled it around one of them, her knee sliding up dangerously.

"Drop me and my knee won't miss your family jewels," she said sweetly.

D0823989

By Gennita Low

Gennita Low

SLEEPING
WITH THE
AGENT

AVON BOOKS
An Imprint of HarperCollinsPublishers

This is a work of fiction. Names, characters, places, and incidents are products of the author's imagination or are used fictitiously and are not to be construed as real. Any resemblance to actual events, locales, organizations, or persons, living or dead, is entirely coincidental.

AVON BOOKS
An Imprint of HarperCollins*Publishers*
10 East 53rd Street
New York, New York 10022-5299

Copyright © 2006 by Jenny Low
ISBN-13: 978-0-06-059124-3
ISBN-10: 0-06-059124-2
www.avonromance.com

First Avon Books paperback printing: January 2006

Avon Trademark Reg. U.S. Pat. Off. and in Other Countries, Marca Registrada, Hecho en U.S.A.
HarperCollins® is a registered trademark of HarperCollins Publishers Inc.

Printed in the U.S.A.

10 9 8 7 6 5 4 3 2

*To Mother and Father;
to my Stash,
so many decoys but only one true one;
and Mike, my ranger Buddy,
whose generosity and patience are unequalled.*

*Love doesn't consist in gazing at each other but in looking
outward together in the same direction.*

—ANTOINE DE SAINT EXUPÉRY,
MY FAVORITE WWII HERO AND VERY WISE MAN

Acknowledgments

Special thanks to Maria "HoF" Hammon and Melissa Copeland, who, like me, didn't sleep; the sea mammals always gave up so much, including sleep; Erika Tsang, my ever-patient editor; and Liz Trupin-Pulli, my wonderful agent.

And always, the ladies at Delphi TDD, who read for me, especially Sandy "Sadista" Still, Mirmie Caraway, Karen King, Teena Weena Smith, and Katherine Lazo. Also to all the members of GLOW World at Yahoo who gave me their support and thoughts whenever I asked their opinions—*ZZZZZzzzzzzzzzzzzz*!!!

Thank you to the great ladies at RBL Romantica, romance readers who know their books!

1

Mountain pass, Macedonia

Love's like riding a wave, dude. Sometimes you fall on your face, even when the ride's incredible, you know? All you have to remember to do is get up, get back on your board, and paddle out and meet the next big one.

Reed settled back against the shrub, one eye trained on the scope, arcing the night viewfinder across the midnight-dark landscape. Dead silence. Nothing moving. He put the scope down and looked up into the clear night sky.

The situation was code yellow, just a notch up from green. His SEAL team was out here in the cold Eastern European terrain going through a few quick practice runs before going out into the mountains of Albania for the real thing. He could hear the lazy banter between members of his team over his helmet intercom.

Reed kept silent. He always paid attention to what was being said but rarely joined in unless necessary.

He had always been like that, and not understanding his reasons, the others at training camp had started calling him Joker for irony. The name had stuck.

He studied the constellations, searching for the North Star. It was Archer who had taught him to read the night sky, Archer who had given him his love of the ocean. Reed had been just a spoilt, wealthy, blond-headed surf-rat taking a break from boarding school when Arch had come along and shown him that there was more to surfing than name brands and bright-print baggy pants.

But Arch had been gone for a long time now. The man who had said those words about love hadn't really followed his teachings. When his lover of almost thirty years had unexpectedly been taken from him, Arch had taken his surfboard and headed out for that "next big wave." Or so he'd said. Except he hadn't come back.

"We'll be moving to Position Two when daylight breaks, over," Jazz, his team commander, said over the helmet radio. He was relating position and sitch-rep—situation report—to Hawk, their co-commander through Satellite. Hawk was still in the military hospital recovering from an injury.

"How's the river? Nice and cold?" Hawk asked.

"Why don't you come and try it for yourself?" Jazz invited. "Oh, I forgot, you're in a hospital skirt and can't escape from the loonie bin."

Reed smiled as he heard the others chuckle. He and his team had visited Hawk just that morning, and after making sure that their commander wasn't suffering too much from his internal injuries, they had all teased him about chasing the nurses around in his wheelchair while wearing nothing more than a white skirt.

"You're just envious."

"Of your hairy legs, yeah, of course."

Reed had the utmost respect and admiration for both his co-commanders, two best friends who seemed to have an uncanny ability to read each other's minds on and off the battlefield. He knew Jazz had been worried all these months while Hawk had gone solo undercover, especially when he'd disappeared and had been presumed dead. But things had worked out in the end. Mostly. Two weeks ago, the bad guy was killed. The team was now going to destroy the weapon caches that Hawk had located before they fell into the wrong hands again. Only one thing was missing—some kind of explosive device trigger.

The Joint Mission between GEM and STAR Force SEALs had two objectives, and only one had been accomplished. Reed wondered about the missing weapon that was so top secret that even his team didn't know much about it. He was sure that even as his team focused on the hidden caches, someone else was looking for the device.

Tonight, they'd had a more difficult time than anticipated at one end of the bridge, where the water had basically turned into cold, stinking mud. By the time they'd made it past the bridge, they'd pretty much been caked with the slime. "Come on, Lieutenant, make an escape. You'd love it," Jazz said.

"Pardon me, sir," Cucumber chimed in, "but I think Miss Hutchens will object."

Miss Hutchens was Hawk's current love interest. Reed wondered how long that was going to last. His commander had a reputation with women—Catnip was one of his nicknames. But after being gone from the team all these months, Reed had felt a change in Hawk during their reunion. He guessed Amber Hutchens had a lot to do with this change.

Hawk chuckled from his end. "At the rate you guys were moving down there, I'd considered coming down to give you sloths a hand."

Reed checked the surroundings again with the nightscope as he continued listening. The practice runs were to familiarize the team with terrain and weather, so whether the code was red or yellow, it meant doing everything—from rolling in mud to setting up lookout points to staying up in shifts—by the book. Still nothing out there.

"Sloths. Like slothful in the Bible?" someone asked.

"He meant sloths, man," Mink's voice came over. "Those creatures don't move more than an inch at a time or something. I read somewhere that it takes them a year to get down from a tree to have an annual crap."

"Man, why don't they just crap from the tree then?" Dirk asked.

Reed shook his head, a reluctant smile lifting the corner of his lips. It was a good thing no one else could hear their inane conversation. This was how his team was when they were semi-relaxed. Conversations like this reminded him of surfing. The ocean, too, had a language all its own, and the surfer had to pay attention to the ebb and flow of the tide as one rode the board and paddled out. Reed shook his head again. It'd been a while since he had ridden the waves. He was missing it tonight.

"Do you think sloths have big balls?" someone lazily chimed in after a quiet lull.

"Ask Cumber," Mink quipped back.

"Yo. Cumber, you awake?"

"I'm jerking off, scumbag. Go bother some other sloth."

"You think if there were a Cumber Sloth he would take a year to jerk off to get an annual big O?" Dirk asked.

The suppressed chuckles came from different directions. There was another silence.

"Yo, Cumber."

"I'm still jerking off."

"I think a Cucumber Sloth would crap and jerk off at the same time," Hawk observed. "Who's on lookout duty?"

"Joker," Jazz replied. "He'll be on for the next two hours."

Joker, as Reed knew everyone expected, didn't acknowledge. He rarely had anything to say anyway. Unless he saw something out of the ordinary, he usually stayed away from conversation of any kind. He would check in every hour.

"Talk to you next Satellite update then, sloth."

"Yeah, don't have too much fun with your girl there, over," Jazz signed off.

Amber Hutchens was also in the hospital, transferred to the UN base in Kosovo along with his commander, still recovering from an almost-overdose of drugs in her system. Reed hadn't met her, but from what he'd heard from Jazz and Dirk, she was beautiful, very smart, and incredibly brave because of her role in saving a bunch of girls who had been kidnapped from their countries. Which made him think of Jazz's fiancée, Vivienne Verreau, who was also beautiful, smart and brave. Where the hell did they find these women?

"Hey, Cumber, you still jerking off?"

"Nah, taking a crap."

"Knock off, Stooges." Jazz brought them back on task.

Even though he enjoyed the camaraderie among his team, Reed liked the silence the best. But then he'd known since childhood that silence was a great tool. One could learn a lot just by listening to adults. People said one thing when they meant something else, and he'd discovered that words could have double meanings, especially in the adult world.

Better to be silent. Pay attention. Watch and learn.

He was good at all three, and with time, he'd also discovered an inherent ability to shoot with an accuracy that had earned him many medals. He'd worked very hard to become an asset in an elite team for the Navy, and then he'd been assigned to the covert Standing and Ready Force, a job he held proudly, something that was all his own doing. His accomplishments had nothing to do with his background, which was exactly how he wanted it.

He had been gone for so long that he couldn't remember the last time he had been home. Was it a year or two? There had been several tours to Afghanistan, Myanmar, South America, and now Macedonia. Of course his family had probably visited those places too during his absence, except that they would have been doing a different kind of touring.

Reed smiled in the dark. He doubted his mother and father would be huddling against a shrub with a muddy jacket to keep warm. Or doing mock firefights, rehearsing with real bullets.

The practice runs tonight had two objectives. One, to reacclimatize the team, since they had just returned from an operation in the tropics. Two, to play out scenarios on how to approach the weapon caches they were seeking to destroy. Now that word had gotten out that Dragan Dilaver was dead, many of his enemies and other mercenary groups had started fighting over territory, as well as looking for Dilaver's hidden caches. The SEALs had an advantage, of course. While undercover, Hawk had befriended Dilaver and had gotten hold of all the coordinates to each weapons drop-off zone. All Reed and his team had to do was canvass each area and look for the caches.

The low humming of a motor alerted him that a vehicle was nearby, heading around the bend where his lookout point was set up. There was a small narrow roadway about ten meters below him, a winding rocky path that led down toward one of the mountain passes, where notorious bands of mercenaries set up roadblocks to collect fees from travelers.

It wasn't that late, and there were still vehicles passing through now and then, none of which looked like the Jeeps or trucks that Hawk had told them were the transportation of choice for gunrunners. Reed radioed in each time, giving details of what he saw through the scope. They'd been ordered not to meddle or start any trouble during their practices, so as not to draw attention.

So far, nothing too unusual. Besides, they weren't going to start anything when they weren't anywhere near the targeted locations.

As a spotter, it could get pretty cold and miserable, especially if the ground was damp or if the weather decided not to cooperate. But this was a SEAL's way of life—long periods of waiting before action, and practice run-throughs were taken just as seriously as the real thing.

Reed adjusted the intercom mic. "Sir, I hear another vehicle approaching. Will see it in approximately sixty seconds, over."

"Keep me updated, Joker, over," Jazz replied.

"Yes, sir." He saw the headlights hit the darkness of the woods first. Then the vehicle turned into view. "It looks like a van. It's slowing down, over."

"Are you sure?"

"Affirmative. It's almost to a stop."

"Team A, code orange," Jazz ordered.

"Standing and Ready, sir," came several answers over the mic. A vehicle stopping in the middle of the night could mean anything in these parts.

"Joker, give us any unusual details," Jazz said. "I want to know why they're stopping."

"Sir, I think you should come here, over," Reed answered as he looked through the scope. This . . . wasn't what he had expected.

Soon he heard sounds near him, and Jazz crawled over to his side. "What is it?"

Reed handed his commander the night viewer. "Women, sir. Many of them. And from what I can gather, they're taking a piss."

Jazz arched his eyebrows at Reed's words. Silently, he turned in the direction Reed was pointing. He looked through the night viewer. The driver hadn't bothered to turn off the headlights, so it was easy to recognize the female silhouettes moving back and forth. "They're armed," he murmured.

"Not all of them," Reed said. "Three of them are. The others come out two at a time and disappear into the bushes nearby. So far, three pairs, so that makes six girls plus those three. Nine."

"Eleven now," Jazz corrected, still looking. "All women."

"Yeah, and not too concerned about how dangerous it is to stop in the middle of nowhere with the headlights shining for everyone to see." Reed could only shake his head. He didn't know who these women were, but it was foolhardy to be driving this late and stopping here on this particular road. He pulled out his night-vision binoculars. "They don't look like tourists either, not with those weapons."

"The blonde standing in front of the vehicle is the leader," Jazz noted.

Reed turned his binoculars on the figure. The woman was taller than the others and held what looked like a small Uzi with the easy assurance of someone who knew how to use it. She was saying something to the two heading back, probably urging them to hurry. At least someone down there knew about the danger.

He adjusted the binoculars, pushing on the zoom button, for a closer look. The woman had shoulder-length blond hair that she was flicking back impatiently with one hand. She turned to look upward in the direction of the lookout point, an uneasy expression on her face. Her eyes were dark as she seemed to stare directly up at him, as if she knew someone was up there. A watchfulness replaced the impatience and she cocked her head, listening to the night, looking for clues.

Reed knew she wouldn't be able to see him and his commander. They were hidden in a natural niche on the side of the mountain, in the shadows of shrubs and trees. But it was still uncanny the way her senses picked up something from their particular spot.

"She can feel us," Reed said.

"She's probably nervous. I would be, too, with so many women under my care," Jazz said. "Bet they're illegals. Wonder what country she's heading to."

Travelers with the right papers and enough cash using the mountain passes could easily move from

Kosovo to Macedonia to Croatia to Albania without being asked too many questions. They could be smugglers, mercenaries, ordinary folks looking for a new life, runaways, even reporters doing some independent work. There was nothing surprising about a group of armed people traveling these roads.

"What do we do?"

"Nothing."

Reed looked away from the binoculars for a second. "Nothing?" he echoed. That was very unusual coming from his commander. Jazz Zeringue had a soft protective core where women were concerned. Usually, he would be the first to run off to help any females in trouble. But then, the women below didn't look like they needed any assistance.

"There's not much we can do. They are plenty nervous right now. What are they going to do if we show up suddenly?"

A group of men. In uniform. In the dark. "They'll get the wrong idea," Reed agreed. He imagined a bunch of screaming women running around in the woods. "So we just let them continue down the pass? They'll meet up with some mercenaries sooner or later."

He returned his attention to the scene. Well, a bunch of women screaming, minus that one. The blonde looked cool and steadfast as she gave out calm orders. The last of the girls returned to the vehicle. Then she turned and nodded to the two with her, and they made their way into the bushes while she stood guard.

"Do you have any suggestions?" Jazz asked. "We're heading off tomorrow, so we can't actually follow these women to their destination. I can radio back, but by the time anyone shows up, these ladies will be long gone. There are hundreds of illegals moving back and forth in these parts, Joker."

Jazz sounded concerned, but he was right. There was nothing they could do. Reed wished he could somehow help the women. He didn't care whether they understood the dangers ahead or not, or that they were armed. They were no match for the fire-power of a group of hardened criminals.

He looked down toward the vehicle for a few seconds. "They must have good reason to be doing this alone," he finally said, reluctantly disengaging his personal interest. It was an easy thing for a sharp-shooter to do, but then, he hadn't needed much training to learn how to switch off his emotions. "I'm betting they know what they're doing and that they're prepared as best as they can be."

"I'll still radio in," Jazz said as he adjusted his scope. "Maybe they have other teams not far from here who can keep an eye on them or something. For the moment, we'll make sure they're safe till they're off."

That was how Jazz was. He would go the extra mile to protect women and automatically expected that every other man, especially in uniform, should be like that too. Reed respected both his command-ers very much; as leaders, they had taught him different things. Because he was a loner by nature, his decisions tended to be about himself. Now that he'd been working in the STAR Force team for a few years, he'd lately found himself asking what Jazz or Hawk would do in certain situations.

He zoomed in on the blonde woman again as she headed out behind the bushes alone. Unlike the others, who had sprinted like scared rabbits, she didn't seem afraid. He couldn't see her expression at this angle, but it was there in the way she held her weapon, the sure gait of her walk, the quick glances back toward the vehicle, as if she knew the girls in there depended on her strength.

In a few minutes they would be on their way, another image in his collection of unexplained interesting scenes during an operation. Maybe it was good that it would be one of the unexplained ones. That way he could write a happy ending for these women. The real stories never gave him any satisfaction.

The woman emerged from the shadows and walked quickly back to the vehicle. She waited till the others got in on the driver's side then slammed the door shut. The van started up. She moved to the passenger side and opened the door.

Reed watched her duck inside and was expecting the door to close and the van to take off. Suddenly, her head reappeared over the top of the van, and the bright glare of a spotlight hit his binoculars.

"Damn!" Jazz said as he and Reed quickly pulled the scopes off their faces. The light wasn't from a regular flashlight but from professional search and track teams. It could pick off reflections from glass and metal, just like sunlight.

The unmistakable sound of gunfire. A spray of bullets hit near the lookout point, some close enough to shake the leaves off the branches above onto them.

"I fucking hate Peeping Toms!" a female voice called out in Croatian just before the squealing of tires. More gunfire. Then darkness again.

Reed crawled forward and looked through the binoculars. The van was zipping down the road at a dangerous speed. Behind him he could hear the rest of his team climbing to their aid.

"What the hell was that all about?" Cucumber asked when they found that no one was injured.

Jazz gave them a brief account.

"Let's see. We're going to report to Hawk that to-night we saw a bunch of women traveling down the road and they all stopped for nature's call. Then one of them turned her Uzi and nearly killed you," Dirk said dryly. "He's going to laugh his ass off."

"At least it was just one person who was onto them," Mink said. Reed could hear the laughter in his voice. "Imagine a whole bunch of very mad women shooting at the two of them and we have to come to their rescue."

"I wonder how she knew," Jazz said, rubbing his jaw. "There wasn't any way she could have known."

"What did she look like, Joker?"

Beautiful, smart, and very brave. Reed didn't say anything.

She wasn't going mad. She was just being herself, that's all.

"That was crazy, Lily!" Marisa glanced at Lily.

Lily looked straight ahead into the darkness. "Drive on," she ordered quietly. They had been on the road for days now, so she knew they were tired. "We'll be with the others soon."

"There was no one there!" Marisa obstinately persisted. "And even if there were, they could have followed us and killed us all."

Marisa was right, of course, about the possibility of being shot at. But that was nothing new, everyone had been right for a long time now. Lily smiled bitterly. It seemed, even with her eyes wide open, that she was determined to live life on the edge. *But she had been sure someone was watching.* Those reflections hadn't been her imagination.

"They were there." She knew she sounded brusque, but she didn't feel like arguing. "I got our first group through safely to Albania without a hitch. Don't you trust my skills?"

"Of course we do, but why didn't we just drive off? What if they had shot back?"

Lily looked behind her. She had ordered the girls to duck down before she'd started her gunfire, telling them not to panic. Most of them didn't seem particularly traumatized by her actions; most of them had seen more than their share of violence during their captivity. Only the few who had been rescued before their imprisonment in the brothels were sobbing quietly.

Once upon a time, she would have shrugged and told anyone questioning her authority to shut up and just do as they were told. She would have replied that being shot at was half the fun. Besides that, she would have hired a few more bodyguards, giving the impression to any mercenaries or gang members roaming the countryside roads that this was just another batch of kidnapped girls being transported to various *kafenas* around these parts.

But everything was different now. She had to do this alone because she couldn't trust anyone. *But could she even trust herself?* "I don't care about 'what ifs,'" she finally replied. "It didn't happen and we gave them warning in case they'd gotten any ideas of coming closer. Look, either you all have to trust me in this or we can't do this at all. I gave you a choice and you chose to follow me instead of go with the peacekeepers. So are you all in or not?"

Lily had left out many parts of the truth when she'd told them what had recently happened. When she had gathered them from the safe houses in which she'd found them hiding, she'd informed them that the authorities had finally taken Dragan Dilaver's illegal *kafenas* apart. The girls had cheered because many of them had been captives in those hellholes, but Lily cautioned there would be many gangs roaming around now, each one trying to be dominant, and they would, sooner or later, reopen similar places, and their clients would still be the same people.

This she knew without a doubt. The way these scumbags ran their illegal trades was the only thing she was very sure of.

They had to leave earlier than planned, she'd told them. She would transport them in two groups to a safe place, where they'd hide until she could get "legal" papers done for everyone.

"You know we'll follow you, Lily," one of the girls said from the back of the van. "You saved us."

There were other murmurs of agreement from behind her. She knew the girls would understand what she was saying. Many of the brothel clients were, in fact, the peacekeepers themselves, because they were the ones with the cash flow to spend in the *kafenas*. There was no guarantee that if the girls went to the local authorities for help they would be safe from corrupt officials who were looking to make some money on the side. That was how they had been transported from country to country in the first place—through illegal channels and corrupted officials.

"Good. Go take a nap now," she advised. "We'll be joining the others sooner than you know, and then we'll be okay for a while."

Lily thought about the choice she had offered them: either place their lives in the hands of the local authorities or peacekeepers, whichever they liked, or come with her and she would do her best to get them to wherever they wanted after they were healed. There were two dozen girls in her care right now, most of whom weren't able to travel without being noticed. They all needed time to lay low and recuperate.

Not much of a choice, she bleakly acknowledged, staring out at the road as the van sped into the darkness. They didn't know it, but by giving her their trust, they had saved her life. She didn't know what she would have done if she'd been left alone, without anything ahead of her. She had nearly—No, she wouldn't think about that right now.

For her sake, she must focus on what was ahead and not let her past overtake her life like it had before. She would deal with her problem after she took care of the girls. That would be her atonement for all the wrongs she'd caused. She almost laughed out loud. When she had left Velesta behind, she had promised to be a different person from then on. She must be doing it right—*atonement* was scarcely a word the old Llallana Noretski would have used.

But then the old Lily hadn't had the problems she had now. She was afraid again. Being on the run. Living life like there was no tomorrow. She'd never thought this would happen again to *her* after so many years. She didn't like the insecurity and fear that engulfed her whenever she thought of the future. It was as if she was back to square one, when she'd been in those girls' shoes.

Lily deliberately pushed those thoughts away again. Later. Not now. Instead, she focused on the girls and the rest of her plans. This was the final trip, with no problems in both runs. At least the first group, the ones who needed the most care, was already waiting for them in Tirana, Albania.

With everyone in one place, they would lay low while she tried to find out what was happening out there. She had already checked on Amber and Hawk. They were alive, thank God. Hawk hadn't failed her. In her madness, she had still found a way to save her friend.

Stop it. You have more important things to think about. Like figuring out the different routes to ensure that the girls get to where they wanted to go. And the downtime would help her recuperate too. She had to get better with time, right? She wanted to thump on the dashboard in frustration. Again her thoughts had circled back to herself.

Lily heard the girls behind her whispering among themselves as their nervousness dissipated. It was good that they had each other to talk to. They could help each other chase away the bad memories for a while.

She wished she had Amber to talk to again. Amber would know what to do with her problem. No one would better understand what they had done to Lily, but Amber was now seriously ill in the hospital because of her. After what she'd done, her ex-friend probably hated her guts.

Lily glanced at the side-view mirror to check whether they were being followed. There had been no telltale signs back there, but she had been on these runs before. Mercenaries. KLA gangs. And this time, it was just her and a bunch of women. Without the presence of any men, they would look very suspicious to anyone who might stop them.

If nothing else, at least she knew how to do this right. Knowing that she had this one mission to do was like a rope thrown over the side of the cliff on which she was hanging desperately. She didn't dare look down below her. Long way down. Maybe she would fall into hell, where she belonged.

That was just her being silly. She wasn't going crazy.

"*Das macht nichts.* I'll find it. She can't be too far if she isn't dead. No matter what, I'll get this operation done so I can get back home." There were nieces and nephews who had never met her whom she wanted to see. There was a nice country dacha waiting for her, with all the things she had missed so much. She tried not to sound too impatient as she interrupted her caller. "That makes two of us. Isn't it your job to find out who activated her and tried to double-cross me? I thought she was the decoy, and it turns out she was the real thing. There I was at the summit waiting like an idiot when news got back to me that my nephew had been killed. What does the CIA have to say about that?"

It wasn't easy conversing in German for long periods any more, and the man on the other side was irritating her. After all, it had been over ten years. Of course he knew her background, and must think that since she was German by descent, that was the language that came naturally to her. But she had been recruited by the Soviets for almost a quarter of a century, so her language of choice would be Russian or Croatian. Nobody, however, knew that. They all still thought the Germans were behind this.

"What, is it so surprising there is a double agent in the Agency?" She wanted to laugh. What did that make her? A double double agent? "I want everything you have on her ASAP. She's responsible for Dragan's death, so I'd like to handle her myself, if you know what I mean."

She studied her hand as she listened. She liked looking at her longer nails. It had been such a long time since she had painted them her favorite pink. "Are you suggesting that I'm too old for the game?" she asked, injecting a note of politeness in her voice. She supposed they had a right to be concerned. After all, she was no longer in her prime as an assassin, but a woman didn't like being told she was too old, even to kill. "My ten years away from the job hadn't diminished any of my skills. After all, I've had to personally take care of a few of your little spill-ups in the States, remember? You owe me this, Gunth. Fax me all you have on her tonight."

She switched the cell phone to her other ear so she could inspect her other set of nails. Damn it, two were chipped. Her voice sharpened as she changed into English. "Tell you what. I'll fly over to where you are and extract what I want from you. Then I'm going to send your favorite body part back to the top." She smiled at the image. "Are you daring me? I may be *old*, but I still love a challenge. And Gunth, I'll remember that you've insulted me. *Verstehen?*"

Greta snapped her cell phone shut. She tapped it against her chin as she stared thoughtfully out the train window, half-listening to the growl and rumble of wheels speeding over steel tracks. Usually, she would be enjoying a good cup of espresso while she sat in her private compartment, doing a little bit of knitting or playing solitaire. It was a good way to relax.

She smiled again. Perhaps she was getting old. After all, she had played being old for so damn long. Her gaze fell on the knitting bag on the seat across from her. The knitting habit came from her other life, when she had projected the image of a harmless, grandmotherly older woman with ever-whitening hair, knitting peacefully in the corner of the bus or train, with her black pearl-handled knit bag. The CIA loved her. Nobody had given her more than a second glance.

Ten years. Maybe she had really begun to believe that she was a sweet old grandma. Even now her hands itched for the soothing motion of one knitting needle looping a woolen thread from another. Loop, slide out, tighten.

Greta looked at her hands. They always said one could tell how old a person was by looking at her hands. She didn't think so. She had nice hands, but with short, unpainted nails and a simple gold ring, they had looked very normal. Now that she was out of DC, her hands were hers again—nicely manicured with long nails that would have looked ludicrous on the old lady in the bus. She frowned. She really didn't want to give up knitting yet, but it wasn't good on her nails.

She put down her cell phone and smoothed her hands across the tabletop. It was that stupid bitch's fault, of course, that her plans were delayed. If everything had worked out right, she would have been on her way home, happily retired—or semi, she hadn't quite decided that yet—and she would have been on her way to meet the nieces and nephews she hadn't seen in over a decade.

Family. She had thought about them often while she had been away. Impossible to have stayed in touch, of course. She had spoken briefly on the phone several times in ten years, but most of the conversations had been too short and not satisfying. If everything had gone according to plan, that last operation would have been a nice wrap-up of her career.

She shook her head. All right, at least for a while. She wasn't quite ready to fade into nothing yet. Let's face it. If she had succeeded in assassinating the current newly elected premier of Slovistan, then the international summit would have been a failure and the powers-that-be would have been very happy with her homecoming. Now, they were just pleased. After all, she had given them ten years of her life. It would have been nice, though, if she had returned with that little present she'd promised them, the tiny explosive device trigger, so that they could copy its technology. It would have been very nice if she had been able to demonstrate its effectiveness with Liashenko's assassination.

But that was the fun of being out in the field, something for which she had yearned when she'd walked into the CIA building and headed to the same office every day. Being a handler to several American traitors was boring, boring work. Not at all challenging. If not for her, these stupid men would have been caught and killed off a dozen times already. As it was, the whole charade at that office had lasted ten years.

She knew she had done well even without this final victory. She was already achieving legend status among the covert world, and especially with the operatives back home, for all that she had accomplished. The whole big scandal in DC right now, with all their internal investigations and Intelligence committee hearings, was because of her doing.

Greta couldn't help but smile at the thought. Ah, that little old white-haired grandma had wreaked havoc for the CIA all right. And it was all her, Greta Van Duren's, doing.

She leaned back in her seat and closed her eyes, savoring the feeling of accomplishment. It would be easy to trace a stupid thing like Llallana Noretski. She was just another greedy loser being used by the agencies.

There were still people in the CIA she could contact besides Gunther. She sniffed at the memory of how supercilious the other agent had been to her on

the phone. As if she were a washed-out old operative, running away from DC. She frowned. That was
not the perception she wanted to end her career with.

She would get the files on Llallana Noretski.
Someone had thought of using her as a human bomb
to kill off an entire summit filled with world leaders.
There must be more to this. They must have something over the Noretski girl. What?

The ambitiousness of that plan had astounded
Greta when she had figured out what was happening.
One hit, she could understand, but an entire board of
world leaders? *That* would have certainly been
someone's career icing. But who? And why?

She was intrigued. That was why she didn't actually want to truly retire. That would mean she would
be out of the loop, and after playing secretary at the
great CIA office, handling secrets back and forth between deputy directors, she was addicted to the
power of knowing everything.

Langmut. One thing at a time. After ten years
dawdling around CIA red tape, she had learned the
patience of the old man at the sea. There went that stupid word again. She opened her eyes. Old. She didn't
want to look old when she returned home. She wanted
to look beautiful and sophisticated, the way she'd
been when she'd been the number-one assassin.

Langmut. Greta released a long sigh, then cracked
her neck to release the tension. She would knit and
think of a plan to teach Miss Noretski and her handler a lesson about double-crossing Greta Van Duren.

2

There's nothing wrong with me.

Lily stared at her reflection in the bathroom mirror. There were smudges under her eyes from lack of sleep, but apart from that, she felt and looked perfectly fine. Just a little stressed out, that was all.

After all, she was living with a bunch of moody teenagers, for heaven's sake. There were enough catfights around here to last her a lifetime.

She welcomed it, which was ironic. She wanted to be alone, had always preferred to be alone, and now she was afraid of it. That was because when she was by herself, she started to think, and thinking made her afraid.

Lily ran a comb slowly through her hair. The back was curling out softly around her shoulders. She needed a haircut; she liked the short, easy style she'd kept for years. All she needed was a pair of scissors and a few quick snips.

She stared down at the scissors by the sink. There was no logical reason for it—she just couldn't make herself cut her own hair. It was as if staring at her own reflection scared her. What if something inside had been programmed that Lily must have short hair? Maybe she was being prepared for another task.

She shook her head and quickly turned on the tap. Leaning down, she splashed her face with cold water, welcoming the sharp icy slap.

It had been over two months since she'd run away with the girls, and except for one time, she still hadn't been able to say the words out loud. The only person who knew about her condition was Tatiana, and even she wasn't too sure what was wrong with Lily. Hell, *she* wasn't too sure herself. She could only remember up to a point, and then everything was a jumbled mass of images. After that she was just . . . herself. Right?

She bit her lip, drawing her teeth slowly over the lower one. How could she explain brainwashing to a teenager when she didn't even know how it had been done to her? But at least Tatiana had accepted the story and had kept an eye on her to make sure she didn't go anywhere without a reason. That was important—she couldn't disappear without permission.

She wanted to laugh at the incongruity of that thought but couldn't. These days, the things going round and round in her head were bizarre. If she was programmed to disappear, how would she or anyone else be able to stop her?

Lily leaned closer to the mirror, looking deeply into the dark irises of her eyes, trying to find answers to her unspoken questions. Who was in there? She felt like one of those people who had multiple personalities. Could she really have undergone some kind of brainwashing? It had taken years before the CIA had activated her, and even though she had somehow stopped herself in time, something inside her was still ticking. What if there were other things she'd been told to do?

The notion horrified her. She blinked back the sudden swell of tears. She had worked so hard all these years to be in total control of her life, and to find out that she had never been—ever—both devastated and pissed her off. Like this crying. She had been doing that a lot lately. As if tears could change her situation and what she had done. As if self-pity would make her feel less lonely.

She knew there was a reason why she had always hated the CIA. Something inside her had been trying to warn her, trying to make her remember. She'd brushed the feelings off, but now she understood that those were *real* feelings—the hatred and the fear. Everything else was fake. Right? She wasn't sure anymore. She couldn't trust her own emotions.

Sometimes she wondered whether she was going through some kind of drug withdrawal. Maybe the CIA had picked her because she was schizophrenic and they had somehow given her drugs to suppress some of her personalities. She straightened from the mirror, blinking rapidly.

Don't even go there. You're driving yourself crazy, thinking like that.

"Lily, are you all right in there?" Tatiana tapped on the door.

Good, at least someone out there was making sure she was okay. That was why she needed this last job, of taking care of the girls and transporting them to their new lives. If she were alone, she would just stand in front of the mirror all day and slowly go insane.

"Yes," Lily replied, quickly applying lipstick. "I'm fine. Thanks, Tatiana."

"Dinner's ready and the others are already at the table."

"I'll be right out. You girls start without me."

"All right, but don't take too long, okay?"

"Okay."

Lily had to smile at Tatiana's concern. Two months ago, the girl had barely talked because of what the thugs had done to her. She had sat in a zombie state in her room, and nothing had seemed to touch her. Now, in spite of still needing crutches to walk, she had become the den mother.

Lily's smile dimmed. It was because of Hawk and Amber that Tatiana had improved. They had somehow known what Tatiana had needed and had drawn her out of her shell.

She wondered how her friends were doing. They should be out of the hospital by now. If Hawk was

the man she thought he was, he would make an honest woman out of Amber quickly. They both deserved all the happiness in the world.

Lily tossed one last glance at her reflection before
opening the bathroom door. Not like some people
who ran around betraying and drugging friends, and
then almost causing a political scandal as a human
bomb at an international summit of world leaders.

Undisclosed location, VA, the following week

"What are two things you like to do?"

Reed looked at the woman across the table. This
was no ordinary interview. Tess Montgomery, or T.,
as she liked to be called, was the leader of GEM, the
organization with which his SEAL team was conducting a Joint Mission.

When she was first introduced to them, his first
impression was that of a glamorous creature—
model tall, with a face that had the classical Renais-
sance lines of a Raphael angel, and red-gold hair that
cascaded in waves that had made him wonder how
she kept them tangle free. No one in the team could
quite believe that this woman knew anything about
covert operations or running a team.

But she had the full backing of Admiral Madison,
the chief commander of STAR Force, the covert
SEAL teams deployed for black ops, so everyone
had kept their opinions about women joining their
team to themselves. It hadn't been too long, though,
before the guys had been smitten by Miss Mont-

gomery. Yet Reed had never felt that he was seeing the real Tess.

With her perfect hair and long nails, he had also felt a bit doubtful at first about T.'s skills, but his skepticism had disappeared immediately at the final Joint Mission conference. T. had arrived looking nothing like the red-haired beauty they had first met. Everyone in the room, except for Admiral Madison, had sat there in stunned silence when they'd realized who it was that had joined them. She had turned blond. It had still been her when she'd talked, but even the way she'd moved and smiled had been different. Since then, Reed had paid closer attention to everything T. said.

Since then, he was always careful whenever he talked to her. "Like, in hobbies?"

Tess leaned back against the leather seat, her tawny eyes thoughtfully studying him. For some reason she always reminded him of a big predator cat eyeing prey. There was just something very feline about the woman, from the way she played her cat-and-mouse games during conversations to the curiosity she always displayed at the new things that she managed to dig out of a person.

"No," she said, giving a shake of her head. The gold hoops in her ears glinted back at him as they swung back and forth. "Let me rephrase. What are the two things you enjoy doing?"

She had been asking the oddest questions. This was supposed to be a final assessment, to make sure that he was ready for the mission ahead, not some personality evaluation. He didn't feel like telling her anything, but Admiral Madison had given strict orders: Answer all of T.'s questions. Still, he hadn't said that Reed couldn't ask a few questions himself.

"How would those differ from hobbies?" he asked cautiously.

T.'s smile made him even more uncomfortable. It was as if she'd predicted his evasive tactic. "Interesting. You're careful and suspicious. Most people would just answer my question without needing to so thoroughly break it down." She clicked the top of her ballpoint pen several times as she continued to study him. "Hobbies take time. Stamp collecting, for example, is a hobby. Or building model trains. Of course, what one likes to do can be part of a hobby."

"So we're just splitting hairs," Reed pointed out politely.

"Yes," she said, "but you started it. What does that say about you?"

He stared back at her. She was right. She had asked relatively simple questions and he had grown more and more reluctant and suspicious. He was sure that she had manipulated the whole conversation, yet somehow it had ended with him to blame. How did she do that?

"Surfing," he replied abruptly. "And dancing."

T. arched a brow. "I get surfing, but why dancing?" She waved away his next words with her pen and continued, "There's nothing wrong with dancing. What I meant was, Reed—since you're a SEAL, it's obvious that you would like swimming. And surfing suits your personality profile; it projects your aloofness. However, dancing needs a partner, and that's completely the opposite end of the spectrum. Very sad to dance alone, darling."

Reed could feel the tension rising behind his neck. He didn't like being psychoanalyzed, especially by strange agencies. And GEM was a very strange agency, consisting of contract operatives that were mostly women, with a lot of government connections. He wasn't sure whether he liked them, even though he was intrigued by the way it was run. Yet he was under orders to undergo this training, if one could call it training. He decided to not be so cooperative.

"You asked and I answered. I don't have to explain my likes and dislikes," he said.

"Defensive, too."

"I'm not—" Reed stopped himself just in time. T.'s expression was watchful as he sat back in his chair. Hawk had already warned him that the woman's mouth was lethal. He now understood what his commander had meant. Fine, he would play her game. Emptying his mind of all thought, he explained, in a soft, toneless voice, "Both require timing. If you don't do it right, then you'll either crash into the water or into your partner."

T. put down her pen. "Thank you for the interview. We may now proceed to the general meeting about your assignment. Lots of notes to take there. Have you studied the files we've given you?"

Again, her sudden change of direction surprised him. He had done nothing for two weeks but read up on Llallana Noretski and what the mole had tried to get her to do. "Yes, I'm ready. Does that mean I pass this . . . test?"

T. smiled. "What, did you think you wouldn't?"

"Failure is not an option." That was why the admiral had insisted on this assignment. They had failed to complete the second objective of Hawk's mission—the explosive device was still out there somewhere.

"Ask all the questions you need at the meeting. It's very important that you understand what you have to do. We know that you've traveled here before, and it's good that you're familiar with the cities and its customs so that you don't come across like a tourist. That's why you were recommended for this operation. After reading those files, what do you think is the most important thing missing?"

Reed didn't hesitate to answer. It was important to him to have this on record. "Llallana Noretski was a young girl of whom the CIA had taken advantage, and in a way, she was also repeatedly raped, just as those bastards had done to her when she was a sex slave. This isn't just about what some traitors have attempted through her, but what the CIA has done to Llallana with their mind-control programs. The information in the file didn't point the finger in the right direction."

T.'s smile widened as she pushed her seat back. She waited till he stood up too. "It's also good to know that the SEAL team's sharpshooter is also a very astute man," she said. "Let's go to the conference room, shall we?"

Reed walked to the door and opened it for her. As she passed him on the way out, she paused and touched his sleeve. She was standing a bit too close for his comfort. "What's the book that's influenced you most, Mylos Reed Vincenzio?" she asked.

He wasn't exactly sure how she did it. *"The Little Prince,"* he said, without thinking, then blinked when she smiled beguilingly at him.

"Antoine de Saint-Exupéry," she murmured and walked down the hall.

As Reed followed, he realized T. had addressed him by his full name, which not even his teammates knew.

Lily stared out the window. Thank God it had finally stopped snowing. The winter weather wasn't helping their schedule at all. She hoped they wouldn't be snowed in too long or she would have to rearrange her plans yet another time. They were very behind as it was.

"What are your plans for us, Lily? What can we do to help? We know you're short of cash, so we thought perhaps we could go out and find some jobs and help with the bills."

Lily turned around to face Sonja. She was right. Cash flow was becoming a problem as time went by. If it were just her alone, she would be all right, but she had over a dozen girls living here and one nurse she had to pay.

When she had run off from Velesta, she had only had time to grab what had been available in Amber's safe. There hadn't been enough passports for everyone, since the batch had been just enough for the group most ready to leave the safe houses. Lily had taken all the cash, too, which had been substantial, but it still wasn't enough. After almost two months, they were running low.

Since then, she had found out that someone or some people had emptied or frozen all the accounts under her name. Probably the damn CIA again. She still had two sources, under another alias. One overseas, so that was currently unavailable. She needed the weather to cooperate so she could withdraw from her second source. It was out of town, and she would have to do it quickly before they found out about it.

She wasn't sure who was doing it to her, but she had several guesses. After all, she was a wanted woman. She had something in her possession everyone wanted. CIA. Hawk. Even Amber.

Not Amber. Surely Amber would know that she needed all the funds to help the girls. Her friend wouldn't be that heartless.

Why not? You let Dilaver . . . Disgusted with herself, Lily shook off the memory.

What did she expect? She deserved everything they were doing to her. She had given Amber to Dilaver. She'd known very well what kind of man Dilaver was; all she had to do was look around her at the girls. She had gambled that Hawk would save Amber, which would have given Lily enough time to finish her task. Had she thought they would understand? Especially if Amber had been . . . Lily squeezed her eyes shut.

"Lily, are you all right?" Tatiana's voice cut into the horrific images in her mind.

Lily opened her eyes. "Yes, I'm just tired, that's all," she replied quietly. The others were looking at her, worry in their eyes. "I don't mind one or two of you working, but not everyone can go out. This is a small town, and we don't want to draw too much attention to us, okay?"

"Okay, maybe two of us older ones will get a job waitressing or something," Sonja said.

"How are we going to get hold of you while you're out of town?" Tatiana asked.

"Leave a message at the hotel if I'm not there," Lily replied, making eye contact. Tatiana would understand. She wouldn't be answering the phone at all.

"Still in English?" Tatiana asked.

Lily hesitated. They had been talking more in English than anything else because so many of them were from different countries. It was also good practice for those who didn't want to return to their homelands and were heading out of the country. After all, English was an international language everywhere. "Yes," she finally said. "Everyone will assume it's a foreigner's message, and if they were tracing us somehow, they would expect one in Croatian."

She was sure those after them didn't know where they were, or they would have been here by now. Still, she and the girls had to be doubly careful. Lily looked at her charges again, some of them too young to be traveling alone to their destinations. But this was what had to be done; she couldn't take care of them forever.

"I'll send messages to Tatiana as often as I can," she said, knowing that some of the girls were afraid that she would abandon them. "Nothing's going to happen to me, so stop worrying. I'll get more money and try to get some contacts about more passports. Before you know it, you'll be spending Christmas with family! Or in America, with new friends. Wouldn't that be something?"

It was surprising how the thought of Christmas could cheer the girls up; the room was immediately filled with babble about holidays and presents. Lily turned away to look out the window again.

They were so young, so easily distracted. A tap on her shoulder. She glanced to her side. It was Tatiana.

"How are you going to find any contacts when you can't use the phone?" she asked.

Lily looked at the landscape outside. Everything was hidden under a thick blanket of snow. For some reason the sight made her tired. "I'll find a way," she said.

There was no way she was ever going near a phone. Not as long as the CIA could set off that fucking trigger in her head. She would be damned if she was ever going to be their little weapon again.

Reed didn't like being the last one to enter the conference room. It gave him a disadvantage, since all conversation stopped and everyone turned and looked at him. GEM had thought one of their own field agents might be better. He knew he was under the microscope, since he was being sent out at the admiral's insistence. He didn't like working without his SEAL brothers, but Admiral Madison had said this was an important mission, so he would do it.

Retrieving the missing weapon was part of Hawk's assignment when he went undercover in Macedonia. Since it was a Joint Mission, he had two tasks: one, to find the weapons caches that the enemy had so the SEALs could destroy them, and two, to locate the explosive device before it fell into enemy hands. However, his commander had only been able to achieve one of the goals; someone had run off with the stolen weapon before he'd been able to get to it.

That culprit had been Llallana Noretski. So now it was Reed's job to get Llallana before she handed the weapon over to someone else. And he would get it done.

Admiral Madison had insisted that it was still his and his team's responsibility to retrieve the device for GEM, their partner in this Joint Mission. SEALs always completed their missions; because Llallana was already familiar with Hawk, they'd needed someone else. Reed had been surprised when he had been picked. He was hardly a good candidate to sweet-talk a woman into giving up a weapon worth millions of dollars.

He soon found out the reason he was chosen. He was the team sharpshooter, one of the best from sniper school. GEM wanted him for a specific reason. He had also included the languages he spoke in his files. He was sure they were aware that he could speak and understand Croatian and had spent a fair amount of time there, enough to know the cityscape.

There were new people present this time. In previous meetings, one or both of his commanders would be present, depending on whether Admiral Madison could do a satellite video link or not. Hawk was here today. This time, he had Amber Hutchens by his side. An Asian woman was sitting at the far end. Probably another GEM operative. The man sitting at the other end of the long table reading some files looked familiar.

The others in the room were operatives he had met in the last few weeks who had given him quick workshops on language, etiquette, and bar manners, which had privately amused him. They reminded him of the private lessons his mother had had him take when he was a kid, except, of course, the one about bar manners. His mother hadn't thought of her youngest son growing up to be a Navy SEAL carousing in a bar.

"Reed, this is Jed McNeil, from the COS Command Center."

The man looked up, and Reed met a pair of startling light eyes in a tanned face. His handshake was firm. Close up, his eyes appeared almost silver. Reed *had* seen this man before—wasn't he the one who'd been some kind of undercover commando with the Triads when they had first had the Joint Mission with GEM? Hawk had filled him in on the various different departments and agencies connected with GEM and COS, how the two agencies had merged two years ago so they could go after a common goal.

"Jed's a part of the third phase of Operation Foxhole to retrieve the explosive device. You'll be in contact with him when you have any information about the weapon."

"Good to meet you, sir," Reed said.

"Call me Jed. We keep things pretty informal here. Have a seat," Jed McNeil said, indicating the chair next to him. "Admiral Madison spoke highly of you."

"Thank you."

T. joined McNeil on the other side. "You've met Miss Hutchens, of course. She's been helping us with building a more complete profile of the target. Amber accompanied Llallana Noretski on several of her trips before, so we've used her information to keep an eye on these routes."

Hawk had told him about Llallana's relationship with Amber Hutchens, how Llallana had sabotaged their weapons search and escaped with the device while Hawk had been busy saving Amber. Reed nodded politely at Amber, who smiled back in acknowledgement.

"Miss Hutchens came on board on the specific condition that you give an evaluation of the target's psychological condition before you take her out."

And that was his assignment in a nutshell. Retrieve device. Kill Llallana Noretski before she was instructed by her handler to do more harm. GEM wanted him for the job because, as a trained sharp-shooter, he wouldn't have any problem looking at a woman and seeing her as a target. He was also fluent in several languages. Another thing courtesy of his mother.

Reed noticed that Amber had noticeably reacted to Llallana's being called "the target." She had looked up sharply at T., then glanced away. Could anyone be tricked by a friend so thoroughly and still be so forgiving? Reed wondered whether he had that kind of generosity in him. He thought of his mother. His father had never forgiven her.

"I don't know how to do that," Reed said quietly. He'd never needed to evaluate a target before. "If she could deceive Miss Hutchens so well, how would I be able to tell whether she's fine or not?"

"Which is why we have Nikki Harden on our team this time," T. responded. The Asian woman gave a slight nod and smile. "Nikki's one of our top opera-tives and has expressed interest in this operation be-cause of our target. She'll be your advisor when it comes to dissecting Llallana's current mental state. Once you've established contact, you have to report to her whenever possible."

So many people to report to. Reed frowned. He had to establish certain points here. "Pardon my question, ma'am, but how is reporting back and forth about a target's personality going to help me finish my assign-ment? I don't know how to care for a mental patient." He didn't want to waste time getting to know Llallana Noretski. Establishing a bond wasn't good for a sharpshooter. He didn't say that out loud, though. "I was under the assumption that once I know the weapon's location, I would retrieve it, and finish up."

He tried to be tactful because of Amber's presence. This was what emotional bonding could bring about—the inability to coldly look a target in the eye and pull the trigger.

Nikki Harden's smile was gentle. "You first have to establish a trust between the two of you, Mr. Vincenzio. There's another way to do this, of course. Capture Llallana Noretski and make her tell us what we want to know, in which case, she might do one of a few things. A, she could still be under the influence of her handler and be ordered to self-eliminate. B, she could lie several times to us while someone she knows is handling the sale of the weapon. Or C, the weapon is already gone and she's just a decoy to distract us. We've evaluated a higher probability of retrieving the weapon if you have direct access to it yourself through her. I hope to help you anticipate any problems you might have dealing with her."

He was a SEAL. He knew how to deal with an enemy. A target. They were requiring of him two very different tasks here.

"Are you a psychiatrist?" Reed asked.

"No," Nikki replied quietly, "but I have had experiences similar to those that Llallana Noretski has gone through and can provide you with insight on the effects of brainwashing and drug manipulation, as well as how the mind deals with fear and mental pain. Do you have any similar experience with these topics so we have a starting point in discussion?"

Reed considered a few seconds. He hadn't thought this assignment would go quite so deep. He wanted to clarify his position before they went too far into left field. "I'm a SEAL, ma'am. We're trained to be mentally strong so we can withstand pain from being in extreme conditions, be it weather or mental pain. We spend weeks in boot camp with very little sleep while our bodies and minds are broken down into survival mode. But I don't feel comfortable in judging whether a woman's head is right or not." He took a deep breath before quietly adding, "I'm not going to play psychiatrist."

"But you do have something to help you understand Llallana Noretski. You can always report to me using your training as a basis," Nikki said. "Is that easier?"

"Yes." He hadn't thought of his SEAL training as anything to do with mental torture and brainwashing. He would have to think about this later.

"Perhaps this will help put you in perspective about your target," T. said. "We have the final recording of her last conversation moments before she disappeared. The man she's talking to, Bradford Sun, was a friend of hers and Amber's. He's the chief of CIVPOL, the UN drug and human-trafficking arm. During this conversation, we were trying to deactivate Llallana. At that time, we only knew that her key trigger line was 'Things fall apart.' "

Reed frowned. "From the Yeats poem?"

Nikki nodded. "Yes. Are you familiar with it?"

"Yes," Reed replied, keeping his expression deliberately blank as T. canted an eyebrow. Boarding school had taken care of a lot of his knowledge of classical literature.

"Pay attention to what happens when Llallana says the trigger line," T. said and pressed a button.

The room speakers picked up background sounds of a car moving. Then Reed heard a woman's voice.

"What am I?" She sounded distant.

"You're a CIA sleeper. They used your anger and hatred and programmed you. They channeled all your emotions into looking for a sister you don't have so you could have a purpose in life, and then they put a trigger in that they could set off when the time's right. All those cell calls you have been taking . . . don't let them use you, Lily!"

"I don't know what you're talking about."

"You don't have a sister. It's you all along! You know this! Stop lying to yourself, Lily."

"Llallana. 'Things fall apart; the centre cannot hold.' "

There was a slight pause, and then the male voice replied slowly,

" 'The blood-dimmed tide is loosed, and everywhere the ceremony of innocence is drowned.' What comes next, Lily? Say it and be free."

Reed found himself holding his breath as he listened. This was a sleeper cell awakening from her trigger.

Llallana's voice sounded faint, even uneasy.

" 'The best lack all conviction, while the worst are full of passionate intensity.' "

The rest of the tape was the male voice calling Llallana's name over and over. The phone then went dead.

There was a short silence in the room. The recorded conversation had been intense and personal, and Reed felt a twinge of pity for Llallana. The poor woman must have been brought to awareness right at that moment.

The files reported the initial conclusion that Llallana had committed suicide because a car had been found wrecked at the foot of a cliff. However, no body had ever been found. Nor was there any trace of the explosive device.

Llallana, or Lily, as her friends called her, was still out there somewhere. And she might be the only person who had the weapon.

"We want to give you all the help you need to bring Llallana Noretski back here alive," T. told him. "This was our agreement with Amber before she'd agree to come aboard. If Llallana's too far gone, and has become too dangerous, then you must eliminate her, Reed. That's why we picked you for this job. You have a reputation of being in control of your emotions at all times, and if you see Llallana Noretski selling that device before you can get to it yourself, you have to put her in your crosshairs and take her out, Reed."

Taking out targets was his expertise. He would do his team proud and finish the original Joint Mission. "Not a problem," Reed said.

3

Stimoceiver, developed in the 1950s by Dr. Joseph Delgado and funded by the CIA and the Office of Naval Research. Current miniature telemetry devices.

Reed's head hurt from thinking about all the implications of what he had been reading for the past hour. The possibility of a person being implanted with a tiny transceiver to control and modify behavior and emotion was science fiction stuff to him, but according to these files, it had been done for decades.

Nikki Harden had told him she didn't think Llallana Noretski had had such an implant put in her, but it was a possibility because of her sudden erratic change of behavior shortly before she had betrayed Amber. Nikki had wanted him to understand how a person could be subjected to mind control and the different ways this could be achieved.

Reed studied the two women in the room with him. Sitting at the far end, Nikki was pulling out different sheets from her files to compile into one for him, quietly asking Amber questions as she was doing so. The two women worked well together as they went through the different cases and possible ways they could save Llallana Noretski. He liked that they both didn't view the woman as just a target.

He went back to his reading.

> Project BLUEBIRD, 1950s program authorized by the CIA. Operation ARTICHOKE, authorized by Deputy CIA Director Richard Helms. Psychological Warfare. Drug experimentation on subjects to create hypnosis, amnesia and also implant posthypnotic suggestion.

The documents gave accounts of subjects being put into some kind of living hypnotic state and given new identities in different countries. The hypnotic suggestions had successfully stayed with the individuals.

> The creation of the perfect sleeper cell: using the subject's past with implanted hypnotic "triggers."

There was no way Reed would have believed that the government could actually be doing this to real human beings, except that in the current world, with so many terrorist acts by supposedly normal people, the term "sleeper cell" had entered the vernacular. If the enemy had been doing this, why not his own government?

And Llallana Noretski was one of them. Or so they said. He didn't really buy all this mumbo jumbo. All his life, he had held a person to be fully responsible for every one of his or her actions and their consequences. Arch might have blamed Kim's death, but it was Arch who'd paddled out to sea, who hadn't swum back. His mother might have blamed his father's coldness, but it was she who had chosen to—

The door slid open and T. walked in, urgency in her stride.

"We've got her location," she said, moving to the panel that controlled the video screens. "She showed up at the bank just as we hoped she would."

Anticipation arose. Action time. He was growing tired of research and reading. He put down his file and swiveled his chair to face the wall. Amber and Nikki joined him at the main table, their attention on the screen.

The video showed that it was nighttime. A woman walked toward the camera, hands shoved deeply into her heavy fur coat. Her head was covered with a dark scarf, but Reed could see the dark hair curling at the shoulders. She looked up. It was Llallana Noretski.

"We knew there weren't enough passports in Amber's safe, so we've frozen most of the accounts she and Amber were using," Nikki explained, "hoping that she'll still be trying to help the rest of the girls to escape."

"She's let her hair grow long," Amber murmured. "Lily's never had her hair that long in the years I've known her. Said long hair tickled her neck."

"Then perhaps she's reverting to her former self," Nikki said. "You mentioned she avoided talking about her sister all that time."

"Well, we know why, don't we?"

"Or maybe she's just trying to hide," Reed suggested. "I mean, don't women just change their hairstyles when something drastic happens in their lives?"

T. clicked the video on pause, freezing Llallana in the middle of withdrawing money from the machine, and all three women turned and looked at him. He stared back. Maybe he should have kept that observation to himself.

Then T. laughed and leaned a hip against the table. "You know, darling, you do say the most interesting things with the straightest face. Is this hair phenomenon just a standard male assumption or from past experience?"

Darling. Reed didn't say out loud that when T. called him that, he was beginning to suspect that it meant her mind was targeting him for one of those weird probing conversations. "Darling" was just the distraction. It was the rest of her sentence he had to be careful of. He was still wondering what she knew about his background.

"You were joking, right?" Amber didn't even try to hide her amusement.

She would be telling Hawk about this later. Reed knew what his commander's reply would be, since he was known for it. "I don't joke," he answered, then he looked at T. "Observation."

"That many girlfriends then, Reed?" T. teased,

patting her hair. "Are you the drastic thing in their lives?"

"No, my mo—" Reed stopped, closing his mouth firmly. Damn, she'd done it again. He didn't want to bring up anything to do with his family. He went back to the subject that had started this. "I was just thinking that since I'm letting my hair grow longer than I like, just like the target is, that maybe she is trying to hide her true identity. Maybe she just doesn't like herself at the moment, or her situation, and so she changes her hairstyle."

The length of his hair was way longer than he was used to. It reminded him of his surf-rat days, when he used to have the wavy blond mane his friends favored. They had been shocked out of their minds when they'd seen him return one day with all his locks shorn off, after he'd joined the Navy. Now, they were back—no longer sun-streaked, and a lot darker, but still the same thick wave.

Nikki and T. exchanged a brief glance. They seemed to agree on something.

"We'll know when you meet her," Nikki said, turning back to the screen.

T. reactivated the video. Llallana made her withdrawal, shoving the cash into her purse. She looked up, straight into the camera. Reed frowned. There was something in her expression. . . .

"This is good," Nikki said. "This might mean she's still somewhat in control of her thoughts, that her trigger hasn't been reactivated, or she wouldn't care so much about taking care of the rest of the girls."

"The girls' well-being was her life," Amber said quietly. "She even went back to take them with her when she wasn't herself."

"Yes. The posthypnotic suggestion reversal worked, but who knows how confused and terrified she must have been at all the memories flooding her head. I wonder why her handler never called her back to re-trigger the switch."

Reed listened as he watched the woman on screen make one final quick sweep of the area with those dark eyes. Maybe it was just the play of shadows, but the lone light from the bank machine seemed to emphasize the ones under her dark eyes. He felt sorry for her. If she understood what had happened to her, as they were telling him she did, then she mustn't be sleeping very well. He wouldn't want to fall asleep thinking something could talk to his brain and trigger some kind of damn switch.

"We don't know what she's doing with the money," T. pointed out. "We have nothing on the girls except for the first group, who we've tracked with those passports."

"She used those passports, T. That tells us something," Amber said.

"I know she's your friend, Amber. I have to play devil's advocate, since we're sending Reed in after her. We don't know what her state of mind is, and he has to keep that in mind in all his dealings with her."

"I know." Amber turned to Reed. "She has a very sarcastic and dark sense of humor. I don't care if they said her behavior could have been modified. That sarcasm and wicked attitude is innately Lily. And if she asks you to call her Lily, you'll know that she trusts you at some level."

"All right," Reed said, his eyes still trained on the screen. "There's someone in that corner. I don't think he's out on a late evening stroll."

The three women returned their attention to the video. "He didn't move from that spot," T. said. "There wasn't any vehicle following her."

"But you can see the license plate from his angle," Reed said. "Can you trace a foreign car from here?"

T. glanced back, her eyes thoughtful. "I'll call in and have that possibility checked right away. So let's say someone else is also tracking Lily. Why?"

"She has the weapon in her possession," Reed pointed out the obvious. "So maybe it's her handler, who wants her back in the fold."

Nikki shook her head. "All he has to do is to call her and activate that hypnotic trigger we were talking about earlier, Reed."

"Then it's someone else, someone who might not know what Lily is," Amber said, "but still knows what she has."

"Greta." T. said at the same time as Amber.

"Who's Greta?" Reed asked. No one had mentioned that name to him yet.

"Too much information for your operation, darling. Rewatch the video. I'm off to start preparations for your trip back to Eastern Europe." She stood up.

"Nikki, you have to brief him about the state of mind of a sexual slave and how that could be used as a basis for emotional triggers."

"Yes."

Looking at Nikki, Reed couldn't imagine the slight woman having lived through such horrors, but she had all but suggested to him that she had been subjected to similar experiences when she'd been captured during an operation. But that was ten years ago. Perhaps there was hope for Llallana.

This was precisely what he wanted to avoid: He was beginning to think of Llallana Noretski not as a target but as a victim.

"What if Greta gets to Lily before we do?" Amber asked.

"You leave Greta to me," T. said. "Reed?"

His reply was automatic. Everything was a state of mind, anyway. He was going into mission mode. "Standing and Ready," he said.

Somebody was following her. Lily tightened the scarf around her neck as she continued walking to the bus stop.

She could feel a presence behind her. Or she was just being paranoid again.

Ever since she'd snuck into the library a month ago and done some research with the public computers, she hadn't been able to shake off the growing sense that nothing was real. Too much information about things that had nothing to do with her world.

She could write the story of her life in a few sentences. A kidnapped girl. Rescued from a brothel. Grown up through shady means to become self-supporting. Now a rescuer of young girls kidnapped by mercenaries.

Not exactly a normal life by any means, but now she could add CIA sleeper cell somewhere in that paragraph. Rescued by the CIA, and, she had thought, freed after a short stay to recuperate. How could she have known that they had messed with her mind? She wouldn't have believed it possible at all if she didn't have these memories now of what she had done, what she had believed to be the right thing while she'd been doing it.

When Brad had made her repeat some lines from some poem . . . Lily closed her eyes briefly at the thought of Brad. Oh God. What she had done to Bradford Sun was totally unforgivable. But the man had tried to save her, had somehow known the code that would release her from whatever it was that was controlling her mind. If only she could remember what she had said. That was the key—some poem. But she had no idea what that was, only that she had said it at his prompting and then . . . everything had turned into a horrifying realization of what was in her possession and what she was planning to do.

She had learned new terms from that website she'd found about sleeper cells. Whatever it was she had repeated was called a subconscious trigger. She bit down hard on her lower lip. They had somehow hypnotized her and inserted it inside her head. How was that possible? She couldn't remember any such sessions with the CIA.

Lily reached the bus stop and walked into the shelter. There were two other people sitting there—an older lady and a man, both reading as they waited for the bus. She sat down at the far end. If she was being followed, then she would either see a car, or someone would join her on the bus.

No matter how paranoid she was, one thing was real. Many people were after her and what she had in her possession. She wasn't sure whether they just wanted what she had or they wanted her, too, but either way, she would be damned if she was giving it to them.

Why would they want you? a voice in her head mocked. *Because you belong to them.*

"I belong to no one!" Lily muttered fiercely, then looked up at the other two people in the station. She hadn't meant to say that out loud. They looked at her curiously, and she gave a shrug in answer, as if nothing was wrong. They went back to their reading.

She looked up sharply at the sound of footsteps. A man stepped into the shelter. He was tall and broad, with a thick mustache. He nodded at them as he brushed off the drifts of snow on his thick jacket. Then he sat down in the middle.

Lily watched him put his hand in his right pocket. If he pulled out a weapon . . .

The headlights from the approaching bus shone into the booth. Everyone stood up. The man pulled out his hand. It was empty.

Lily lined up behind everyone and got on the bus, heading straight to the back. She could watch the other passengers in front and also look through the back window to make sure no vehicle was following.

She should have taken a taxi, like she had when she'd gone to the bank, but funds were low enough as it was. She wanted to kick herself for not having anticipated that her bank accounts would be gone. After all, she was dealing with the CIA; they had those kinds of powers. She blamed it on her lack of sleep. She really, really needed a good night's rest.

But at least there was this one account. And the one overseas. She'd been so relieved when the library computer had confirmed that they were still active. God knew what she would have done if she had been totally penniless.

If it were just herself, she would have gotten by, but she had a big responsibility. She could relax a bit now that she had the money in her hands. She had secretly been worried that her card wouldn't work, and that there would be nothing in there. As it was, she would have just enough to purchase the passports and pay some bills. She frowned. She needed to think of a way to make money to pay the usual under-the-table fees to the relevant officials.

The big man with the mustache turned and looked around. Lily kept her eyes on his hands, unconsciously holding her breath as he pulled out something from his coat pocket. It looked bulky.

It was a cell phone, one of the bigger types that had gone out of style a few years ago. *"Ya, hallo?"*

Lily exhaled slowly. She hadn't been this jumpy since she was on her own with nothing but the clothes on her back. She must pull herself together or this wasn't going to work. Right now she needed to be very logical about what she was going to do. She had a lot on her plate. A group of girls was waiting patiently for her to get back. Illegal passports to purchase. She glanced up at the man still on the cell phone. And trying to find a way to get around the phone problem. It was so damn stupid not being able to use one. How on earth was she going to explain that while she made her deals?

Oh sorry, can't call me, I'll call you.

Yeah, that was going to make the illegal traders less suspicious of a woman asking for so many pass-ports. Before, Amber had been able to do it through her information channels. Now that she had to do it face-to-face, the traders would probably want a good reason for the sudden change.

Lily became aware of the man on the cell standing up abruptly, still on the phone. He headed for the exit as the bus came to a stop. See? He wasn't following her after all. There were a few more passengers in the bus, but they weren't paying attention to her. Everyone appeared normal.

Except her, of course. She was the odd person here. *Show of hands, people—anyone here a sleeper cell?* She grinned at the thought of standing up and actually asking that. *And oh, anyone here own some special kind of bomb?* She had one.

She felt herself grinning. She was probably the only woman in Pristina who fit the description she just gave. If she looked at the positive side of things, it couldn't be easy for those looking for her to go around describing her. Let's hope so.

Lily got off at her destination, then walked around for a few minutes to make sure the bus wasn't followed. The roads were eerily silent as she trudged across the median. She caught sight of the restaurants with their bright lights on and suddenly remembered she hadn't eaten dinner yet.

She could get room service at the hotel. She stopped. No, she couldn't. She would have to use the damn phone. Shit.

Maybe she'd come down to the café later. Reaching her hotel, she looked up at the lit sign, which she hadn't noticed before. Welcome to Pristina, it said.

"Welcome to hell," she muttered, then walked quickly through the foyer into the lobby. She smiled at the proprietor-cum-desk clerk. *"Dobro dan."*

Let's hope she still had some charm in her to persuade the nice gentleman to help her make a very special call.

4

Hey man, there's got to be more than just loving to ride the waves, you know. For me, it's a quest. I go out there practically naked, just me and my board. The ocean hides everything, son. Sharks. Undertows. You're out there paddling and then, just like that, it can get you. You can't be a surfer and be afraid of what the ocean can do. You're alone and you catch a wave and ride your board like a magic carpet all the way back home. I love that feeling, man! Especially when I see that little curl of a wave on the horizon and I know it's going to grow for me as I paddle hard toward it and that if I time it right, it's going to rise up and challenge me. Wooooohoooo! You know what I mean? Son, there's nothing like that perfect wave crashing all over you. And that's what the right woman can do for you, too. Now get out there and get laid.

The corner of Reed's lips quirked at the memory of that particular conversation. He'd been fifteen and horny. Arch had been a rather unconventional father figure, if nothing else. He had taken Reed to a rather wild surfing party and . . . Reed looked at his surroundings at the moment. Yeah, this place had a lot of Arch in it.

The right woman in a place called The Beijing Bombshell in Pristina, Kosovo. It couldn't get any more surreal than this. The Beijing Bombshell was the hottest underground place in town right now, catering to a very exclusive clientele. One needed to pull strings to get into the club—money, influence, illegal trading, or in his case, *veza,* the Croatian version of returning a favor from the past.

T. had told him his identity—an ex-peacekeeper, MIA, now in the arms-dealing business. "You're still American, darling, so just be yourself," she'd said. "You know your weapons, so there should be no problem with discussions about types and quality. We've set up your MO for months now, so they've heard of you."

"They know me?" Reed had asked.

"Not you. The person you're going to be. They've done business with you before, but not in person."

"Ah, understood. What about name?"

"Funny thing, that. We used the initials R.C. for our fake setup, and you're Reed. So you can stay Reed."

Reed remembered the expression in T.'s honey-colored eyes only too well. The woman could speak volumes with just one look. "So do they call me R.C. or Reed?" he'd asked.

"Whatever you like." She'd shrugged. "It's *your* identity now. Make it personal."

That was the first thing they'd told him at the training workshops. He had to make it personal or it wouldn't look real. "Okay. Reed to my friends, R.C. for business," he'd said.

"Now, darling, you have to tell me what R.C. stands for," T. had said.

Reed had thought for a moment, then said solemnly, "Really Cool."

T.'s face had lit up with amusement. "That," she'd said, "was pretty funny, Joker."

But the Joker never joked. Not in public, anyway. Reed leaned back against the bar lit up with neon lights, which shot colorful electronic pulses to the beat of the music. He soaked in the strange atmosphere of blond Asian women strutting around in bustiers and fishnets, cavorting in and out of the arms of men that looked as if they had either come out of the theater district or a street fight, depending on the state of their clothing. T. had told him that was one of the club specialties—all its women wore Marilyn Monroe blond wigs. It had become such a rage that even the women who came to party had begun to dress up that way. On the weekend they came by the hundreds, partying while making deals involving drugs, weapons, and other illegal activities. All to the beat of some kind of techno tango. The owner was a very eclectic man.

Reed was here to meet with him. He looked around again. Men were openly caressing lines of women, choosing their companions for the night. Some went for the petite Asians; others preferred the taller, more voluptuous, heavily made-up Caucasians. He was supposed to mingle with the crowd so the owner could see where he was, but he really didn't have any desire to go over there and make a play for any of those girls.

There was a dance floor in the middle, lit up by disco lights and littered with dancing couples. The oddest thing about it all was the music. He had noticed it the moment he had walked into the club but only now realized that it wasn't just one song like that. Every song was pure old-fashioned South American music with a techno-beat. Right now everyone was *ole*-ing to a lone female in the middle stripping to the beat of "Kiss of Fire" sung in accented English. The moment she pulled down her bustier, she disappeared behind an excited group of three or four men. Reed looked away. That's when he caught sight of her.

Everything clicked into place. He had studied Llallana's photo many times in the last month and had felt drawn to her somehow, that he had seen her somewhere before. But her short dark hair had thrown him off.

"I see her," he said, knowing his mic would pick up his voice.

"Are you sure?" Nikki asked, her voice surprisingly clear over the noise. "Our scouts haven't seen anything."

"She's blond too, you know," Reed pointed out.

"Ah. So how can you be sure that's her you're looking at? I believe the women are all heavily made up at this club."

"She isn't." He didn't say he'd seen her in that blond wig before. He straightened up. "She's heading toward Johnny Chic's office. Someone's blocking her path, bothering her. Should I intervene?"

"Is she in trouble?" Nikki asked.

He didn't think so, but he didn't care for the way the man had one arm across Llallana's shoulders while the other reached for a more intimate grope. Reed was about to head that way when suddenly the man was backing away from her, hands held up pacifyingly. The lighting wasn't good enough to see, but he guessed that she was holding a small weapon against the man's chest. She had quick hands, he noted.

"She's knocking on Johnny's door. Can we trust him to do exactly what we've told him?" Someone tucked her hand under Reed's arm and he turned, finding himself eye to eye with T. His eyebrows lifted as he silently studied her before politely saying, "That's a nice wig."

T. patted her platinum blond hair. "Darling, I have had better compliments than that tonight."

He bet she had. Her costume left nothing to the imagination—some skintight, black lacy thing that molded to her gorgeous form. She wore see-through black lace stockings and high heels. Again he wondered at this woman who could put on disguises like outfits. He cocked his head. "Nice garters."

"Hmm. You're hurting my feelings."

"Why are you here?" he asked.

"To distract you."

Reed stiffened. "Why?"

T. flicked a lazy finger at his shoulder. "Because, darling, despite your cool and collected demeanor, a SEAL is ingrained with honor. You would rush your cute ass over there and save Lily if she got into trouble while negotiating with Johnny."

He narrowed his eyes at her. "What's he going to do to her?"

T. considered him for a long moment. "Suppose he asks for sexual favors from Lily? Are you going in there to stop this whole thing because of your sense of outrage?"

"Lily would kick Johnny's bloody ass first."

It was hard to have a conversation with so many women in his head. "Amber said—"

"I'm wired, too," T. said with a smile. "I can hear what Amber says."

She leaned over, way too close. He suddenly realized she had covered the button mic with her thumb. "We don't know how desperate Lily is," T. said quietly into his ear, "and whatever choices she's making now isn't any of your business. Johnny Chic will do what he's agreed to do, but don't expect sleaze like him to help us out by the book."

Reed covered T.'s hand, and she didn't resist him as he slid it off the button. "I understood the idea was to get her desperate enough to come to me," he said, with emphasis, "not to get her so desperate that she would actually sell herself."

T. smiled again, her red lips pouty and totally at odds with her words. "My assignment doesn't include evaluating the target's mind-set, darling. Yours does. So you keep what she does in mind as *you* decide whether to cancel her or not."

His hand tightened. "You're playing with my head again. Stop putting suggestions in there."

"I think he's onto your NOPAIN, T.," Nikki chimed in.

"Just doing my job, darling," T. mocked. "Now, I just know that a Vincenzio dances very well. Did you know that the tango was a dance started in the brothels, signifying the intimacies of a whore and her pimp? Johnny Chic knows how to make fun of everyone in his own way. Shall we?"

Reed let her lead him toward the dance floor. How much did she know about him? He couldn't ask her anything while these damn recording pieces were on them.

It was much easier for Lily to come here than she'd anticipated. She didn't think she would have been able to do it if she had just been herself. The old Lily wouldn't have walked through here without hurting someone. She really hated these places.

However, tonight she was here for another reason. She tried not to look at the huge two-way mirror that filled up half the wall; instead she concentrated on Johnny Chic.

She had imagined Johnny to be some tall, fat slob sitting in some brothel, making his oily living doing illegal trading. Instead, a trim man with a small mustache greeted her from the desk. She couldn't place a finger on his nationality. He looked very exotic, almost Asian, but not quite. When he stood up, he wasn't very tall at all, maybe about five-three at the most.

His eyes were too bold, as if he was imagining her naked, and she wanted to reach across the desk and grab him by his snazzy tie. Biting back a rude comment, she instead tried her best to smile.

"You aren't what I expected, Ambrosia," Johnny said, his accent tinged with an Italian or South American flavor.

Another thing for which to apologize to Amber. She had used her friend's code name to get Johnny's attention. "Yeah well, vice versa," Lily said.

"Are you blond under that beautiful wig?" he asked.

She chose not to give him an answer. She smiled again. "I've brought the cash for the passports."

"Oh yes, the transaction." Johnny's attention seemed to be fixed on the two-way mirror. He swayed to the muted music piped through the speakers. "Oh, but we have great dancers tonight. Look."

Lily gave the mirror an impatient glance. She wanted to get out of here as quickly as possible, but this was a different world than her usual transportation of kids over borders, and she had to play by the rules. It was a strange place, with too many weird people in here.

There was a half circle around a couple who seemed to be in a world of their own as they danced to the rhythmic sway of whatever this music was.

They were well matched—the man was holding the woman close enough to be obscene, yet the woman seemed to be able to turn and swirl without bumping into him.

"The tango is so beautiful to watch, isn't it?" Johnny murmured. "Especially if it's done right. Look at that. He holds her like he owns her, and he does because he's the master and she's his slave. Yet he gives her a little room and she's a spitfire, following his steps."

Lily didn't want to hear about masters and slaves. "You've just made me dislike this dance," she told Johnny, unable to hide the wry tone of her voice. "Shall we get back to business?"

Johnny Chic shook his head, his eyes still on the couple out there. "You can't dislike the tango till you actually dance it, Ambrosia, my dear. Ah, look, look! He's definitely a good dancer. He controls his lady so well."

He gave a long sigh of pleasure and, squeezing the five fingers of his hand together, he kissed the tips loudly, while his hips moved suggestively to the music. "Tell me, Ambrosia," he added, "why are you here in person? Usually we deal through our couriers. You give me the information and I supply what you need, so this is indeed a surprise."

He stopped and turned toward her suddenly. Lily met his gaze squarely.

"I'm passing through," she said smoothly, "and needed this done as quickly as possible. Besides,

I've heard about The Beijing Bombshell for a long time and wanted to check it out. It's everything I've imagined."

He beamed at what he thought was a compliment. "It's all about me," he said.

"Is that right," Lily murmured.

"Oh, yes. Surely you already know, with your excellent sources, that my mother was imported from China by my Argentinian father?" His gaze narrowed a little as he questioned softly, "Don't you?"

She had to be very careful. She plopped down on the sofa and crossed her legs. His gaze slid down, following the movement of her hands as she smoothed the silk stocking. "Johnny," she chided. "Are you trying to test me? I don't share information unless there's a bargain, you know that. Now, I want my passports."

"And what is this hot information you will give me in return, besides the cash?" He took a few steps toward her. "You always give me some information to seal the deal, Ambrosia."

Her mind was careening wildly as she looked up calmly. She didn't know that. She had thought Amber had gotten the passports with just cash. Stupid, stupid, stupid. Amber had dealt with information; of course she would have used it as a means to get other illegal things, such as passports to help the girls.

She didn't have anything that she wanted to share with him. Certainly not about a sleeper cell on the loose. She wanted to laugh out loud wildly.

"I've heard," Johnny continued, coming even closer, "about a secret weapon that everyone's after. Have you heard of it?"

Not *that*. She wasn't going to use that as a way to get the passports. Was she? "Of course," Lily said. Ambrosia wouldn't be able to deny knowing about this weapon if it was such hot news. Lily shrugged. "There's nothing gainful about it till someone finds it. It's lost or gone."

Johnny looked a tad disappointed. "I thought you might know more," he said.

"I will sooner or later," Lily said, "and I can forward that information to you when I do. But I really need what I came for right now."

"They're on my desk."

She got up, trying not to walk too eagerly. She hated the way he was looking at her butt as she headed toward the desk.

"This package?" she asked, turning around. When he nodded, she added, "Can I check the goods out?"

"Of course. They are the best out there, as you know."

She opened the box. Picking up the stack of passports, she counted them. And recounted. She turned to face Johnny again. "This isn't the number I ordered. There are a few missing."

"Yes," Johnny smiled. "That guy dancing out there offered me a great deal for four of them just before you arrived. That's all I have for you."

No way. She couldn't leave without all the passports. "Then I'm not giving you all my money," she said.

Johnny shrugged. His eyes turned crafty. "Of course, if you would let me see whether you're really blond all over, I'll personally get R.C. to give you those passports. I can't kill him, you understand. Bad for business. But you can negotiate with him."

Lily looked at R.C., and then she smiled. Messed-up head or not, she really felt good about fulfilling this urge to beat the crap out of Johnny Chic.

Reed swiveled his partner one last time. She turned, kicked one leg out, swiveled back into his body, and slid down the length of it as he deftly caught her weight in one arm while he leaned over her. The music ended. The crowd clapped enthusiastically, some yelling lewd suggestions.

Reed looked down at Tess for a second. Her eyes half closed, she didn't push away, as if she were still in the middle of the dance. He straightened, bringing her up slowly. The music had already restarted.

"Supremo, darling," T. said, scarcely out of breath. She fluttered her eyelashes teasingly. "A girl would fall like a sack of potatoes for a man who can move like you."

They were just moving slowly to the music now. "She's heading this way," Reed said.

T.'s gaze didn't move from his face. "On the other hand," she said, "a girl would be easily devastated to know you were looking at another woman while moving like that. It's very interesting, though, how you seem to know that she's near when there's a crowd all around her."

He couldn't explain it either. He had been watching for Johnny's door to open even while they were dancing, and was disappointed that it took the whole dance before Llallana reappeared. He hadn't wanted her to . . . He quickly compartmentalized his thoughts. T. was watching him way too closely.

"What next when she's here?"

"Tell her no, whatever she offers, unless it's the right offer, of course." T.'s expression shifted, turning serious. "If she does, you know what to do."

Then a flirtatious smile appeared and her face resumed its bold, come-hither look as she led him off the dance floor. The woman either guessed right or her timing was excellent, because she bumped right against Llallana Noretski. Reed suspected the latter.

"Oh!"

T. somehow managed to pull him forward, using the momentum of their two bodies to knock Llallana off balance. The collision caused Llallana to stumble backward hard, and Reed reached out and curled an arm around her waist, pulling her against him. T., however, was still holding his other hand, and she followed his thrust forward. She swung into Llallana again, pushing into her target's back and sandwiching her between them.

It was like part of a dance, Reed thought as he absorbed the combined force, closing his arms around the women for balance. Again, somehow, T. was already stepping away, and he found only Llallana in his hug. He looked down at her. Her upturned face, cushioned against his chest, registered a startled realization at where she was and then an awareness of their closeness.

"Hey, watch where you're going!" T. yelled out in Croatian. "And find a man of your own!"

He could have released her but he didn't. "Are you all right?" he asked, his Croatian halting and a bit off-key, just the way he'd been practicing. "Sorry, I didn't see you."

The dark eyes glared up at him. "Too busy with other things," she said, in English. "I have to talk to you, R.C."

He liked the way she deliberately used his name. Of course that would get a gunrunner's attention immediately. The music had gotten louder again and he could barely hear her, so he let her feel his surprise by tightening his hold on her. He noted that she didn't try to move out of his arms. "Not too busy for you," he said in English, and in one smooth turn, he had her back on the dance floor. "Care to dance?"

"Hey!" T. cut in. "What about me?"

"Does she work here?" Llallana asked Reed, ignoring T. as she put a hand on his chest to let some space between their bodies.

"Sort of." He slid his hand down to the hollow in her back, gently adding pressure. Her bare skin felt hot and smooth. "She's been given to me to dance with tonight."

Llallana turned to T. "Johnny Chic wants you in his office. Right now."

"For what?" T. stood there, hands on her hips.

"I've bound him really, really tightly and he needs someone to undo all the knots," Llallana explained in a sarcastic drawl. "He's also not wearing any pants and I wouldn't want any of his guys to walk in and embarrass him. You'll make points with him if you go and help him now."

Reed glanced over at T. He could have sworn there was a tiny smile in those eyes. "You go, babe. I'll make sure you get your tip tonight." He turned back to Llallana. "Of course, if she goes, you'll have to take her place."

When he had seen her from afar that first time, he had sensed something different about her. She had impressed him with her alertness and, especially, the bold way she'd warned off danger.

"I don't take the place of anyone," she said, leaning closer.

Although he hadn't recognized her in the photos in the GEM file, he had gotten an impression of a woman who knew what she wanted. Now, meeting Llallana Noretski up close, her vibrancy hit him like a wave. The careless way she tossed her head back as if nothing in the world bothered her. The challenging attitude, the boldness in her eyes, the small smile that was both mocking and amused.

He was intrigued by the package she presented. Maybe he was intrigued because he knew more about her than she thought, or maybe she presented it because she needed his cooperation. Either way, he wanted to know whether it was just a façade. What was the real woman like inside?

"I want to talk to you, not shout out every sentence. Can we go to a table?" Lily asked as she motioned toward the tables.

Reed shook his head no. He had to wait for T.'s go-ahead signal that everything was A-OK before he could start talking. It was easy to find distractions in a place like this, so everyone had agreed to let him play it by ear.

He liked the way she felt in his arms. The music was a little slower than the song before, with a heady, melodic beat that was sensually inviting. She didn't know the steps to the tango, but the way she subtly swayed against him was sexy, like a woman who had secrets to tell. He deliberately pulled her closer, then, inserting one leg between hers, he dipped her. He suspected that in real life, the woman didn't like being kept off-balance, literally or figuratively, yet she allowed him to hold her that way for a few beats, her dark eyes flashing challengingly as she looked up at him. As he slowly straightened back up, he slid his hand from her neck down to her upper back, taking away her support and thus not allowing her to get out of position.

It was a move most professional dancers used to show the mastery of one partner over the other, as the male controlled the female's upper body. In a choreographed dance, the woman could use her arms and legs to express her emotions. She could curl one limb around her man's leg to show a rebellious streak. She could hold on to the partner's shoulders or lapels to signify a need for him. Or she could totally relax her entire body, flinging her arms out trustingly, and allow her master to do what he would.

Because it was a dancer's move, he had expected Llallana to grab him out of instinct, like most people who didn't expect the falling sensation would. Instead, she did all three—she took the leg that he had trapped between his and curled it around one of them, her knee sliding up dangerously close to his balls, while at the same time she grabbed the opening of his light jacket with one hand and pulled hard enough that he had to bend lower or cause the both of them to fall down. Through it all she relaxed her entire body so that her back arched up to meet him, demonstrating amazing upper body strength on her part.

Totally intriguing.

He found himself staring down at the smooth silky expanse of skin that sloped into gentle mounds. He could see her nipples through the dark, tight material. They were hard and erect, barely covered, and he had the sudden urge to bite on the top and pull it down to reveal them for his eyes.

"Drop me and my knee won't miss your family jewels," Llallana said sweetly.

Suddenly, Amber's laughter pierced through his focus on her. "That's Lily all right," she said, her voice coming so clear through the hidden listening device that he was sure her friend could hear her.

"Oh, by the way, R.C., don't forget she's skilled in martial arts. She *will* kick you if you drop her."

Damn. He'd forgotten that he was miced. Reluctantly, he slowly straightened up, keeping her leg imprisoned, his hand gliding back up to behind her neck. Her face was flushed and her eyes sparkled. Another time, another place, he would have finished this dance, and they would be naked. The image of Llallana Noretski naked came too easily.

Reed gave himself a mental shake. He shouldn't have danced. It brought out too much of himself.

"Now we'll look for a table," he said.

They weaved around other writhing couples. She pointed to a booth in one corner and he nodded in agreement. T.'s voice came through the mic as he headed in that direction.

"Reed darling, she's tied up Johnny Chic like a hog, with his pants in a knot at his feet. The man isn't happy with her treatment of him." T. laughed huskily. "He swears, though, that he told her exactly what we wanted him to say, so you can do everything according as planned."

Reed moved back to allow Llallana into the booth. Instead of sitting across from her, he joined her on the same seat. She turned to face him, her eyes glaring a warning now.

He smiled at her for the first time. He was really enjoying the way her eyes were so expressive. Despite the cold, hard facts he had read about her, there was so much contradiction about this woman. He certainly couldn't see any sign of the calculating woman who had led her friends into a trap. And she hadn't given in to Johnny Chic's sexual demands, which, for some reason, made him feel lighthearted all of a sudden.

He could sense the anger coming from her, as if she was impatient about all this but needed to bide her time to get what she wanted. That was okay. He understood waiting. He did it a lot in his real job.

The booth blocked out a lot of the noise from the music. After all, this club was also a place to discuss business. "Something tells me you're going to dash out on me right after I give you what you want," he said as he slid in a little closer. "This is just insurance, Miss . . . ?"

When she remained silent, he lifted a brow inquiringly. "Usually I do business with people who have names. Besides, you obviously know mine." He put out a hand. "Hi, I'm R.C., but you can call me Reed. What can I do for you tonight?"

5

Maybe it was because she had just been
in his arms, or because it had been a few months
since she'd allowed herself to be this close to another man, but Lily was keenly aware of Reed sitting
so near. She suddenly realized how much she had
avoided this kind of proximity with a man—not that
it had been difficult, as she had been on the run with
a bunch of teenagers and young women. But she
knew it had been mostly out of fear of her own
memories.

She had been running from herself and it had been
easy, because as long as she had had the cash to see
to all her charges' needs, she hadn't needed to have
contact with anyone from her old life—the friends
she'd abandoned, her shady business "acquaintances." In the back of her mind, she'd known she
would have to deal with her own fears sooner or
later, but she had been willing to make it as late as
possible.

But now, because of this passport situation, she'd
had to go back to her old life, which included dealing

with the kind of people who reminded her of what she was. And what she was, no matter how she avoided the truth, was very simple. She was Llallana Noretski, a woman of dubious background with shady motivations. Just like everyone around here. She drank down the glass of wine she had picked up on the way to the table.

"You can call me . . . Ambrosia."

She almost gave him her real name. That would have been stupid, since she was sure she was on several wanted lists.

However, the rush of just being the old Lily while dealing with Johnny Chic had brought back a bit of her old swagger. She knew how to deal with people like that. At that moment, when she had been smacking that lecher around, she had suddenly felt exhilaratingly free. Almost normal, in fact. She had walked with confidence toward R.C., the man Johnny had pointed out, with her focus on getting those passports from him. What could be so tough? She was used to dealing with gunrunners too, right? It felt good to just go with the flow again and not be suspicious of everyone's, as well as her own, actions.

Then, this man had surprised her by keeping her on the dance floor. That had been totally unexpected.

"That's unusual," Reed said. "Is that your real name?"

Lily studied the man sitting so close to her. She hadn't been held by a man since . . . "No," she said abruptly, "but does it matter?"

"It does to me," he said, cocking his head, his gaze quizzical. "I like to know whom I'm dealing with."

"Our meeting is business, not a date, so whether I'm called Mary or Ambrosia, what difference does it make?" She really should just get down to business, but it felt so good to spar with someone again. She hadn't realized how starved she was for interacting with people. It was difficult to have long conversations with her girls because of their age, and the nurse helping them out asked too many questions that she didn't want to answer. "How do I know R.C. is your real name?"

"Call me Reed," he corrected. "And yes, that's really my name. I like to be myself because it's easier. Being two or three different persons at the same time seems so unnecessarily difficult, don't you agree? I might confuse myself with myself. That wouldn't do."

Lily searched his face. He was too close to the truth, although he couldn't possibly know. He was just flirting. She had seen him doing it with that other woman with whom he'd been dancing—the same intense look in those eyes, the same tilt of the head, as if he was just enjoying being with a woman.

She hadn't really wanted to dance, but that look had changed her mind. It had had such a strange effect on her—enjoyable and uncomfortable at the same time. He made dancing into some kind of personal revelation, as if he wanted to see the woman inside her, and, again, to her surprise, her body had responded.

She didn't need to look too closely to know that Reed, if that was really his name, was easy on the eyes. Tall and, as far as she could tell from the lighting, blondish or light brown hair, the kind of face at which a woman would look twice. More than twice, she admitted as she studied him. It was the eyes— she was drawn to them. There was an easy smile on his face, but his gaze remained watchful. Killer eyes. She'd seen that look in men who lived at the edge of danger . . . like gunrunners.

"Like what you see?" he interrupted her thoughts.

Lily blinked. She probably shouldn't have stared at him this long. She didn't want to give him the idea that she was interested in anything but business. "I was talking to Johnny Chic," she said, ignoring his question, "and he told me you bought some passports from him."

"And if I did?"

"They are mine," she said. "I ordered them from him."

Reed shrugged. "He took my money, so they are now mine."

"You don't understand," Lily said. "I ordered those passports in a batch, and Johnny sold part of my order to you."

He shrugged again. "So? Order from him again."

"I need them now. Tonight. I'll pay you for them." She narrowed her eyes at him, although he wasn't smiling, and added, "with cash, not favors. I don't think you want to end up like Johnny."

"I don't think you can afford me, Ambrosia."

It was stupid. Why did she want to hear her name on his lips? "How much?" she insisted. "Look, I really need the passports."

"I saw the batch he took mine out of," Reed said, stroking his chin. "There's quite a few of them. Surely you don't need that many, unless you're going around the world a few times. Why do you need so many of them?"

Lily shook her head. "My business. How much did you pay Johnny?"

"I'm into weapons, sweetheart, what do you think the exchange rate was?"

She should have guessed. A few months out running around in a daze appeared to have slowed her thinking process down, too. She needed to be smart here. And persuasive. "Look, Reed," she said, smiling and looking directly into his eyes, "what if I pay you double the street price that Johnny charges for those passports? You can get new ones and have some pocket change. I really have to have the ones in your possession right now."

"Why?"

"What difference does it make why?" she asked, frowning, feeling exasperated.

"Curiosity, I guess. Like I said, that's quite a few you ordered. You aren't one of those child smugglers, are you? Selling babies and kids to desperate couples overseas, that sort of thing. I really hope not."

Lily stared at him in disgust. How dare he think that of her?

"I don't do business with human traffickers," he continued, his eyes still watching her in that intense way that pulled at her insides, "although you don't seem the type that would sell girls to men looking for mail-order wives. But then one never knows."

"You think I'm running a sex slave ring?" Lily asked slowly.

It was getting really annoying the way he kept looking at her like that. It was as if he was waiting for her to do something.

"Why else would you need so many passports? How much do you make per child? No wonder it's urgent for you . . . someone must be paying a lot for these kids. Young girls are the premium, aren't they?"

Rage boiled over rational thought. Without thinking, Lily reached out and grabbed him by the front of his jacket. If she hadn't been sitting down, she would have kicked him and beaten him to a pulp. The idea that he thought that she would do that to girls and children . . . that she would take advantage of . . .

He didn't resist when she jerked him forward angrily. Instead, he braced himself by putting both his arms on the wall behind her, trapping her face between them. She stared up, suddenly aware that his lips were a few inches away from hers. His gaze held hers, alert and watchful, with a hidden emotion she couldn't quite understand. Her heart was thundering in her head, and she fought the aggressiveness that had risen so suddenly. She had to stay in control. Maybe it hadn't been a good idea to think she could be herself again.

This flower is a very complex creature.

Reed really didn't understand it, but sometimes he thought Arch still talked to him. One of the first things Arch had given him was a book called *The Little Prince,* and ever since his friend had died, Reed had found himself hearing quotes from that book. Lines would pop up out of nowhere and it would make sense.

"Let me make it very clear, mister," Llallana said, her hands still on him, "I don't sell or abuse women and children. As far as I'm concerned scum who do should be hung, drawn, and quartered. What I do with the passports is my business, but it has no connection with . . ."

She paused and bit her lip. There was consternation on her face. Reed understood. She had caught herself in a lie. Her business did have something to do with human trafficking, but her reluctance to lie to him was intriguing.

He looked at Lily Noretski and again thought of that flower in the book, which had appeared out of nowhere, demanding all of the little prince's attention. Lily caught his attention like no one ever had, with that outward exotic beauty and those thorny secrets. Being near her like this, he had the strange urge to make her tell him all her fears so he could take them away from her.

"Maybe, maybe not," he said softly.

She didn't know it, but he was her guardian and her executioner. He had to make sure she wasn't a danger to society, that she couldn't be used by those who had programmed her mind. It was much easier to just follow orders and sight a target through the crosshairs of a weapon, but Lily had somehow slipped under his skin and made herself more than that.

So cool. So confident, treating him as if she knew exactly how people like him behaved. He wanted to push her, show her the passion that he knew was there. And thanks to GEM training, he knew exactly how. He knew her weaknesses because they were in her CIA files, so he had used them against her to see whether she still had the same core beliefs.

He was a bit surprised at himself, actually. He was enjoying this charade more than he'd thought he would. *Be careful, Joker, emotions blind people.*

"Isn't there any way I can convince you?" she asked, pulling him closer.

The heat of her anger was very real. The passion in her eyes, the dangerous edge to her voice, the spontaneous way she'd struck out at him. He let her slide her hands inside his jacket, molding her hands down his chest, curious to see how far she would go. At the same time, he felt like a bastard because he didn't like manipulating her. But he had to know.

There was total silence from his listening partners. He realized that they were observing him as well as Lily, gauging his actions and reactions. Hawk had told him that their organization's idea of teamwork was a far cry from the SEALs'. They would let him do anything and everything he wanted, as long as they achieved their objective. He understood now that that meant they wouldn't interfere with him unless he asked them to.

Her hands urged him to come closer. He didn't resist her.

"Let me find a way," she murmured softly, her breath brushing his lips.

She kissed him tentatively, almost as if she was afraid of the act itself, then, when he didn't respond, she deepened the kiss, slipping her tongue into his mouth.

He was very conscious of his silent eavesdroppers. They were all women and didn't need to see to know what was happening. He pulled away a little. Lily slid her hands lower. He went still. He hadn't thought she would . . .

But there was no time for thought as he felt her tugging at his shirt. Her tongue tangled with his, becoming bolder. She tasted sweet, with a hint of wine. In spite of himself, he wanted more, his tongue taking the initiative, chasing hers as he found more sweetness in her mouth. He felt her hand going lower still, pausing at his belt for a second, before bypassing it for the zipper.

His body responded like lit dynamite. Her tongue was too insistent, her hands too damn clever.

This time Reed resisted the urge to continue. He moved his hands from the wall and placed them on her shoulders, forcing her back as he broke away from her kiss.

Her eyes were so dark that he couldn't see the pupils. "What's the matter?" she asked. "Don't you like this?"

Too damn much. "Your hands are in my pants, lady," he told her. "I think you can tell I like it. But I can also tell you're just manipulating me, and that I don't like. If you really want to convince me, I prefer to do this sort of business somewhere quiet, with less distraction, and with me calling the shots."

Her eyes narrowed. "I could hurt you right now."

"Then you won't get my passports."

Their eyes locked for a few seconds. "I haven't traded cash for my passports yet. Johnny's holding onto them till I come back with yours," she told him. Her hands moved leisurely, and she smiled at his response. "You wouldn't be saying no if your underwear hadn't been in my way."

He had a feeling she was right on that point. He had been warned that because of her past, Lily was a woman who wanted total control of every situation, including sex. He had been prepared, yet he hadn't expected his own attraction to her to be so deep.

He gently dislodged her hands, wondering whether he could zip up his pants sitting down. "Somehow I think you always get your way with men," he said.

Her smile disappeared. "I used to," she said. Rubbing her hands on her thighs, she added, her voice wry, "I must be losing my touch."

It was that odd humor of hers that popped up suddenly that got to him. The woman hid everything behind a smile and a sarcastic comment. He caught her hands and brought them to his lips. He kissed her knuckles softly. "Let's go to Johnny's office," he said.

As he followed her from the booth, he couldn't help but notice the long length of her legs and the sway of her hips. For sure, a stack of passports wouldn't easily fit in that outfit she was wearing. He hadn't the faintest idea how he was going to bring the conversation from sex to weapons, especially when his own body was having ideas of its own about which was the more important topic. He opened the door to Johnny's office for her and indicated that he would wait outside. He wanted to show her that he wasn't that interested in her business with the other man.

She sauntered in. "*Dobro*, Johnny," she said in Croatian, "good to see you decent."

Reed hid his amusement. *The flower is a very complex creature . . .* She was a combination of fragility and strength, trying to camouflage her softness with a thorny outside. Maybe if he took the time, he could get her to tell him more about what was going on inside her head. But he didn't have that much time.

She reappeared quite quickly, a bag in her hand. His amusement grew. Johnny must have learned his lesson from their last encounter.

Lily gripped the bag in her hand tightly. She must be out of her mind. She had no idea what she was going to do once she and Reed were alone. What had possessed her to kiss and touch him like that?

She was playing with fire, being as reckless as she

used to be when it had come to doing business on the shady side. Allowing herself so much free rein had summoned back all the things she wanted to keep out of her life—her wild mood swings, her runaway tongue.

She looked up, startled, when Reed reached out and caressed the side of her face. "He didn't give you any trouble, did he?"

She shook her head, surprised at his concern. "Just a little mad about being tied up before," she said, then smiled and added, "I don't think I'm welcome here any more."

The way she was going, Amber would be losing all her information business clientele. Another wrong she was doing to her friend.

"You weren't planning on coming back anyway," Reed said, surprising her with his seeming ability to read her mind.

She studied him surreptitiously as they walked through the noisy crowd again. The lighting close to the entrance was brighter, and she could now see the amusement in his eyes. That riled her up. Did he find her attempts to seduce him *funny*?

She frowned at her strong emotional reaction. Why did he have this odd effect on her? She was too aware of him, especially when he looked at her. She had this uncomfortable feeling that he could see right through her lies, which was silly. She was, if nothing else, very good at hiding her pain from everyone. But he had managed to unnerve her just now—so much so that she'd almost lost it when he'd mentioned that she might be connected to the human trafficking trade.

Her rage had been like a sudden full blast of heat from the furnace. Her only outlet had been either violence or—

The next thing she'd known, she'd found herself kissing Reed—a total stranger—trying to make him lose some of his damn cool. And in the back of her mind, she'd known she'd just been doing what she had always done in the past whenever she'd felt the need to exert control: used her sexuality to beat them at their game.

Only this time, the man had resisted her, wouldn't give himself to her. She was aroused. That he was too was pretty obvious. Remembering the proof of *that,* she shoved one hand into her pocket. She couldn't help wondering why he had stopped her, something no man had ever done before.

She had come to her senses then. Now she wasn't sure what she was going to do next. She'd deliberately kept her relationships as brief and noncommittal as possible, and even though she understood why now, it was still something she wasn't proud of. It had been so easy in the past; if she had felt a bit out of kilter, or if she had seen one too many sexually battered girls, she'd gone out and found someone to sexually dominate. It was as if she'd won a battle, if not the war. She closed her eyes for a second. Except the last time she became intimate with a man, she had felt something more . . . and then, the cell phone had rung. . . .

Cold air beat at her face. They had made their way to the entrance, by the coatroom. She gave the girl her claim ticket.

"Are you parked nearby?" Reed asked.

"I took the metro," she said.

"I came in my car," he said. "It's not parked very far from here, by the bridge."

He was so matter-of-fact about it. "Who said I'm coming with you?" she asked, annoyed.

He helped her into her jacket. "Changed your mind? I thought we had an agreement."

She turned around, cocking her head to one side as she buttoned her coat. "Really? And what's this agreement?" Men assumed so much, she mused.

"That we're going somewhere private. That you'll let me call the shots," he said, his voice suddenly low, with that American drawl that was both sexy and arrogant.

She hadn't been able to tell before, but his eyes were a mixture of blue and gray. Everything about this man was a mixture. The dance exhibitionist and the polite boy who opened doors and helped women into coats. The hot desire in his kiss and the reserved coolness in the way he'd pushed her away.

"I don't let anyone call the shots," she told him.

"Then we have a problem, since you want something from me," he said. He bent and lifted the weight of the bag dangling in her hand, bounced it several times, and added softly, "and you have something I want."

Lily had spent most of her life in the company of men who gave crudity a whole new meaning. No one had ever aroused her interest with such a simple suggestive line before. But then, in the past, she hadn't been willing to give any man what she had.

It occurred to her that she wasn't feeling the usual disgust that always popped up when a man talked to her this way. She searched his face, looking for an answer. That's when she noticed the traveling red dot that was moving along the wall, then across his chest, looking for a target.

She didn't have time to shout a warning. Lily pushed Reed to one side as hard as she could, and they both crashed against the entrance door.

Reed slammed into hard wood. Someone who had been behind him screamed in pain. A quick glance. He registered the splatter of blood on her clothes before people got in the way. The noise level rose as some of them realized the woman had been shot and everyone started to panic.

He took hold of Lily's hand so as not to lose her, and, pushing the door, he got out of the crushing humanity. Others followed them into the cold night air.

"How did you know?" he asked, his breath coming out in puffs.

"Someone's using a laser sight."

Another person screamed. Reed immediately

tugged Lily back into the crowd. Someone was target shooting, and he had a bad feeling it wasn't random.

"Run," he ordered.

"Where?"

Somewhere dark, where they wouldn't be easy targets. "We're sitting ducks if we stay out here," he said and began to run into the dark alley by the club.

"That wasn't us, Reed," Nikki's voice suddenly came in his earpiece. "Are you sure you're the target?"

"Yes," Reed replied. "They were standing close to us."

"What?" Lily asked as she kept up with him.

"I said two people were hit. Do you think we're being followed?"

"I don't know," Lily answered.

But Reed wasn't really talking to her. If someone was after them, he was going to need Nikki's and Amber's help to protect Lily. Except for a small firearm, he didn't have any other weapons on him.

"T.'s checking the situation right now."

He looked back. The distinct glare of a flashlight lit up parts of the darkness.

"I think my question just got answered." He took out his weapon. He didn't appreciate being on the other end of a hunt.

"I have a small weapon too," Lily said. "There might be more than one assailant."

"Stay behind me," he said, hoping she would be one of those females who didn't get riled up at being told what to do. He didn't want anyone in front of him when he sighted his target.

She didn't say anything. He slowly moved forward, gliding along the wall, watching the spotlight move closer as it searched one side of the alley and then the other. He pulled a crumbled piece from the wall. He counted to ten as he gauged where the target was, then threw the piece in the opposite direction. The beam of light immediately swung toward the sound.

Reed dove forward and did a body roll. He started shooting, the blasts from his semiautomatic reverberating back and forth against the alley walls. The flashlight did a crazy flip and landed on the ground in several bounces as his bullets connected. His target was down; gasps of pain echoed eerily.

Reed got on his feet and bent to pick up the flashlight. His target, a male, tried to get up. He stepped on the man's arm as he shone the light on the man's face. He didn't recognize him. "Who are you?"

"We're sending T. out there to pick him up," Nikki said in his ear.

Lily came up beside him. "I don't know him."

As she bent down to inspect him, another shot rang out and she yelped. Reed immediately tossed away the flashlight. He couldn't see where she had been hit; not wanting to waste time, he swung her over his shoulder and took off in the opposite direction from the shot. He hoped no one was on the other side of the alley.

"Another shooter," he reported, running as fast as he could. He hoped T. was okay. "Are you all right?"

"I'm alive," Lily said, "but it's hard to breathe upside down, Reed. Put me down."

"In a minute." He looked around when he reached

the end of the alley. He slid Lily off his shoulder. "Tell me where you've been hit."

"No time. Let's get out of here first." She started running across the street. "You said your car is parked somewhere. Anywhere near here?"

"See that little bridge? Over there." She seemed to be running fine. Reed caught up with her. "When we reach the other side, dodge around the parked cars for protection."

Spoken too soon. The words had scarcely left his lips when a car skidded into view, moving at a speed that spelled *Coming at you, stupid*.

"Run, run, run!" he yelled.

They raced hard toward the bridge, their shoes clacking on the wet cobbled road. They had almost reached the other side when the car accelerated even more, its tires screeching like banshees. It was coming straight for them.

Lily veered off to the left. The car careened in her direction.

"Get away while you can!" she yelled. "They're after me!"

As if he would actually abandon her and let some car run her over. Reed followed in her direction and grabbed her hand. They reached the edge of the embankment. There wasn't any option left at this point. They plunged into the darkness together.

6

I'm going to die.

Years ago, egged on by her older friends, Lily had jumped off the highest diving board at the local swimming pool. She remembered the feeling of indecision that split second before the running leap into the open air, twenty meters above the water. She hadn't known anything but the doggy-paddle at that time. She'd almost drowned.

She felt herself tumbling in the air, her stomach left somewhere above her, her hands flailing and grasping at nothing. She thought she heard herself yelling, but she wasn't sure, since everything was masked by some loud drum beating in her head.

The splash into the water was painful. The water was icy cold, soaking through her jacket immediately, as she sank deeply. She opened her eyes. She couldn't see anything. Her hair was caught on something. Holding her breath, she clawed at the darkness, kicking hard with her feet. It was a losing fight—her clothes had become too heavy.

Her breath released in desperate bubbles as she

pulled at the jacket on her body. She took in several inadvertent mouthfuls of water and choked. In desperation, she reached up and found air. Her hands were above water.

Air! . . . She kicked as hard as she could. *Come on, Lily, kick harder.* But that precious air was out of reach and her strength was disappearing fast. The water felt like thick molasses. She took another swallow of water, and, choking, out of air, she sank.

Something pulled hard, and suddenly Lily's head was above water. She gasped as air filled her lungs. She coughed out water. Oh God, air. She struggled to stay afloat.

"Hang on, don't struggle." She recognized Reed's voice, even though she couldn't see anything. "I've got you. Just let go. I've got you."

But she was sinking, and her body refused to obey as she panicked. She desperately clung to the body next to her, thrashing at the water that seemed determined to pull her back in.

"I've got you," she heard a voice keep repeating. Why couldn't she see anything? Why couldn't she move? She had to get out. She didn't want to die. She pushed hard at Reed, trying to climb on top of him.

Somehow, he evaded her. She sank into the dark water again. Oh God, no. Then she was pulled back out. Reed was behind her this time and she couldn't get at him. Exhausted, she finally went still.

She didn't know how long it took them to reach the riverbank. A voice was murmuring in her ear, but she couldn't make out the words. Then she was hauled up against something solid. She opened her eyes. There was light and she could see again.

"Shhhh," the voice said.

She coughed out water, her hands finally finding something she could hang on to. She laid her cheek against it as she tried to calm her racing heart and thoughts.

Reed's body covered hers from behind. It was strangely comforting, even though she couldn't really feel anything. "Shhh . . ." he repeated. "Stay quiet. I don't know what happened to the car that was coming at us. They could be up there looking for us."

His voice was so unflustered, the quiet words cutting through her emotions. Lily drew in more air, her breath coming out in short little gasps. Stay quiet. She could do that. Even though she felt like screaming and crying.

She drew in another breath. She was in danger. She hadn't felt so helpless and afraid in years, when those men had . . . Her eyes opened wide. Oh no. She wouldn't go back to those memories just because she was frightened. She clenched her fists around the clumps of roots and plants. *Pull yourself together, Lily.* She willed her breath to stop laboring.

"I don't hear or see anything," Reed said, after what seemed like an eternity. "There isn't time to be careful. We've got to get out of the water or freeze to death. Here, step on my knee and climb out."

Lily tried to pull herself up, but her soaked clothing impeded her. She found Reed's braced knee in the water and used it as support, climbing out slowly. Her water-clogged jacket weighed about a thousand pounds. She stood up on land and stared at the puddle forming at her feet. She had lost one shoe.

She heard Reed climbing out behind her, and she turned slowly, like some old, dawdling woman. Mud and dirt plastered every inch of him. His clothes were an unrecognizable brown. She probably didn't look much better as she watched him peel his jacket off and struggle with his jeans.

"What . . . are you doing?" Her teeth were clattering.

"Trying to get the car keys out of my jeans," he said, working his fingers into his wet pockets. She realized that she had spoken in Croatian and he was answering in English. "We're right under the bridge, so my car isn't very far away, if it's still there."

Lily marveled at his absolute control, as if he jumped from a bridge and swam in a muddy river all the time, whereas all she seemed to be able to do was admire her dirty clothes. She hugged herself. It was chilly.

She heard sirens in the distance. "Do you think someone called the police?" she asked, reverting back to English.

"Probably. There were some shootings at the club, remember?" He pulled out the keys. "Got them."

"I don't want them to find me," she told him. She didn't want to explain anything to the police.

He looked at her. "If they're at the club, they'll be searching the alley soon."

She remembered the man lying there. She shook her head. "I can't be seen."

"Nor can I," he said. He offered her his hand. "Come on."

There was nothing else she could do. She took his hand and trudged up the steep riverbank, her shoeless foot slipping on the icy parts. She concentrated on each step, trying to ignore the bite of the cold. She shivered involuntarily.

It took all her strength to climb the steep bank. They finally reached the street level and stood in the semidarkness. There was no sign of the other car.

"There's my car. The blue one. Hang on a moment." Reed looked around. "We'll have to hurry over to it. Just in case."

She understood his unspoken warning. Someone might be out there lying in wait for them. *For her,* she corrected. She had to keep her wits about her. Someone was after her. She nodded, then, looking at the vehicle he'd indicated, she took in a deep breath as she gathered up all her remaining strength.

"I'm ready," she said.

They ran—she hobbled, really—toward the car. He opened the passenger door and she tumbled inside. He was beside her in seconds. Moments later, they were out on the road, with the heater on full blast.

"Where were you shot?" he asked after a few minutes.

She shrugged. "I don't know, but my shoulder hurts like hell. It can't be serious, since I'm still talking."

"You're shivering and your teeth are clattering. Your body's concentrating on getting your body temperature back to normal right now."

She glanced at him. "Are you a doctor now, too?"

His eyes gleamed at her through the mud. "I want you to slowly ease out of your jacket, then your clothes."

She suddenly realized her clothes were probably destroying the interior of his car. "I'm sorry," she said, "your car—"

"Ambrosia, your not catching a chill's more important at the moment. Take off the damn coat."

"I can't. My shoulder hurts." It was throbbing really hard now. She couldn't think straight, couldn't focus on anything at all. Wet coat. She played with the zipper. Cold. She moved closer to the heater. She kept tugging at the zipper, but it was stuck. Her foot . . . she could feel her foot again. "Where are you taking me, by the way?"

"Somewhere safe. Lie back, close your eyes, Ambrosia. I'll get you out of your clothes myself."

Lily leaned back into the seat. It actually felt good to be told what to do. She released a sigh and gave in to the pain and exhaustion.

"Call me Lily," she muttered, closing her eyes. She thought she heard him say her name aloud before she drifted off into welcome nothingness.

Greta had forgotten how easy it was to curse in German. Just add the word *shit* in front of everything. The person on the other end of the cell phone wasn't happy with her report. She wasn't too happy herself, but she had better control of her vocabulary than he did.

Finally, she snapped the cell phone shut. She would deal with that later.

She coldly looked at the scrawny idiot who was being held up by her two men. According to reports, he was the powerful owner of this club. He didn't look that powerful. He was so skinny she could break him in half. "Talk," she ordered.

"I don't know anything."

"They tell me you broker deals. This," she said, giving the office a sweeping glance, "club's just a front. So, tell me what you arranged between the two of them."

Johnny Chic studied her for a moment. He didn't appear to be afraid of her or her men. "I do broker deals. You must be new around here if you don't know who I am. How did you get into my club? And how dare you cause trouble? My backers won't appreciate the police sniffing around here tonight. A woman who's trying to break into our kind of business should be more careful who she's threatening."

Greta had half a mind to kill him. But she'd been warned that Johnny Chic had many friends in the weapons business and that killing him off would anger a few important people whose deals might be underway. Damn that *Scheisskerl*, Gunther. He had given her just enough information but not enough. She realized now, a little belatedly, that he wanted to get her into trouble. Men and their little power games.

This was what ten years out of real action could do to someone. She had wrongly assumed too many things.

"I'm only interested in the blonde and the man," she said.

"Every woman here is a blonde. That's a club rule," Johnny politely pointed out. He smiled. "I love blondes."

She'd noticed everyone here with that strange blond wig. The loud booming music outside had given her a headache, and this man was wearing her patience thin. "I'm talking about the one who came into your office. Lily Noretski."

He shrugged. "I talked to nobody by that name." He looked up again. "That name sounds familiar, though. I've heard it somewhere before. Perhaps you could tell me a bit more about your situation and I might help you out, but first, you have to get these goons off me. I don't like being manhandled."

Greta met his direct gaze, trying to gauge how much trouble this man was going to cause her. Since right now she needed information from him, she would let him have the advantage. She nodded at her men to let him go. Johnny brushed imaginary dust off his shirt then went to sit on his couch, crossing his legs and reposing back, with his arms stretched across the back of the sofa. She didn't like the satisfied glimmer that had entered his eyes.

"It's been a particularly rough night," he said, a strange smile on his face. "I have a feeling I know who you're talking about, but you're dealing with

Johnny Chic and you've insulted me by coming to my club without dyeing your hair or wearing a wig. For that, any information is now going to cost you double. Your causing trouble at my club will add another twenty percent surcharge. And, for roughing my new clothes up, there'll be another ten percent fine."

Greta narrowed her eyes, taking a few steps toward the man sitting in front of her. "Don't threaten me."

He shook his head. "I don't threaten anyone. This is my business. You're in my world so you've got to do things my way. Kill me and you won't get out of here alive. And even if you do, whoever hired you won't be happy because my backers will come after all of you."

"You don't know who I am," Greta said softly.

He shrugged. "The cameras in this place will identify you to my handlers. Kill me and they'll know everything about you within a few hours." He smiled again. "But I really don't use threats in my business. Treat me with respect and I'll broker a deal for you."

Greta walked around the office while she decided on her next steps. She didn't want to, but she had to compromise. The police were out there looking around. It wouldn't be long before they found the body in the alley. Fortunately, she had gotten there before Lily and her companion had gotten a name. She didn't want anyone to know about her just yet.

The fact that the police weren't swarming into this club right now hinted at how much pull Johnny Chic had with the local law departments. Maybe she hadn't lost everything yet; maybe Gunther had been lying about Lily selling the device. These new covert games were the absolute *Scheissdreck*. A sense of frustration edged her temper. Ten years ago, no one would've dared to play with her like this.

She turned back to Johnny Chic, plastering a smile on her face. "I apologize," she said pleasantly. "I've been rude, but I didn't understand. I don't need you to broker a deal, just answer a few questions. Would it soothe your ruffled feelings if I told you that my agency will pay you what you ask and double, *if* the information you give me is correct?"

Johnny smiled back. "My information's always correct. And yes, the terms are accepted. If you'll make the necessary calls and wire the cash right now to the account number I'm going to give you, as soon as I have confirmation, I'll answer all your questions."

Of course she wasn't going to call headquarters and ask for money. Gunther would be waiting for that piece of news. No, she wouldn't give him that kind of fun. She'd just have to use some of the money her poor dead nephew had left behind in their joint account.

"Of course. Just write down your price and account number," she said.

She looked at the note he passed to her. It was an exorbitant amount, but it had taken her this long to catch up with Llallana, and she wasn't going to walk away empty-handed now.

Greta made her call, knowing very well that she was on the losing end of the deal here. However, she felt that she deserved this loss for not being prepared. She hadn't wanted Lily to be killed off yet, and these people Gunther had sent were obviously not following her orders. He'd wanted her to fail, wanted her comeback to be tinged with failure.

No fucking way, as an American would say. She'd spent ten years in the States observing how Americans messed up their lives when it came to preparation for the future. She'd always had a future goal in mind, and she would get it.

She finished the transaction over the phone. One quick transmittal and all that money gone. Sometimes she hated modern technology. She gave Johnny a brilliant smile.

"All done. Now, shall we talk?"

She would take care of Gunther later.

Reed pulled into the underground garage and headed to the back. He wondered briefly whether he had done the right thing, then, glancing at the woman beside him, decided that it was the best option until he could contact T. and headquarters. That was, if T. was all right. The last time he had been able to communicate with Nikki, she had said that T. was going into the alley to investigate. When someone had shot at him and Lily, he hadn't stayed long enough to warn T.

The mic button on his jacket had disappeared in the river somewhere, and Nikki's end had been silent since that jump off the bridge. The receiver must not have liked water.

No phone, no sign of T., no communication, and possibly two snipers hunting them down. Not to mention the vehicle that had gone after them. If he had been alone—he glanced at Lily beside him—he could have gone into hiding and waited, even with his drenched clothing. But he didn't want to risk Lily's catching pneumonia. Besides, he still didn't know how serious her injury was.

Without a phone and with an injured woman, this was the first place that had come to mind; he knew he could enter without any questions asked.

She had remained unconscious through the drive. Damn. Not only had she been immersed in icy water but she'd also almost drowned. Her body was still in shock from the experience, as well as the loss of heat.

"Lily?" he called out, but she didn't even stir.

He stopped at the executive parking spots and parked right in front of the private elevator. No one was around.

Leaving the car on, he pulled at the door release, looking over at Lily again. She was out like a light. He frowned at the red stain mixed with the muddy streaks on her clothes. Damn it, how seriously hurt was she? Leaning over, he touched her cheek. Despite the heat being on, she felt like a block of ice.

He gave a curse and got out of the car quickly. There was a security box by the elevator, and he punched the required code, then the password. It asked for him to swipe his special ID card through the slot, but of course, he didn't have it on him. So he punched the No button. A moment later a voice came through the speaker.

"Can I help you, sir?"

"Get Petr on for me, please," Reed said.

"Yes, sir."

Out of habit, he checked the area while he waited, although he had made sure no one had followed him here. This particular part of the garage would usually be quiet.

"Mr. Vincenzio?"

"Yes, it's me, Petr, and I don't have an ID card to get into the elevator," Reed said. "Can you come down and accompany me up, please?"

"Of course. I'll be there in a few minutes. I'm sorry, we didn't know you were coming."

"It was a last-minute thing," Reed said dryly. "By the way, Petr, bring down a blanket, and I'll need someone you can trust to move the vehicle I came in."

"Yes, sir."

Reed went back to the car and waited, keeping a worried eye on Lily. She hadn't stirred. He thought of her struggling out in the water, almost drowning out there. He understood the fear. Being in water in pitch darkness took a lot out of one, especially after a jump like that. She hadn't been afraid of the height—she had made that jump without any hesitation.

He'd gone into the ocean at the darkest hours before, so the unexpected late-night swimming hadn't been a shock to his system at all. Training came like second nature. In the ocean, he'd had to rely on his underwater compass to tell him whether he was going up or down, but tonight, he'd just kicked and allowed himself to float to the surface. He was just glad that it hadn't been shallow water, or they'd have been dead meat already.

After his eyes had adjusted to the darkness, he had quickly realized that Lily was in trouble. Everything had been a blur as he'd gone into search mode, looking for telltale signs of splashing. He'd turned one way and then the other, feeling the freezing water more and more, trying to figure out the most likely place she'd have landed. For one sickening moment, when he'd thought she was gone, something very unusual had happened—a strange but familiar tightness had squeezed his insides.

If he hadn't been so focused on finding Lily, Reed would've stopped to register and analyze it. He hadn't felt this way since the first time, when he'd been assigned to a child hostage situation and he'd had to take out the target before the hostile killed the hostage. He had failed.

When he'd spotted those hands above the water . . . he couldn't describe the sense of fierce relief that had engulfed his whole being as he'd swum hard toward them. Nothing else had mattered. He'd just wanted to get her out of danger.

The elevator door opened and two men came out, one of them holding a box. They stopped short at the sight of him.

"Are you all right, Mr. Vincenzio?" the older man asked, a concerned look entering his eyes.

"I'm fine, Petr. Sorry for dropping by so suddenly. Now you know why I couldn't walk through the lobby," Reed said wryly. He opened the passenger door. "Thank you for coming down so quickly."

Petr took in the whole situation at a glance and, nodding at the man standing by him, he took a few steps forward. "Do I need to call a doctor?"

"Not yet. I'll let you know when I get to the suite. I'm afraid I'll be muddying the carpet up a bit."

Petr nodded briskly. "Yes, Mr. Vincenzio. Here's the blanket. Carlo here will drive the car out to the service station."

"Thank you."

Reed slowly slid Lily out of the car so he could gather her into his arms. Petr helped him wrap the blanket around her. At the touch of her cold body, the older man exchanged a glance with him. Reed knew he probably hadn't missed the blood either.

"Go ahead, Carlo, and call me when you get back," Petr said, then followed Reed into the elevator. He punched the floor number. After a few moments' silence, he added, "Here's the keycard to the suite and elevator, sir. I'll send up a fresh change of clothing and hot cocoa for you—and the lady."

"Thanks again, Petr. I really appreciate your taking care of things." Reed frowned worriedly at Lily. He'd never seen a woman in such deep sleep. He was pretty sure she hadn't fainted in the car. "Be on call, just in case I need medical help."

"Yes, sir. I'll also inform your father that you're here."

The ping of the elevator signaled their arrival at the floor. Reed paused by the open doors. "Not yet," he said. "I'll call him myself after I've taken care of my guest, if you don't mind. In fact, Petr, shut off the phone system till I say so."

"How would you get hold of me, sir?"

"From the elevator box downstairs."

"Of course."

Reed didn't want any interruptions for as long as possible, especially from his family.

The suite was more a spacious penthouse, with every possible amenity to make life very comfortable. His family used it for short stays as well as a guest suite for business clients.

He strode past the elegantly decorated living room into the master bedroom. His shoes were probably leaving mud marks on the white carpet. He'd forgotten how huge the place was as he walked into the adjoining bathroom, which was the size of a small bedroom.

Hesitating a moment, he lay his bundle down carefully on the small lounge chair by the tub. She mumbled something as she stirred.

"Lily," he called softly.

She looked so frail cocooned in that blanket. When she didn't answer, he went to the shower stall, looked around, and turned on all four of the sprays. There was a tiled seating area at the back wall for use when the bath was converted into a steam room. He played with the spray positions, so that the spray from the shower heads would hit back there. As he waited for the water to heat up, he took the opportunity to get out of his soggy shoes. He knelt before Lily and took off the one shoe that was left. He hesitated, wondering what her reaction would be when she woke up and found herself in the shower with him. Only one way to find out.

He got up and opened the door to the shower. Steam poured out. He went back and gathered Lily into his arms again, stepping into the stall. Spray from four different directions hit their bodies.

He shook the water out of his eyes, then headed for the back ledge. She made a small sound and wrapped her arms around him, tucking her head under his chin. Reed looked at the muddy rivulets streaming off their clothes onto the tile. He could smell the river in their clothes. Maybe it was better Lily didn't wake up.

He had to hand it to Petr. Beyond the initial show of surprise, his father's regional assistant hadn't asked anything about his disheveled appearance. Petr had always had that unruffled demeanor that was butlerlike. In his quietly efficient way, Petr administered Reed's father's hotels in the Eastern European division.

It took a minute or two before Reed actually felt blood flowing back into his legs. Used to hostile conditions in his job, he had ignored the bite of the cold. He checked Lily's face tucked against his collarbone. Her cheeks were flushed, her wet eyelashes incredibly dark against her skin. He slowly reached out and wiped the dirty smudges off her face, the pads of his fingers moving over her nose and her lips. Funny how vulnerable she looked when she was out like this. His hand combed her hair away from her face.

"Cold," she mumbled, her voice a soft echo in the stall.

"I know," he said.

There was no getting around it. He had to get her out of her clothes. Being in the icy water and wearing wet clothes had made her body lethargic. It was natural for the body to shut down and go to sleep. Besides, he couldn't put her into bed in these clothes.

His hand reached around to the back of her top, and he slowly slid the zipper down. She stirred as the water hit her bare skin.

"I'm taking these dirty clothes off," he said to her, hoping she could hear him. She didn't say anything.

He paused. She wasn't wearing a bra. He took a breath, then started to peel off the wet dress.

"Hurt," she told him.

Her shoulder. Like it or not, he had to see how badly she was injured. And to do that . . . he pulled her top off her shoulders, sliding her arms off him so he could see her front. There was a nasty crimson gash on her forearm, but it wasn't bleeding profusely. The bullet must have grazed her when she had leaned down to look at their assailant.

Get her clean first, then take care of the wound. Reed pulled the rest of the fabric down to Lily's waist, trying to ignore the soft skin revealed underneath. Water washed over her as he tried to take the top off. He pulled it lower, his fingers working around the edges, concentrating on the flesh rather than what part of her body he was touching. He then realized that it was the kind of dress a woman had to pull over her head.

Reed looked down again. He couldn't keep his eyes from wandering. Her breasts were high and small, her nipples pink and erect. Drops of water settled on each areola, shimmering as they grew in size before toppling over, running down the sides of the soft mounds. He closed his eyes, took a deep breath.

"Dress," he told himself firmly. "Off."

He gathered her upper body against his bare chest as he worked with the zipper in the back. The damn thing just wasn't coming off easily. All the while he could feel her slick breasts against him, sliding up and down, as he struggled with the top. He thought of the pink, erect nipples. Not good. His jeans were growing tighter by the second.

He tugged harder and heard the material tear. It came off easily then. He ran a tentative hand over her shoulder, wiping off the red and brown streaks. He caught sight of the bar of soap sitting on the dish nearby. He paused. This was going to be harder than he thought.

He looked down at Lily again. Okay, he could skip soaping the front. She would understand. . . . The thought made him smile wryly. He looked lower and shook his head. Whatever happened to underwear? He could see right through the thin material of her dark panty hose. There were tears here and there, caked with clumps of mud. Those had to come off too.

Water splashed on his head as he leaned forward and hooked his thumb under the material, tugging it downwards. He'd never taken panty hose off a woman before. They didn't slide off like he'd thought they would. His hand went lower. He closed his eyes and pulled hard. He could feel the clingy material pulling away and felt the bare skin with his knuckles. He patted the area awkwardly.

You can't get her clean if you don't open your eyes, Vincenzio. Besides, he had to carry her out of the bathroom sooner or later.

It's just a human body. He had seen naked women before. Reed opened his eyes. And wished he hadn't. He was never going to get out of his jeans in this condition.

7

Lily had never felt such bone-deep cold
before. All she wanted to do was go back to that nice,
deep sleep. It had been the best she had had in
months, the kind of sleep that had no dreams;
dreams where she was always running.

Water. She was drowning all over again. She was
too exhausted to fight. Maybe that limbo feeling was
her dying or something. But the water wasn't cold
like before, it was deliciously hot. She could feel the
steam in the air as she breathed. She stirred.

Ouch. "Hurt," she said.

Someone was holding her very close. She could
hear a heartbeat thudding against her ear. She
wanted to open her eyes, to investigate, but even that
seemed like an impossible task. Her eyelids felt as if
someone had laid weights over them.

She felt hands on her, moving over her body
slowly. Someone was tearing off her clothes. An awful thought entered her mind. Maybe she was back at
the brothel. Maybe she was being . . . no, she didn't

want to wake up. She retreated back into the darkness again. It was always easier to be unconscious.

But the heartbeat pounding under her ear kept interrupting her sleep. It was strong, and it was beating faster. The water beating down on her body felt like a shower. What was she doing showering? Wasn't she in the river?

Snippets of memory entered her consciousness again. She remembered the car, the river, and then the awful cold. Reed. She opened her eyes to slits, peering out.

Her face was buried in someone's bare chest. In fact, from the way she was positioned, she was sitting on that someone's lap. She frowned. In a shower.

A hand slid up the length of her thigh, moving over her hip bone. Her body shuddered at the sensation.

"I know. I'm sorry your shoulder hurts," a voice said above her. It was Reed. And his heart was pounding like he was running. "Almost done here."

Lily realized he was talking to himself, that he wasn't aware that she was awake.

"Just a leg. Thigh. Kneecap."

A hand caressed her thigh and her kneecap. It was softly rubbing her skin. She had sensitive thighs and had to resist the urge to squirm.

"Other thigh. Other kneecap."

He was washing her. And naming her body parts while doing it. She frowned and was about to say something when she went very still. That hand had moved up higher. The sound of his heartbeat was echoing like thunder now. She felt her teeth biting down on her lower lip as he slid his hand between her thighs, the water feeling very warm. She bit down harder as the hand nudged intimately. There was a pause. The hand didn't move, as if Reed had encountered some problem.

Finally, it moved, sliding downward. Her leg was lifted at the bend of the knee and braced against the wall. Her legs parted. She heard a cough. Then his hand was pulling at something clinging to her skin. *Her leggings.*

"Inner thigh," the voice above her muttered. "The . . ."

There was silence. He moved, and her face was buried deeper into his chest as he leaned forward to . . . oh, my God. He could see everything.

"The . . . the . . ." He seemed to be at a loss over what to name the part, but his hand continued to pull off the rest of the legging under her. "Damn you, come off, will you?"

She could actually feel his sigh of relief when the material under her gave way. He moved away, and she stiffened again when water splashed onto her . . . ahhh . . .

She must have made a sound.

"Lily?"

She wasn't going to be caught awake with her legs spread open and hot water splashing right at . . . ahhh . . . She almost groaned aloud.

He moved again. Oh no, he blocked the water. Thank God. But her body certainly didn't agree. She kept her eyes closed as she felt herself lifted and then placed on a hard surface. She was on some kind of a seating area in this shower room. There was silence again. She knew he was looking at her, trying to see whether she was conscious. Hell no, she wasn't going to open her eyes and look into his.

"Lily?"

She didn't answer. Couldn't. Not when seconds ago, she had almost . . . Finally, after a few long moments of inactivity, she peeked. His back was toward her, his head bent in fierce concentration. She realized suddenly that he still had his jeans on and was trying to get the things off him.

Spray hit his body, and she could see how dirty his back was as brown rivulets ran down his equally muddy pants. He finally pulled the jeans down, squeezing out of the tough denim. Her eyes opened wide at the sight of his bare ass followed by muscular thighs.

"Fucking thing," he muttered, as he pulled and tugged.

She closed her eyes quickly, then couldn't stop from peeking again. She wondered whether the man was as magnificent to look at from the front. The back muscles of his calves stood out in cords as he finally freed himself from the jeans. Kicking them aside, he picked up the bar of soap and began to briskly lather himself.

He soaped his hair and face in the careless way only a man could, then turned to face one of the shower heads, his eyes shut. Lily was given a whole frontal view for a full five seconds. She caught sight of a wide, athletic chest that narrowed down at the waist. Magnificent pecs. Magnificent abs. Her eyes traveled lower. And a magnificent something protruding rather obviously.

She closed her eyes again, knowing that he would look in her direction as soon as the soap was gone from his head and face. It was good that the bathroom was steamy, because she certainly didn't feel cold any longer. In fact, her whole body felt flushed all over.

The water shut off. She heard him moving about, pushing the shower door open.

She was scooped up against a bare chest. She was very aware of her nakedness against his. He smelled clean. She had the insane urge to lick his skin, to taste him. He carried her out of the bathroom, where the air wasn't as steamy but his heat penetrated her cooling skin. She heard his strong heartbeat, and it was still at galloping speed.

Then she felt him lowering her gently. She swallowed as she felt his penis pushing hard against the side of her thigh as he laid her down on something soft.

"Jesus," he muttered, unceremoniously dropping her body onto the bed.

"Ouch!" she said, her eyes flying open.

He jumped back as if he had been burned. "Your shoulder. I'm sorry. I tried not to touch it, but—"

He stopped when he realized she was staring at his nakedness. He looked down at the obvious, then turned around and walked out of the room without another word.

Lily continued staring. Nice back. Nice ass. And up close, nice . . . front.

What was wrong with him? He was acting like some horny teenager.

Reed dried his hair with a towel and threw it with the pile of clothing on the bathroom floor. Nothing had gone the way it was supposed to.

Instead of negotiating with Lily Noretski about a missing weapon, instead of finding out whether she had sold it and whether she was still under the influence of mind control, he was naked with her in his family's penthouse suite. In his father's hotel. And his mind certainly hadn't been on missing weapons or sleeper cells.

He pulled another towel off the rack and wrapped it around him. He wasn't going to use the excuse of having a naked woman in his arms. He had trained himself to be unaffected by emotions, especially by feminine wiles. Not that Lily was practicing any feminine wiles on him.

He released a sigh, tucking the knot securely. That was it. She had been soft and pliant. She had really needed him to take care of her. His emotional distance had been culled from years of listening and watching his mother's calculated play on his emotions, and nothing about his mother was pliant in the least. But Lily hadn't been playing that kind of game—she had been direct at the club even though she had lied about her identity. She hadn't fooled him one bit with that tough girl act. There was something vulnerable about her, almost fragile. He had no idea how to stop the feeling of tenderness that engulfed him when he had her in his arms, like a helpless kitten left in his care, knowing that she needed him, even though she wasn't aware of it. It did strange things to him. Must be some entrenched genetic makeup in the male to take care of someone so lost and on her own.

"The flower . . ." Oh, stop fucking thinking about the stupid book. He had to get out there and act like who he was supposed to be . . . a former soldier running illegal weapons, doing one last final run for profit. He also had to make the woman lying on the bed in the other room think she was safe with him. He took the bathrobe off the hook. She was safe from everyone but him.

Lily was under the spread when he walked back into the room, not that it helped. He could remember every part of her shapely body, the long legs, the . . . ah, better not start naming body parts again. That was what had gotten him in trouble.

"This is for you," he said, showing her the bathrobe.

She looked at him, her eyes settling briefly on the towel around his lower body before quickly going back up to meet his. "Uh, where are we?"

"My best friend loaned me his hotel penthouse," Reed lied. "This is the only place I could think of at the time where I know we'll be safe."

"Safe . . ." She thought for a moment, her forehead furrowing. "I'm trying to remember everything. You saved me in the river. Thank you."

He nodded. "A bullet grazed your arm. How do you feel?"

"It hurts like hell," she admitted, glancing at the wound, "but definitely better than having one inside me."

"Yeah." She was so matter-of-fact, as if she had been shot at before. "Will you let me look at it and clean it up?"

Color tinged her cheeks, but again, she surprised him with an impish grin. "Why not? You've cleaned me up everywhere else."

His lips quirked. No games, always to the point. "Believe me, you wouldn't want to be wearing any of your clothes."

"Okay." She shifted under the blanket. "How long can we stay here?"

"Not sure," he said honestly. He had to make communication with several parties as soon as possible. "Actually, I've got to go tell someone we're here, so after I've taken care of that arm, I'm running down to make sure no one barges in on us or something."

"Are you sure we're safe here? Can't we just call someone?" She looked at the phone by the bed.

"Since I didn't tell anyone, the phone line's dead." This time he had to lie.

"Your friend trusts you so much that you can just pop into this place without calling him?"

He walked to the table where Petr had set the medical box. "Yeah," he said easily, taking out what he needed. "I'm very close to him. Someone like me has to have a place away from the usual fun and games, you know."

"I've never met a gunrunner without a hideout," she said from the bed. "This is nicer than most, from what I've seen."

He headed back to her. He could see she wasn't sure how to take him. He sat down by her, on her injured side. "So you associate with gunrunners a lot?"

"Some," she replied noncommittally. "Business only."

"Are some of them after you? The car was going straight for you." He unscrewed the bottle of iodine, then wet a big swab of cotton with it. "This is going to sting. Who wants to take you out?"

She tensed and winced at his first touch. She was damn lucky. It was the closest call to a bullet hole he had ever seen.

"Who's after you, Lily?"

Her frown deepened. "How did you . . . oh yeah, I told you." She sighed. "I don't know."

He glanced up. Her gaze was on her arm, so he couldn't look into her eyes. "Are you sure?" he asked gently. "You knew they were after you."

She shrugged. "It could be any number of reasons."

He examined the gash. "They're going to look for me now, too, you know. If you're hiding anything, let me know."

She finally looked up, her expression sober. "Don't we all have secrets? As soon as I'm able, I'll be out of your hair."

Not taking his eyes away from her, he pulled away the seal to the gauze. "You're forgetting something."

"What?"

"You need something from me."

She stared at him, her expression freezing. He knew she had just realized what he had known since he'd brought her here. "The passports . . ." She closed her eyes. "Oh my God, they're gone. I was holding onto them when I jumped. . . ."

Her shoulders slumped. She stayed that way as he continued to take care of the wound. He waited, knowing that she was running through her options. Even though the original plan hadn't included all the passports being gone, it was helping him tighten the screws on Lily. Still, he felt a twinge of reluctance to bring it up right now. It couldn't be a good feeling to be slowly forced into a corner.

"This is going to throb for a while. I have pain medication if you have trouble sleeping tonight," he said quietly. When she just shook her head, he added, "I'm going to tell someone we're here. Will you be all right alone?"

She nodded. "I'll be fine." She looked disinterestedly at her bandaged arm. "How long will you be gone?"

"Half an hour to an hour. I've got to get us clothes and food."

"How are you going out? Not in that towel."

"I'll make do with the bathrobe."

She frowned. "It's going to look weird."

"It won't. Lots of vacationers around here. I'll be right back."

He took the robe and went back to the bathroom. When he came out, he brought her a glass of water and some more towels.

"Will the phone be working when you get back? I need to get hold of somebody."

"I'll try to see whether I can get a cell phone."

"Okay."

He gave one last backward glance at the bedroom entrance. She looked lost in thought, lying there on the propped-up pillows, looking up at the ceiling.

"Lily?" He felt a need to comfort her, to take away that worried look. "It's going to be all right."

Lily looked at the shut door, listening for the sound that would tell her Reed had left. But there was nothing. She frowned. Maybe it was one of those heavy doors that closed slowly.

She looked around the bedroom again. From the ultra-huge bed she was in to the intricate furniture to the beautiful artwork hanging on the walls, it looked and smelled expensive. One of her many jobs dealt with art pieces, some of them stolen. Through the years, she'd learned to recognize the real from the fakes. Many of these were originals. This friend of Reed's had lots of money.

Which reminded her . . . She ran a weary hand through her damp hair. What the hell was she going to do now? How could she have forgotten about her bag? Granted, the passports would still have gotten destroyed, but she hadn't even given them a thought. Instead, she had been in that shower admiring a man's naked body.

She was totally useless. When she wasn't thinking, she reverted back to her stupid, silly self, the one who would forget, just because a handsome body happened to be in front of her, that other people were depending on her.

There was a time when she'd have immensely enjoyed the whole ridiculous experience. She wouldn't have minded sitting up and taking that bar of soap from Reed's hands. There was a time when seducing a man had been downright easy and she would have done it just to know that she could conquer that male body.

"Lily, you can't be like that any more," she muttered, picking up the towel Reed had left on the bed and starting to dry her hair. "Can't let your emotions take over."

She was afraid. If she let herself go, how long would it take before she forgot, and then before she knew it, she would pick up a cell phone. . . . She threw the towel on the floor in disgust. She couldn't use one, so how was she going to reach Tatiana?

Leaning over on one side of the bed, she touched the phone. Once would be okay, wouldn't it? Her finger hovered over the speaker button, but she was unable to push it. She took her hand away. She couldn't chance it, not until she got the girls away from her.

Lily sat up and kicked off the spread. She had to get out of here, get back to the girls and rethink this whole situation.

Pain shot up her whole side when she put weight on her arm as she got off the bed. Gasping, she fell back, tightly holding her bandaged arm as her body absorbed the shock, and waiting for the stars floating in front of her eyes to disappear. Minutes went by before the pain subsided. She hadn't realized how tender the areas around her neck, shoulder, and arm were.

Slowly, she made her way out of the bed, carefully sliding off the side. She let her injured arm hang loosely, trying not to jar it any further. Cracking the bedroom door slightly, she peered outside.

Reed was nowhere to be seen. She opened the door wider and hesitantly stepped outside, her bare feet clinging to the soft carpet. Her mouth gaped open as she took in her surroundings.

The place was incredible. The living room looked like one of those settings in an expensive magazine. Fireplace. Dark paneling. Even a whole wall filled with books. A plasma TV hung on the wall.

She walked through each room, looking at everything. Picking up the notepad by the phone, she read the letterhead and frowned. Hotel Palazzo, with the address. She walked to one of the windows and parted the drawn curtains a few inches.

She looked down. The street was way down there. She turned back to the living room, looking left and right for the main entrance. It was nowhere in sight.

She walked around the place again, checking all the doors, but they all only led to closets or a powder room. Finally, she paused by the phone table again.

This looked more like a foyer, with its coatrack and little table placed in a narrow, well-lit space. The wall opposite had panels of mirrors from ceiling to floor to create the illusion of space. Pausing, she looked at the light switches on the wall. One of them looked like a wall intercom, with a numbered pad.

Walking over, she examined the mirrored wall carefully. Part of it was recessed. She took a few steps back, looking at its height and width. Here was her door. She ran a hand along the creases. It looked like it could slide open, but where was the handle? She glanced at the pad with the numbers on it, then at the door again.

A coded doorway that she couldn't open. And oh, one more major problem. She stared back at her reflection. Without her clothes, she was totally at Reed's mercy.

"She's going to want to get out of this place soon," Reed said, sitting back in the leather chair.

He knew that Lily wouldn't just lie there and wait for him to come back. She would be checking out the suite and, of course, looking for the obvious—a door out of there.

The suite used an elevator to get around the hotel. It was designed for private use, for special guests— sometimes a politician who wished to have a few quiet days or a family friend. His family had a lot of international connections. Reed had been here several times when he'd been given off duty after a mission in these parts and hadn't felt like flying home.

He liked it here, where he was neither Joker at his job nor Reed at his family home. He was just "sir." Almost anonymous, although he was sure his father always knew he was here. Not that the old man bothered him or anything.

Right now, he was in one of the private offices on the top floors, on phone conference with Nikki and Amber. He suspected there were others listening with them. Like Jed McNeil.

He told them his location, but not the connection. They hadn't asked the obvious question—How had he been able to secure a suite that quickly? Instead, everyone concentrated on the events after the first shot. He related how they had jumped off the bridge and had had to get out of the cold, as well as Lily's injury.

"You're making progress if she told you to call her Lily," Nikki observed. "Think of some excuse to keep her there for a few days while T.'s gone."

"Where is she?" He was glad to find out that the operative chief of GEM was alive and well. He had been afraid that she might have walked into the alley and had gotten shot.

"She's taking care of things. By the way, we talked to Johnny Chic after the shooting. We have a name."

"The shooter went after Johnny, too? Who is it?"

"It's Greta. She was the double agent handler and mole in the CIA who disappeared this year."

He knew about Greta only from the CIA files they'd given him. She had worked as the secretary for some kind of CIA task force for a decade while in actuality she'd been the real leader behind a network of double agents.

"Isn't she about fifty years old? I didn't see anyone her age at The Beijing Bombshell." Of course, with everyone being blond and heavily made up . . . A thought occurred to him. "Should I tell Lily who's after her?"

"What's your reason for telling her?" Nikki asked. "You aren't supposed to know her background, remember?"

"I won't tell her immediately, but if I offer to check around and talk to my sources or even tell her I've talked to Johnny, and then bring up Greta's name, maybe she'll open up and tell me her story."

"That might buy you and us the time we need," Nikki agreed. "It's very important you gain her confidence in this matter, Reed. Time's running out for her. And with Greta after her, we don't know what plans she has for Lily."

"Understood." If Lily was still susceptible to her mind trigger, he would have to go to Plan B, something he didn't want to think about right now. "She's still concerned about her girls, and I'll have to think of a way out of that problem, too, now that her passports are gone."

"She gets very, very upset whenever those girls' lives are in any way endangered," Amber interrupted. Reed thought she sounded a little upset herself. "If she gets that way, especially if she starts attacking the system that couldn't help the girls' plight, I'm afraid that means she's still under the influence of whoever was controlling her. She grew more and more volatile the last few times we were together. I remember she would yell at Brad and wouldn't let him get a word in."

"She did ask for me to get the phone working or to bring a cell phone," Reed told them.

"That could be just normal concern," Nikki said.

"Or an embedded command to get orders," Jed's voice came on quietly.

"You'll have to watch her actions very closely the next few days, Reed, as well as get her to talk. She might sound almost detached when she talks about her past experiences. That doesn't mean she isn't hurting inside. She's just dealing with the pain through compartmentalization, talking about someone else," Nikki continued.

"She's pushed all her experiences into a make-believe sister," Amber said.

"That's another problem. Part of her memories have been rearranged by previous hypnotic suggestions. Depending on which level, it's going to be tough to work her out of it," Nikki said.

"Levels?"

"There are five levels for CIA hypnotic embedment," Nikki told him, "with level five being the deepest. These are the sleeper cells who could live ten or fifteen years with an identity created just for them. When the right time comes, their triggers are activated."

"That sounds like Lily, doesn't it?" Amber asked soberly.

Reed didn't want to think about levels of hypnotic embedment. He preferred to deal with one problem at a time. Right now, it was to get Lily to talk. Then he'd decide whether she was lying.

"What's Bradford Sun's relationship with Lily?" he asked. He had been curious before, because the man in that phone conversation had sounded as if he'd cared for Lily a lot.

"As you know, he's the chief of CIVPOL," Amber replied. "He was also Lily's lover."

Oh.

8

The phone rang and rang. Lily stared at it. She was so tempted to pick it up and answer. Who would know she was here, anyway? She should answer it.

What if it wasn't Reed but his friend or someone looking for either of them? It rang again, insistently calling to her. She reached out and placed her hand on the handle.

This was ridiculous. Her heart was racing maniacally. She was afraid of a stupid phone, how ridiculous was that? She, who had done so much. . . . She closed her eyes. *She who had betrayed friends precisely because of a damn phone manipulating her.* She didn't know what or how, but something about phones had made her do the very things she abhorred most. *She had sold Amber for her own misguided agenda!*

Lily released the phone handle and backed away from the hall table, staring at it as if it were some wild, dangerous beast about to leap at her. She turned and caught sight of her image reflected in the wall mirror.

Her dark eyes were wide with panic. Her hair, still uncombed, was sticking out every which way. She was clutching at her towel. She looked like . . . a raving maniac. She took a deep breath and sighed as she studied herself. Had she really been reduced to this—a raving lunatic who couldn't handle a phone ringing? How was she going to accomplish this final task if she couldn't communicate with anyone?

She needed to get hold of Tatiana, to tell her that she might be a few days late. She had left them enough cash for food and other necessities but not enough in case there was an emergency. She hadn't anticipated this delay.

The girls would understand, of course. They hadn't complained about their predicament—anything was better than what they had gone through—but she also realized they were beginning to talk amongst themselves about her odd behavior. She hadn't told them the whole truth about what had happened between Amber and herself in Velesta, so it was understandable that they were confused about why they were running again. She had just told them that it wasn't safe anymore, and they'd taken her at her word. Fortunately, they'd believed her when she'd told them Amber had had to leave with Brad for a vacation because Dilaver was getting suspicious. Because she'd saved them when they were kidnapped, they now trusted her implicitly. Because they all wanted to go home or get out of this country, they'd pinned their hopes on her.

Before, Lily would have relished this responsibility. She'd loved defeating those bastards from whom she had saved the girls, even to the point where she'd had to deal with illegal stuff herself. Getting the girls out of their clutches had been her ultimate goal, and she hadn't particularly cared how she'd done it, from moving stolen art for her customers to selling information. It had been like fulfilling a destiny, and it had calmed the vortex of fury inside her.

She couldn't explain to her friends, especially Amber, how angry she was sometimes. The fury was blinding to the point where she couldn't think properly unless she had some girls safe and sound in another country. She had lashed out sometimes, uncaring who she hurt, and when things went her way, she would have that calm in her soul again— for a while.

Then one day, something in a phone call from Brad had done something to her. She couldn't explain it, but it was as if a door to some bulging closet had opened inside her mind and every dirty little secret she'd ever hidden had tumbled out. In an instant she had regained her memory about what she really was.

"But what are you?" Lily asked aloud.

What did sleeper cells do when they malfunctioned? She didn't understand what had gone wrong, but something had stopped her from finishing her deadly task a few months ago. It had had to do with a phone call, but it hadn't been like the others. That was all she remembered.

She had wracked her brain at night trying to piece the events of the last few months together, but everything was a blur. Only the memory of her fury stood out. She had been so close to breaking point, and no release was coming because . . .

She frowned. "Because I couldn't get some of the girls out quickly enough," she muttered. She sat down on a nearby chair, wrapping her arms tightly around herself, trying to remember all the notes she'd made from her library research. Some of the terms she'd jotted down hadn't made sense at the time. "Mental pressure valve for emotional release . . . the girls functioned as a pressure valve for me, then."

She closed her eyes fiercely, shaking her head in denial. No, no, no! She refused to believe that. She cared for the girls' safety, more than her own, and her need to take care of them wasn't just something some stupid mind doctors had put in her head so that she could get relief from her emotions. Her need . . . her eyes flew open, and she glared harshly at her image again. That was the point, wasn't it? She wasn't supposed to know, and it was fine and dandy as long as she had some kind of release for the buildup in her mind. The more girls Amber had saved, the more bordellos Brad's department had raided, the more her frustration with the system had grown . . . until she blew up.

She was getting a headache trying to make sense of this. There was no one to talk to, and her mind kept repeating the same old same old until she felt like screaming. But one thing was very, very clear. She had to find a way to get the girls out of here, away from her. It seemed that the more frustrated she was, the more dangerous she became to everyone around her.

"I'm a mental pressure valve, that's what I've become," she announced.

Her image in the mirror started to vibrate, and with a silent swish, it slid open. Lily found herself staring straight at Reed in a T-shirt and shorts.

She looked mad as hell. Her eyes had that look in them that women got when they'd been left stewing and thinking too much by themselves. Not a good omen.

Reed walked out of the elevator, turned, and pulled out the trolley that was behind him. Maybe a hot beverage would put her in a better mood.

"This is all the food I could get them to make at this hour," he said. "I called up several times to see whether they got the phone working. Did it ring?"

She had her arms around her as if she were cold. "Yes, it did," she replied stiffly.

"Why didn't you stay in bed? It would have been warmer." He pushed away the mental image of her wandering around the suite just wearing that towel. "Why didn't you answer the phone?"

"I . . . didn't know who it was and didn't want to let anyone know we're here." She looked at the trolley. "Are we really staying at Hotel Palazzo, then?"

She must have come across something with the hotel's logo. "Yes," Reed said, coming over to her.

He frowned slightly when she backed away in the chair. "What's the matter? You're acting nervous all of a sudden."

"You locked me in," she accused.

"Of course not," he said. It was technically a half-truth. He'd known she wouldn't have been able to get out of the suite without a security code. "I thought you would be asleep. It's very late, you know."

"You still should have said something about the elevator."

He took a step closer. "Were you planning to run away?"

Her eyes were jewel-bright. "How? In this towel?" She jerked at his touch to her forehead. "What are you doing?"

"To see whether you have a fever. You look flushed." He wanted to divert her attention. She wasn't a stupid woman, and it wouldn't take her long to figure out that he was going to keep her a prisoner for a while. "You feel slightly hot. I called up to ask for your dress size so I could leave that with the concierge. He's going to make sure they deliver some clothes for us tomorrow."

She blinked. The challenge in her eyes dissipated a little. She looked down at her towel. "Oh. Will they actually get clothes for us?"

"There are perks to a private suite," he told her. Like telling Petr to take care of certain details. "Anyway, I did bring up another T-shirt, but that's all I could scrounge up. Come on, you have to get back to bed. You're running a slight fever." Her forehead felt hot, and he realized her eyes weren't bright with anger, but with fever and exhaustion. "You're sitting out here in a towel after that splash in the river, Lily. Asking for bronchitis, aren't you?"

"I'm fine." She carelessly threaded her fingers through her hair. She put her hand in his and pulled herself out of the chair. "Okay, I have a headache and I feel like shit."

She did look like she was in pain. "Take a couple of painkillers," Reed advised.

"No."

They walked back into the bedroom. She hesitated, looking at the bed.

Reed looked at it too. "I'll take the couch," he said. "Just for tonight, you understand. When you're better, that's another story. We have a deal, remember?"

She looked away. "It's a big bed. We can share. Besides, we don't have a deal, since I lost all my passports."

He deliberately reached out and caressed her neck. "But that means you need the ones I have even more," he told her. He had something she wanted, and he intended to keep pushing her. Her skin felt tantalizingly soft. "And I like the idea of keeping you naked while you think about those passports in my possession."

Her eyes narrowed, even though her telltale pulse under his thumb was telling another story. "I may be feeling like shit, but it doesn't mean I can't kick your ass."

He had always liked her fearlessness. She never backed away in the face of challenge, not in the middle of that mountain road six weeks earlier, not during a shoot-out, not here, when she was in a locked suite with barely any clothes on. And each time, he'd wanted to reach out and hug her, and shield her from danger. He gently stroked the thudding pulse. He knew he was making her think he'd touched more than her neck in the shower earlier.

"We can discuss more in the morning, how about that? I'm too tired right now after having taken care of you all night." As he'd known, reminding her that he'd saved her took some of the fight out of her. He suddenly scooped her up in his arms. He looked into her startled eyes and added, "You're running a fever and you're favoring that injured arm. It's got to be throbbing like hell, but I've a feeling you're going to stand here and argue all night if I don't put you into that bed."

He walked to the bed and climbed into it with her. "Now, I'm going to get the painkillers and you'll damn well take them so you can have a good night's rest. And if you argue, I'll force them into you. You can kick my ass tomorrow."

Her face was mutinous. "I—oh!"

Reed froze. The knot in Lily's towel had loosened, and the two sides fell open. With his body literally covering hers, she couldn't cover herself. He didn't move away, couldn't take his eyes away from her body. This time, it felt even more intimate than when he'd had her naked in his arms earlier. Then, he'd been concentrating on the task of cleaning her. Now, all his attention was on the woman.

He had wanted to kiss the tops of her breasts when they'd been dancing and he'd dipped her. Now he wanted to bury his face between the rounded softness and lick the creamy pink of her nipples till they reddened. As he watched, they hardened into small pebbles under his gaze. All he had to do was lean down and he would have one in his mouth.

"Stop looking at me like that," she said, her voice very hushed.

He looked up from those tempting mounds. Her face was flushed—with desire or embarrassment, he couldn't tell. She made a small movement, pulling at the towel. Part of it was trapped under his knee, and that was what had loosened the knot. He didn't shift his weight.

Instead, locking her gaze with his, he removed her hands and held them against the bed. Her eyes widened, but she didn't fight him. He bent down lower, blowing softly on her skin. She arched, a small gasp escaping her lips. "Take the painkillers," he said softly.

"Are you . . . threatening me?" she whispered.

"It's an ultimatum," he said. "Take the painkillers and I won't do this."

He blew on her skin lightly again, this time moving lower toward her belly button. He wanted to taste that too. He wanted to explore the hidden parts he had inadvertently touched in the shower. To press home the point that he intended to carry on, he trailed the tip of his tongue down the slope of her stomach. She gasped again.

"Oh . . . you win, you win. I'll take the damn pills." Her voice came out in a husky groan.

Because he knew he wouldn't stop if he continued, Reed sat up. "Too bad. I'd hoped you would let me continue."

Lily seemed at a loss for words as she lay there with her hands still imprisoned by his. Her expressive eyes spoke volumes, though. He released her. She lay there quietly as he tucked the sheets around her.

He went out and returned with the trolley and two pills. He sat beside her, and for a moment he thought she was going to refuse him again. Then she obediently took them with the glass of hot milk he gave her. He kept silent. She sighed when he adjusted her pillows, betraying how tired she really was.

He climbed into bed and turned off most of the lights using the control panel by the night table, plunging the room into semidarkness. It would be several minutes before the pills took effect.

"I thought you were going to use the couch," she said.

He had been going to, but Reed the gunrunner wouldn't have done such a gentlemanly thing. At least, that was the excuse he was going to use. "I changed my mind," he said, then turned on his side to look at her. "Sorry, but the bed looked more tempting."

Especially with the woman in it. She must really be out of sorts or very comfortable being naked because she hadn't once asked for the T-shirt he'd brought up. He thought about her sore shoulder. Maybe she couldn't even put the shirt on herself but hadn't wanted him to see how much pain she was in. She'd rather go naked than tell him.

Stubborn.

There was another short silence. The pills must have acted quicker than he'd thought.

"Reed?" Her voice was slightly slurred.

"Hmm?"

"I like you naked, too."

He smiled wryly. Stubborn and always wanting the last word. He wondered whether she would have admitted that if the medication hadn't loosened her tongue.

He listened as her breathing slowed. Tonight—last night, he amended, after glancing at the alarm clock—she had revealed more of herself than she'd intended. He smiled wryly in the dark. *Keep your mind out of the gutter, Vincenzio.* He meant the passports. She'd given him an idea of how important they were to her. He couldn't help but wonder about her desperate need to help those girls. She couldn't be all bad if her sole desire was saving helpless women who had no one to turn to for help.

But that was the problem. Lily Noretski wasn't bad because she was someone's victim, too. He just had to find out where she'd hidden the device before she became *his* victim.

Reed stared into the darkness. Never ever get emotionally involved with the target. It only made his job tougher to do. His eyes closed. His awareness of the naked woman sleeping beside him heightened.

Too damn late.

* * *

Dammit, Lily Noretski was just getting a bunch of passports, not trying to get a buyer for the device. Greta continued knitting furiously for a few minutes. She finished the row, changed hands, and started again. She dropped several stitches.

"Scheiss!"

She stopped, clicking the needles together, as she looked at the pattern. It was just a minor mistake, something she could fix in minutes, but she seemed unable to calm herself, which made her madder, since she loved knitting because it calmed her down whenever she was stressed.

This wasn't stress. Stress was keeping up the pretense of being a secretary at the CIA for ten years when she was more than that. She had done that without a complaint, so this one tiny mistake—she looked at her knitting—wasn't a problem.

Although Greta didn't want to admit it, Lily hadn't been that easy to find without her old sources. The CIA, with all its excellent monitors and paper trails, had truly spoilt her. That girl had seemingly disappeared from the face of the earth until Gunther had revealed that his mole had received some information. Finally! Greta had almost given up.

It seemed that Lily was actually here in town and had been seen making several withdrawals from banks. Then she had contacted Johnny Chic, whom Greta had discovered was a well-known underground middleman who owned a club named The Beijing Bombshell.

Greta made a sound of disgust at the thought of the slight, mustachioed man. What a twisted mind, to have a business that actually made all women behave like sex kittens and dress up like his Marilyn Monroe fantasies. And people actually paid him to get into the club. He'd chided her for not having worn a wig. As if she was going to actually don one and parade around him in fishnet stockings. She didn't cater to male fantasies; her forte had always been to kill, not seduce.

First, she had to straighten Gunther up. He had started this. If he hadn't misled her with certain details, she wouldn't have concluded that Lily was making a sale. But the information had been deceptive—an illegal trade negotiator like Johnny Chic setting up what had looked like a meeting between a gunrunner and Lily. When her spotter had said she'd been carrying a bag with her as they had gone out of the club—a bag big enough for the device—she had given the go-ahead signal to get rid of the gunrunner. The idea had been to isolate Lily so they could nab her and the bag.

Here was where everything had gone down the drain. Greta's hit man had missed his target and those two had run out of the entrance. Then the other man assigned to her hadn't followed her exact orders.

She didn't want Lily dead yet. Obviously Gunther was trying to sabotage her job. That sniveling, ambitious piece of garbage! Did he think she would allow that to happen? Her homecoming was more important to her than he'd ever know, and she wasn't going to let someone like him win.

Greta got up and walked to the kitchenette in her small *pensione*. A good cup of coffee. Maybe a good soak in the bathtub. She glanced at her watch and sighed. No time for the second option. Ah, for the good old days in the States, when she would spend hours relaxing in a tub of bubbles. It was something that she definitely missed now that she was back in the game.

She filled the small kettle with water and set it on the burner. Some habits were tough to get rid of, especially when she had cultivated them for a decade. She looked over at the small sofa where the knitting sat. She just couldn't give up knitting, not yet, anyway. Besides, after this final grand entrance, she would be officially retired, so she would have plenty of time to indulge in knitting and bubble baths.

She smiled indulgently as she waited for the water to boil. Funny how she, of all people, looked forward to retirement. Americans thought about it all the time, and she had somehow gotten that into her thinking, too. But she did want to meet some of her family and settle down in the dacha the government had promised her. Nieces and nephews to play with and spoil, wouldn't that be nice? Shopping for teddy bears and electronic games . . .

She frowned. That big sum of money she'd had to give Johnny Chic had set back her wealth a bit, but what she'd found out had given her an entirely different picture of what was going on.

One thing was for sure. She couldn't trust Gunther any longer.

Greta turned off the stove. She poured the hot water from the kettle into her cup. Really, what she needed to do was take a quick trip to see Gunther and make him talk to her. She smiled again. He thought she was too old to take him on. She would show him. Bullying an old lady.

She carried her cup back to the sofa and sat down comfortably. This whole place was too small. A few steps and there was the living room. A few steps and there was the bed. Disgusting. Her dacha would have a lot of room. She could knit in one and have coffee in another. She would have a dressing room as large as her bedroom.

She laughed. She was getting so silly. First, she had to get this job done, to show them she was still worth their respect. She didn't just want to retire into anonymity; she wanted them to come to her for advice, maybe give her a small position in training some of the newer operatives.

Greta shuddered. Okay, maybe not. She hated the idea of competition. She was the best, and that was why they'd given her this monumental task that had lasted for so long. She had delivered, time and time again, for them and their cause for ten long years. She hadn't enjoyed the work—although the money they had transferred into her account was nice— because she preferred a more active role than mere mole handler.

She thought of Gorman and the network she had nurtured. "Oh, more than a mere mole handler, my darling Greta," she murmured softly, bringing the cup to her lips. She took a long sip of coffee. "That network almost crippled the damn CIA."

She laughed triumphantly and lifted the cup in a victory toast. She had done a great job. She deserved everything that was coming to her. They were going to give her a nice dacha once she delivered the explosive trigger device.

After all, she was Greta, not some sniveling pencil pusher like Gunther. She was going to go home a legend. Of course she had to up the ante. She was going to show them how the device would work, perhaps with a timely assassination. She tapped her chin thoughtfully. Who in Europe wasn't popular with her agency right now? Most important of all, she wanted to demonstrate that she hadn't lost a step during all these years of absence from the scene.

Greta shrugged. Vanity was a strange thing. She was a woman, after all, and knew they might look at her as a washed-out has-been, if she wasn't careful. She was way over the age of a regular assassin, but . . . She. Wasn't. Regular. That was the point.

She could have kicked herself for not having anticipated certain problems, though. Like someone with an ambitious eye, looking to use her brilliant idea to further his own position within her agency.

She hadn't figured out all the details yet, but one fact stood out. Gunther had somehow managed to get Lily to help him out a few months ago. What did he have on her that had made her so willing to sacrifice her life? He'd gotten that woman to betray her friends, steal the device, and head for the summit almost without a hitch.

That was what pissed Greta off most—that she had been so out of the loop. Wasn't she the one who had arranged for the weapon to be dropped off in Macedonia? Wasn't she the one who had successfully gotten her nephew to keep it hidden till she'd been able to get out of the States? Then why all those lies about using a decoy when Lily had been more than that? Perhaps Gunther was a double agent like her.

Greta had thought the target had been one person at the summit, not a whole group of international leaders. To have Lily walk into a roomful of political leaders during an art exhibit unveiling . . . it would have been a coup for Gunther if she'd finished her task. A whole group of very important people blown up in front of all the international news cameras.

Greta shrugged again. That had been massive vanity on Gunther's part. Lily had obviously changed her mind after getting her hands on the device. Good for Greta, bad for Gunther. Without Lily and the device, of course Gunther had to cooperate with her again, but now that the girl had resurfaced, it was a waiting game. Actually, Greta was surprised that Lily hadn't attempted to sell the device earlier. And now, at the club, it was passports that had exchanged hands, not the missing weapon. What was happening here?

She finished her cup of coffee and looked down at her knitting. She was going to make that trip to Gun-

ther. Then she was going to find out more about this
R.C. who was with Lily Noretski. She hadn't been
able to run after them that night, not with having to
take care of the downed man and then being shot at
by someone else from behind. Gunther's orders
probably. She frowned. He was going to regret that
so much.

Too bad her nephew had been killed by that damn
SEAL. Dilaver would be useful just about now. He
could ask around for her about this R.C. and maybe
set up a meeting. She could use a weapons dealer
right now, someone she could trust, and she had
trusted her nephew. She exhaled, feeling a bit regret-
ful that she hadn't had that much time with him before he was killed. That was why it was essential to
get this job done, so she could spend more time with
her relatives.

Passports . . . her eyes narrowed as she stared into
space thoughtfully. Why had Lily purchased so
many of them? Gunther was withholding something
about Lily Noretski.

Greta picked up her knitting, squeezing the soft
yarn in her hands. This was going to be the prettiest
blue-and-pink shawl. She loved the swirling pattern
she had designed. She planned to add a fringe at the
edge when she was done. She knitted, methodically
moving the needles, sliding the stitches from one to
the other.

Gunther first. Then Lily. And if she had to get rid
of a gunrunner or two in between them, so what?

9

A slow prickle of awareness woke Lily from a deep well of sleep. She tried to hang on to the darkness. It was so peaceful where she was—the deep, dark slumber where dreams didn't interrupt. But the more she tried, the more her mind awakened, as if her spirit were moving from room to room, turning on the lights.

"No, not yet," she muttered. She hadn't had such great sleep forever.

"Not yet, what?"

The sleepy male voice woke her up completely. Her eyes flew open. "Shit," she said, as she stared up at the ornate ceiling above her. Everything was coming back. "Shit, shit, shit."

"Is that how you greet your day?"

She turned her head slowly. Early morning was slipping through the window panels, giving her just enough light to make out Reed lying on his stomach, his face snuggled between a strong-looking arm and a pillow. His eyes were closed and his eyelashes looked ridiculously long. She looked at the hand resting by his face. That hand had touched her . . . everywhere. She quickly glanced down.

"Shit," she repeated and tugged hard at the sheets trapped under his body.

His eyes finally opened into a sleepy half-slit. She couldn't help it. Every time he looked at her, her heart skipped a couple of beats and heat stirred in the pit of her stomach. It irritated her, since he looked so calm while he was affecting her this way. Did the man ever get excited about anything? Too late she remembered that she *had* seen him excited. She didn't want to think about that while she was lying in bed. She pulled at the sheets again, trying to cover herself.

He lay there, looking at her, not saying anything as he watched. Irritated, she turned on her front, further twisting the sheets around herself.

The corner of his lips quirked. Lily glared at him. She knew that he liked making her feel uncomfortable. She hoped he hadn't woken up before she had and seen how she'd kicked the covers off. Not that he hadn't seen it all already. Damn it, she could feel the heat suffusing her cheeks. Hopefully the room was still too dark for him to see her embarrassment.

Slowly, Reed stretched his arms over his head, arching his back like an animal getting up after a nap. He rolled over. She stared at the way his T-shirt stretched tautly across his chest as he repeated the motion. The heat coming from his body curled her toes. He sat up, propping the pillows behind his back.

"What were you dreaming about?" he asked.

Lily frowned. "Nothing, why?" It was the best sleep she'd had in ages. She hadn't had a good night's rest since Velesta.

"You said, 'Not yet,' and then cussed." He flicked his hair back with his hands. "Bad dreams?"

How could she explain that she'd wanted to continue sleeping? "I can't remember," she lied. "And the cussing was because I found you in bed."

He regarded her for a moment. "You're still mad about the painkillers," he said.

"No, I'm mad because you forced me to take them," she said. And she had been turned on by his method. She really wasn't mad. The medication had really helped, but he'd taken advantage of her exhaustion, and she didn't like it that she'd given in so easily. "You threatened me."

"Do you feel threatened now?" he asked.

Lily held her breath as he slid closer until his body was inches from hers. One moment she was on her front, trying not to be conscious of his body; the next, she found herself flipped on her back, staring up into his shadowed face. Lily blinked, startled by his quickness. He threaded his hand through her hair and held her head still. The look in his eyes had quickly changed from lazy sleepiness to banked heat. Her heart started thrumming that odd little staccato again.

"Do you like taking advantage of injured women?" she demanded as he leaned closer. She watched his mouth with the fascination of a caught prey. Everything about this man fascinated her. "You've been manhandling me since last night."

"It's becoming a habit," he said, and closed the gap between their lips.

He kissed her softly, his lips moving against hers. She tried to turn her face away, but the hands in her hair held her where he wanted her. He didn't force his kiss on her though. His lips trailed to the corner of her mouth, and she jerked as his tongue licked the little crease there.

"Sto—"

His mouth immediately covered hers again, easily gaining access, and the taste of warm male invaded her senses as his tongue slipped in and found hers. She felt a delicious shiver dance through her body as he sank into her, tasting her as if she were a delicate sweet that needed to be savored slowly. He deepened the kiss and her mouth opened further. Intoxicating moments went by as his tongue tangled with hers. The man . . . could kiss.

His mouth lifted, and she groaned as he trailed sensual kisses down the side of her face, following her jawline to her earlobe. She caught his scent, a heady mixture of clean male and some kind of cologne, before his tongue invaded the shell of her ear. She gasped and jerked again, but those hands were still in her hair, holding her still as he explored the erogenous zone. She realized, too late, that she should really struggle in earnest.

Too late. His tongue drove her crazy as he teased her sensitized ear. She pushed ineffectively against his hard chest as she gurgled out whimpering noises.

"Reed!" she managed to pant out, desperate for the torture to stop. She felt weak as a baby.

He finally relented. He released her hair, sliding his fingers caressingly over her warm cheeks. "That's much better than 'shit,' isn't it?" he asked.

Lily tried to catch her breath; her left ear was still tingling. She was horrified at how weak she felt from just one stupid kiss. She'd never felt this way before. Usually, in the morning, she would be the one taking advantage of the sleepy man with her, not the other way round.

His head dipped again, and before she could reply, his mouth recaptured hers. This time he wasn't slow or tender. He kissed her firmly, as if he had a right to her mouth. She couldn't help herself; she responded equally fiercely.

He lifted his head. The glow of the morning brightened the room. Through her haze of desire, she noted that his eyes were more gray than blue, a shade that blended in with the shadows.

"Why do you keep doing that?" she asked, wishing her voice didn't sound so husky with need.

"Doing what?"

"Catching me by surprise."

His hand reached for the sheets. "Because then I can see the real you."

Her mouth fell open. He couldn't know. . . . Again, thoughts disappeared as he took his time untangling the sheets from her body. *Do something, Lily.* But she could only lie there, watching helplessly. He pulled back the sheets, revealing her body to his eyes. There was plenty of time to resist, but she couldn't seem to breathe, let alone say a word. Once again she was naked. The silence stretched as his eyes roved over her. He seemed to take pleasure just from the sight of her.

"You're fully awake now," he said. "Not out from the cold, not out from exhaustion. No medication."

She bit down on her lower lip when he finally touched her. Maybe she was still feverish. She felt hot all over. His hand moved leisurely from her breast to her rib cage. She sucked in her tummy when his thumb tickled her belly button. Her once-relaxed limbs were taut with anticipation.

"Open your legs," he whispered.

"I don't even know you," she said softly. "Just because you saved me doesn't mean I have to sleep with you."

He smiled for the first time, and her breath caught in her throat. With the pale morning light behind him catching the gold glints in his dark hair, and with the sensual curve of his mouth so temptingly close, he looked unearthly beautiful, like one of those mythological bad-boy gods paying a visit. And, from the look in his eyes, with something very naughty in mind.

"We already slept together, sweetheart," he told her, leaning closer. His hand moved over her lower tummy. "Now I want to just wake you up slowly."

Her lips parted as his hand delved lower still. She didn't seem to have any will to stop him at all. "Why?" she said, then closed her eyes as his hand slipped between her thighs. Every one of her senses zeroed in on the knowing glide of his fingers as he turned her into a useless puddle of emotional need.

His breath was warm. "Tell me you're awake and willing, and I'll tell you why."

Her legs parted on their own accord. She was pretty sure he could tell she was only too willing.

"Why?" she asked as his fingers continued their sensual exploration. She inhaled sharply as the tingling sensation built into a tighter knot.

"When I first saw you, you were blond and beautiful," he told her. "Now you're brunette and beautiful. And it's your natural color."

That startled her eyes open again. He was looking at where his hand was causing such havoc. She'd forgotten about her wig. She must have lost it in the river. Right now . . . she didn't really care where the hell her wig was. . . .

"So I wonder who this Lily is who won't tell me anything about herself?" he continued. "You're so beautiful outside. What are you like inside? Can I get to know you? Make you tell me all your secrets?"

All the while his fingers glided against her erotically, his timing slow and perfect. Lily looked down

at his hand nestled so intimately between her legs. A
fire was slowly consuming her, making it hard to
think about anything.

Secrets? She had plenty of secrets, but sex
wouldn't get any secrets out of her. She moaned
softly as a finger invaded her softness. Would it? Her
whole being screamed for release as he seemed to
stretch each pleasurable glide to eternity. She pushed
her hip up to meet those fingers, a silent urge for him
to go faster. He did. Just a bit. A long sensual pull upwards, leaving her aching for more. Paused.

Lips swallowed her moans. Tongue invaded her
mouth. She responded eagerly as she followed the
glide down. Faster. Please. Another mind-blowing
pause. She almost died. Then it began again.

Ravished. That was what it felt like he was doing
to her. When she'd first met him, she'd expected seduction, but this was more than that.

She could handle seduction. One had to be innocent or untouched in some form to be seduced, and
she was far from that. So she had been reasonably
sure he'd fail if he had seduction on his mind.

But she hadn't counted on fighting her own attraction, too. Not another gunrunner. And she certainly
hadn't expected to be lying here naked, aroused to
the point of no return, without even a whimper of a
fight.

His lips trailed down her chest. A hot tongue surrounded her tender nipple.

Lily whimpered.

A hand slid under her, arching her back, bringing

her breast fully into that hot mouth. It felt like when he was dipping her, but this time, it was a sexual tango, with his tongue and fingers doing all the dancing.

Her head rolled back helplessly as he tortured her other nipple. His finger stroked faster. Finally.

Ravished. Beyond thought. Just an urgent, urgent need, one she'd never felt before. This was . . . untouched territory.

"Trust me, Lily."

That was all she heard as she hung on to the handsome stranger seducing her. With a last choked cry, she let go.

There's a devil inside all of us, dude. Sometimes he just makes us do things to get us into more trouble. Where do you think that expression came from?

Somewhere in heaven, Arch must be laughing his ass off, because Reed had found that devil inside him. On the one hand, he kept warning himself not to get emotionally involved, and then he abruptly turned around and did just that. On the other hand, he wanted to protect Lily from everything, which was, of course, not possible when the woman didn't trust or know him.

A naked, achingly beautiful woman in bed, one whose secrets he needed. He didn't have the time to nurture any trust, nor was this the place to start something normal. Maybe it was just genetic, he didn't know. He just knew, innately, that to get what he wanted, to achieve what he hoped for, he needed to bond quickly and intimately.

As a SEAL, Reed had learned not to second-guess himself during times of action. Never, at a crucial moment, wonder whether it was the right thing to do. Sight the target. Pull the trigger.

He just knew he wanted to touch this woman again, that to penetrate her most secretive layers, he would have to go after her when she was least expecting it. He was a man after all; he could feel her attraction and her desire. They seemed to be communicating with their bodies more than with words, and so he had followed instinct and made his move.

She shuddered in his arms as she climaxed, and he went ruthlessly after her pleasure, prolonging it. A woman giving herself in intimacy was at her most vulnerable, and he would deepen this bond the only way a man could, by pleasuring her in the most memorable way.

He loved the way her nipples puckered in his mouth as she strained against him while another wave of pleasure hit her body. His own body ached to climb on top and sink inside her. He nibbled gently and she groaned.

"Reed . . ."

"Trust me," he repeated. She was wet with need. He inserted a finger inside her. Wet and tight. She moaned again as he opened her slick folds, sliding his finger against the hidden nub and gaining an involuntary shiver when he found it.

"Reed, not yet . . . too sensitive . . ."

"I'll make it good," he promised. He wanted to start her fire again. It was like riding an incredible wave and wanting more. His cock strained inside his shorts, wanting out. "Are you on the pill?"

She shook her head. "No."

His cock was going to be an unhappy camper. "I don't have any condoms."

Her dark eyes smoldered with emotion. "I want you inside me," she said. Her hands reached down to join his. "You have to stop. I can't think when you're teasing me."

"Don't you like it?"

"I . . . yes, but . . ."

"Then enjoy it, Lily." He liked seeing her this way.

"What . . . about you?"

"Later," he told her. If his cock could kill, he would be a dead man now. "I'm a very patient guy. Now shut up . . . where was I?"

"Reed!"

He ignored the growing heat in his own pants, concentrating on the woman instead. She squeezed her thighs together and came violently this time, her limbs thrashing as she sobbed.

A beautiful, delicate flower. With thorns. They were woeful protection from him right now. And for that reason alone, he wouldn't give in to his own needs. Later.

"What are you thinking?" she asked, lying quiescent in his arms now.

He smoothed the hair from her brow. "I was wondering whether calling down for them to deliver condoms would give the hotel staff more sordid tales to tell. After all, they're going to have lots to talk about once they clean the bathroom and see those muddy clothes."

She stared at him for a moment, then laughed, a small, hiccupy chuckle. "You say the funniest things, you know that? I can't believe this is happening."

"What is?"

She was quiet for a moment, then she raised a hand and ruffled his hair, as if she wanted to make sure he was real. "No man has ever made me come before sex," she said quietly. "In fact—"

She was lost in thought for a moment. He remembered Nikki and Amber mentioning that Bradford Sun and Lily had been an item. He wondered whether she was thinking about her ex-lover. That cooled his rampant desire. He didn't want to make love to her while she had another man on her mind.

"Let's eat," he said. She frowned at his change of subject. "What do you want for breakfast? I'm starving."

"Reed, can you do me a favor?"

"Sure, what?"

"Make a call for me."

"I got a cell phone for you. You can make the call while I order up some food."

"No." Her voice had turned forceful. She bit her lower lip. "Can you . . . do it for me?"

He didn't want her communicating with anyone anyway, but she was making his job of keeping her out of circulation from everything too damn easy.

"Sure," he said. "Who do you want me to call?"

"Just a girlfriend. I want her to know I'm okay."

The girls. But why wouldn't she talk to them? "Why can't you tell her yourself?" he asked, casually outlining the bone structure of her face with his forefinger.

She moved restlessly. "I don't feel like telling her the passports are all gone."

That made sense. She probably didn't want to worry the girls, wherever they were. He recalled how young some of them had looked when he'd spied on them.

"I see," he said. He bent down and kissed the tip of her nose. She needed him to do this, so here was his chance to push that emotion home. *Make her need your help,* Nikki had said, *but always make sure it isn't free, or she'll get very suspicious very quickly.* "So what do I get in return for this favor?"

Her beautiful eyes narrowed a fraction. "You're demanding payment for a phone call?"

He had to make her start thinking of ways to get him to help her. "Why not? You came to me to bargain about certain items in my possession. I still have them, you know, and you just told me you don't want your girlfriend to know about the set that you just lost. I figure that means the value of my passports has gone up since last night." Leaning over, he placed his hands on each side of her face, effectively trapping her. "I like you naked, Lily, but you already know that."

"So you're saying that you're playing some kind of power game with me?" she asked, her voice turning frosty.

"Hey, would you rather I lie about my intentions? Do you think if I just go about helping you, you won't be wondering what I'm up to? This way, we're clear where we stand, right?" He came closer. Feeling her feminine warmth, he could feel himself getting uncomfortably hard again. "I'll take care of you, sweetheart. I'll make that call. Maybe even jump off another bridge to save your gorgeous ass. Believe me, I don't run around diving into freezing water for nothing."

He almost winced at using half-truths to cover the real truths. He must have learned that from his mother. He didn't like himself very much for doing it this way, but he had to get Lily to start thinking about how he could help her.

He was breaking many of his own rules, but in Lily's case, he was—literally—not himself. As far as he was concerned, the original operative plans had gone out the window. This wasn't going to be a quickie job, not when someone was after Lily and, most probably, the weapon, yet there wasn't enough time to just wait for her capitulation.

Saving her life had given him a small foothold into Lily's willingness to trust him. He knew, from her files and after meeting her, that it was going to be extremely hard to get her to open up to him. It would be even tougher since she was on the run now. He had to get her to consider him as more than someone with whom she was stuck.

She wanted his passports. He could tempt her by offering more.

"I don't have any money," she said, interrupting his thoughts. "Not the amount that'd interest you, anyway."

Reed grinned. "Good girl. I knew you wouldn't think that sex would buy what you want." He looked down and sighed. "Although I'm really, really tempted."

That, at least, was the truth. He had never wanted a woman more, and he'd never been more tempted into forgetting about missions and assignments and just letting his raging hormones take over. But even the devil couldn't make him break the most important rule—protection or nothing.

Lily's hands slid up his arms and squeezed his shoulders lightly. "Once upon a time, I'd take that as a challenge, Reed," she said. "But right now, all I want is to take care of my business and disappear."

"Which is why this game's so interesting to me, you see," Reed told her. "You need me right now. I like that."

"I don't need anyone."

He cocked his head. "Oh yeah, who's going to get you clothes? Who's going to make that phone call for you? Who's going to help you get passports?"

Her eyes lit up. "Are you? Going to help me get passports? How?"

Reed shook his head. The seed had been planted. Let it take root in her thoughts. "I might have an idea or two, but let's eat first. I'm starving." He rolled and got off the bed. *You're a stupid SOB.* He ignored his very angry libido yelling at him. "Coming?"

Pink suffused her face as she slowly sat up. He'd chosen the word deliberately. "I don't have anything to wear," she reminded him.

"You can have the T-shirt I brought up," he told her.

He picked up the phone to call room service, trying not to imagine how he was going to down his food while she sat across from him in a T-shirt and nothing else. His gaze followed Lily as she walked off to the bathroom. Better than her in that damn towel, Vincenzio.

"Yes," he said. "I need some food sent up, please."

What he really needed was a cold shower.

10

"*Buffy the Vampire Slayer?*" Reed asked as he clicked the cell phone shut. "That's you and your girlfriend's favorite television show? Do they even show that here?"

The call itself had been to the point. "Tatiana," if that was her real name, had sounded as suspicious as a mother whose daughter hadn't made curfew, except that she'd sounded all of sixteen. Once the password had been confirmed, however, she had just asked for the message. Strange how she hadn't seemed concerned enough to demand to speak to Lily.

"Yes, to all your questions," Lily said, food in mouth.

Reed hadn't realized how hungry they'd both been until they'd dived into the plates of breakfast food without any conversation. He was used to going without for a long time and eating at odd hours, so his body had learned to ignore the usual hunger pangs until the smell and sight of food came within touching distance. He felt bad. Lily had probably been famished and he'd spent all morning . . . *Stop thinking about the damn T-shirt.*

Dammit, what the hell was wrong with him? He hadn't had so much difficulty concentrating before. The woman was tempting him every time she walked past him in that thing. Sitting at the table beside her was worse. His knees kept bumping into her long bare legs. And of course, he knew what she had under that scrap of clothing. Not a damn thing.

He drank down his juice in one gulp. "Why did your friend need to ask a secret question, anyway? It's pretty juvenile, if you ask me."

She looked up from the apple she was peeling. "Who's asking you? Besides, Tatiana *is* a very young girl. She thinks this is a great way to let her know it's really me."

"So every time you call her, she asks, 'What's our favorite TV show?' and you answer her?" There was something wrong here, but Reed couldn't quite put a finger on it yet. "Can't she recognize your voice?"

He watched Lily as she carefully sliced the apple into sections, as if it were very important to get every cube the same size. A password. Juvenile, but effective. Those girls were young, so maybe something like a password would appeal to them. But what kind of danger did they think they were in, that they couldn't even communicate on the cell phone without a secret code? They were escapees from thugs, not operatives involved in spy games.

"Want some apple?" Lily asked. Without waiting for his answer, she offered him a piece with a fork.

She was trying to distract him. He leaned closer, taking the fruit into his mouth. Their eyes met as he tugged it off the fork. The tart and sweet taste of apple filled his mouth as he continued watching her. She put a piece in her mouth, licking the juice off her lips. Fine, she wanted to tempt him, he'd bite. Time to push her again.

"Now that we've reassured your friend you're okay and going to be late going home," he said, getting up, "let's hear your other plans."

She looked around the room, then shrugged again. "It depends on what your plans are."

He settled onto the nearby sofa by the fireplace. "So you're placing yourself in my hands?"

"What choice do I have? First, I don't have any clothes." She came over to join him. "And don't give me that look. I can read your mind."

"That'd be an easy thing to do," Reed said wryly. "All you have to do is keep reminding me you don't have any clothes on."

"You see? That's so male. I said, 'I don't have any clothes.' You're the one who tagged 'on' at the end of the sentence." She leaned back, drawing his eyes to her legs again. "Once you get me something to wear, we can go to my hotel to pick up the rest of my clothes."

"And then?" He wanted to know all her options. His own were simple. Nikki had said they needed time as they gathered information. All he had to do was stall long enough for them to find out the identity of the person who'd shot at them, as well as whether there was a price on Lily's head. In the meantime, he was to work at finding out what was on Lily's mind. So far, he hadn't seen any evidence that suggested she was confused or afraid, which meant he had to get even closer to her. Quickly. He tried to distance his emotions by mentally going through what he knew of her. He watched her hands as they smoothed the hem of her T-shirt. Not working.

"Reed, I thought you said you'd help me get more passports. I know you have something in mind. What is it?" She crossed her legs, exposing even more of her thigh. "I don't have the cash. If you can't help me, let me know now. I don't beg."

"I can only help so much, sweetheart," Reed said. "Look, I'm a gunrunner. I can make another deal, but if you know the business at all, you know these things take some time. I sold my last batch to get the passports so I can get out of this hellhole, so currently, aside from my own personal stuff, I'm running on empty. All I can do right now is go to Johnny to get some information, find out whether he has a buyer that's in need of something hot on the market, and maybe cut you into the deal. Maybe."

She tucked a stray strand of black hair behind her ear as she studied him thoughtfully. "What do you want from me?" she asked quietly. "Besides sex?"

He shook her head. "That isn't part of our deal. I can have that from you right now and you know it."

She arched a brow. "Confident, aren't we?"

He was dying to get his hands on her again, but hey, he was willing to play the waiting game a bit longer. After all, he still didn't have any condoms. But that didn't stop him from getting off the sofa.

Her eyes widened when he kneeled down in front of her. "Want me to demonstrate?" he asked. He put a hand on her knee. He felt her tightening to keep her legs together. "I have time."

"I . . . don't," she said, a slight tremor in her voice. "This isn't fair. I'm here like some kept woman while you play your stupid game. Are you going to help me or not?"

She was right. It really wasn't fair, and Reed had no idea what this was leading to. But he wanted this woman to give herself to him freely. He wanted to do her in the most carnal way till she let all her defenses down.

"If I still say maybe, would you open your legs for me?"

Temper darkened her eyes to jet black. "You're a damn crude American, you know that?"

Yeah. But only with her. "It's important to me," he said.

"Why?" She covered his hand with hers but didn't stop him as he slid his hand under her shirt. Her thighs were warm and smooth. "Why is it important that you seduce me? You don't know me."

"Exactly. But I want you badly, enough that I'm actually thinking about doing one last run. I was going to enjoy myself with one wild weekend, you know, sort of like a celebration to the end of the old me. Then you came swaggering into my life." He shrugged. "Providence, maybe?"

"Providence," she repeated slowly. "That's a mighty big word from a gunrunner."

But it was an easy subject for Reed. And he could be honest about it. "They say things happen for a reason," he said, feeling the tensing muscle in her calf as he ran a teasing finger up it, "and so I'm always trying to find this reason. Take your dropping into my life, for instance. Is it simply just because of what I have, or is it just a means for providence to bring you right here?"

She shook her head, as if she wasn't sure what to make of him. He didn't blame her. He had never spoken like this to anyone but Arch. Even his SEAL teammates had never seen this side of him. He was Joker, the quiet one, always the listener.

"So what do you want to prove with me?" she asked.

"I want you to say yes to me in spite of the fact that I might not help you." Why the hell would that be important to him? He didn't know. It shouldn't matter, as long as she told him where the weapon was . . . but somehow, he didn't want that to become part of this attraction for her. He wanted her to want him for himself. "So, I'm being honest. I like the idea of my final celebration being with a woman I didn't pay for. I want to make you cream up because you want to. What's wrong with that?"

She started laughing, just a little wildly. "'Cream up'?"

"Yeah. Like this." Nudging her knees apart, Reed bunched the T-shirt in one hand and shoved it up.

"Reed!" Her voice was breathless, panicked.

"Stop me if I'm not doing it right," he told her and reached for the fruit he really wanted to taste.

Lily couldn't believe this was happening. She had lost it. She never let a man take the lead in sex. She never let a man take over, period. It was a point of pride for her that she was the one in control, that her partner was helpless and weak. Yet for the third time this morning, this man had broken through her resistance by just touching her.

A woman he didn't pay for. He didn't know how seductive those words were. To give to someone freely again—was it possible?

Her past had made it impossible for her to act normally with men, so she had tended to avoid relationships. She'd had men wanting her before, had walked away from them without any problems. So why couldn't she do it now?

Providence. She was at the end of her rope. He didn't know it, but he was the only hope she had left to help the girls. *But why not for you, too?*

His shoulders nudged her thighs further apart. She pulled the ends of her shirt out of his hand and pulled it down, covering herself. His hands, however, remained where they were. She made a final attempt to escape the temptation of giving in to her needs. "Reed, we can't spend the whole morning doing this. So much to do . . . I want to get my clothes and . . ." She lost her train of thought as his hands reached further up under her T-shirt.

"The stores downstairs don't open till ten, so I can't get you anything to wear till then anyway," he said in the most reasonable voice. "Then when we get your things, I'll have to get some cash and weapons, since I lost those in the river last night. We can't see Johnny till late in the day because that's how he conducts business. Plenty of time, Lily."

She sucked in her breath as his hands roamed freely over her tummy, on her thighs, teasing her with his thumbs. "This is insane. Last night—"

"Last night changed everything," he said, his voice low and seductive. "Don't you agree? You're getting wet. Why don't you just sit back and relax?"

Relax? Was he nuts? She stared at him, then laughed. "What am I going to do with you?" she asked. She was supposed to be urgently running around town, getting the necessary papers to get her girls out, and here she was being tempted to enjoy what fate brought her. "There's got to be more on your mind than my body!"

He shook his head. "Right now? Nope, not a thing. All this arranging will take a couple of days, you know. So why not just relax here with me? I think you're just a control freak. When was the last time you just lay back and let someone take care of you?"

She continued staring at him. Lie back, relax . . . let everything float for a few days. She had been on the run for months. How she would love that. But the girls . . . there was nothing she could do without getting the passports, and this man, with his secretive gray eyes, was her chance to quickly get more. She knew he would help her even though he kept playing this stupid game.

She *was* tired of thinking for everyone. She *was* tired, period. And for the first time, she wasn't having that dreaded feeling of anxiety hanging over her. She should be afraid of this man, but she wasn't.

She didn't fully trust him, of course. He was a gunrunner, after all, with the same arrogance and for-the-moment attitude of someone who lived on the edge. He intrigued her with his air of mystery, spouting philosophy with such ease while his eyes undressed her. The way he was trying to get her to do things his way told her he wasn't someone she could just play with. Plus, he wanted her.

And, she admitted, she wanted him.

Why was it so easy to let go with him? "And what happens in a few days?" she whispered.

His eyes gleamed at the knowledge that she was giving in. "Who knows? I can't promise you anything. Maybe I'll let you go, maybe not."

She frowned. "I wasn't talking about myself."

His mouth curved. "I know. You're obsessed with the passports. I want you to think of you and me in terms of you."

She shook her head. "I've no idea what you're talking about."

She watched, fascinated, as his hands reappeared from under her shirt. He slowly pushed the material upward again. "Just think of it, Lily. A few days of pleasure. Just for yourself. No worry about passports, no girlfriend you have to report to, no vehicles trying to smash you to pieces. Just you and me, alone. What's wrong with that?"

This time she didn't stop his descending head. She gasped at the touch of his lips. Time for herself, he said. She couldn't think of a single argument to counter his clever tongue.

The devil was an insidious piece of . . . Reed nodded curtly at Petr. He didn't feel like talking to anyone right now.

"Have you called your father yet, sir?" Petr asked.

"Not yet. Why? He doesn't like to be disturbed in the States at this hour anyway."

"He's actually on business in Prague."

Hell. That was close enough for a visit. "He hasn't mentioned anything about coming down here, has he?" Reed asked carefully.

"Not that I know of, sir, but I'm sure he can jet down here quickly for any family plans," Petr informed him without any telltale sign that he knew that would be the last thing Reed wanted. "But I wanted you to know because I'm sure he'll call me today sometime."

It was Petr's way of saying that Reed's stay wouldn't be a secret any longer. The man was one of his father's most trusted assistants. Of course Petr would have to tell his employer that his youngest son was staying at the suite.

"Will you get hold of me after you've talked to him?" Reed asked.

"Of course. Sir, wouldn't it be better if you called him yourself?"

Reed didn't feel like explaining anything to his father, and he had a feeling it would be one of those long conversations about his lack of ambition and his need to go talk to his mother. After all, he hadn't talked to her since . . . he couldn't remember when he'd last had any words with her. Had it been after Arch's funeral? Maybe once more after that, who knows.

"Just let me know when he calls, Petr, that's all. Tell him I'll be staying at the suite for a few more days. If it's inconvenient, I'll find some other place."

"Yes, sir."

"By the way, Petr, are the stores down in the lobby open yet?"

"I think they're just starting their business day."

"If I place an order with them, can you pick up the items and deliver them up to me? Thank you."

Once he was alone, Reed stared at the portrait of his father, which was hanging over the mantelpiece in the office. This must be a recent piece, since Reed had never seen it before. His father had always been a handsome man, with the dark good looks of his Italian ancestors, and old age had given him a distinguished air. Or maybe the artist had somehow added that layer, like artists tend to do with important subjects.

He massaged the back of his neck to ease the tension that always seemed to appear whenever he thought of his father. Or anything to do with family, for that matter. It had been a while since he'd sat down to talk to the old guy.

He should, at least, make a cursory call, but superficiality escaped him right now. There was currently enough deception around him that he didn't think he could sound artlessly pleasant in any conversation with his father. He thought of Lily on the sofa upstairs. Her response to him was real. Her answers rang true so far. If that was the case, then he was the one doing all the deceiving here. He was surprised at how hard he'd had to fight his instincts. It had always been his nature to accept things as they were and move on when deception got in the way; he hadn't thought that would interfere in the course of a mission, though.

One thing was for sure. He couldn't fail Admiral Madison in this Joint Mission with GEM. The latter had fulfilled their part of the bargain by letting his SEAL teammates destroy the caches of weapons that Dilaver had hidden. This device that he was trying to get from Lily was the only thing that GEM wanted and that his commander, Hawk, had been unable to secure. This was the last chance.

Reed sighed. Well, he'd always wanted a last chance in which things went right. With his parents. With Arch. Ironically, it seemed the only thing he was pretty good at was shooting things down, without giving them a last chance, so to speak. He thought of Lily again. Last chances were always powerful and meaningful.

Dude, quit thinking like that or life will drown you, man.

As it did you, Arch, my friend, as it did you.

Reed dialed the secured number to contact Nikki Harden. He had to report—without too many details, he hoped—that he'd managed to get Lily to agree to spend a few days with him and to outline the new schedule of events.

The woman was like an addiction. He hadn't wanted to leave her in the suite.

And you haven't even made love to her yet.

He wanted to, desperately, but he wasn't that far gone yet. He wouldn't do it without protection. He'd be out of his mind to play with fate like that.

"It's Reed," he said, after he was patched through. Not that they didn't know it already. "I'm to accompany her to get her belongings at her hotel. I need some weapons. Is there a place I can pick some up without trouble?"

There was a slight pause. Reed could hear some discussion in the background. "I can deliver them to you," Nikki said.

"You mean, meet me in person?"

"It'll give me a chance to see Lily in person, too."

He'd forgotten that Nikki was working with him to evaluate Lily's mental status. He wasn't sure he liked the idea. "How do we meet?"

"Like all spies, of course—at the park." Nikki's voice was amused. "You know how they exchange goodies there while reading some paper on the benches."

"Or feeding the birds," Amber chimed in. "Don't forget the dark sunglasses, even in winter."

The women were making fun of him. "All right. What time and which park?" Reed wrote the venue and time down on the pad in front of him. "Do I introduce you to her?"

"Yes. The usual cover, but we'll use a car instead of walking around in the cold. During the conversation, I'll be telling her that someone's after her, then when you get to Johnny Chic, he can confirm this again. Make a good bargain, Reed, so she can see you as a gunrunner who can help her sell that weapon."

He didn't want Lily to just see him in that role, but at least there really was someone after her. "Any news about the dead body in the alley?" he asked.

"He's a former East German operative. I know, there's no such thing as East Germany, but there are certain factions who've hired many of those who used to work for the other side. He's been inactive for a while, so we're working on the angle of a network of operatives who's been called back. Johnny Chic talked to Greta last night, so whoever shot our dead operative also works for her."

He was glad that one detail had been confirmed. Lily wasn't working with Greta. Not now, anyway. "Is she behind this whole thing with the sleeper?" Reed asked.

"That's what T.'s working on. Amber's looking for information for us, too."

"Why don't we just pick Greta up?"

"Easier said than done. We don't know where she is, for one thing," Nikki said. "We do know that since Lily failed to follow instructions, Greta's been looking for her and the device. Keep an eye on Lily, Reed."

"I will. One more thing. If Greta's the one who activated Lily's sleeper status, and Lily was stopped from following through the last time, then she can do it again, right?"

"Yes, and there won't be anyone to stop Lily this time. Brad managed to get hold of her this one time and somehow got through to her." Nikki paused. "You're her last chance, Reed. She can't outrun Greta and the others after her."

Last chance. Hadn't those words just popped up in his head a few minutes ago? Reed bit his lower lip thoughtfully. "In all honesty, she appears to be really alone," he told Nikki.

"She's always worked alone, Reed," Amber said. She'd been very quiet throughout the conversation. "She doesn't trust anyone. The thing about Lily is that she seldom talks about herself. It took her four years to tell me a little bit, and most of it was programmed lies she'd told herself, anyway."

"But she doesn't lie about her need for those passports for her girls," Reed countered, giving some details about the phone call to Tatiana.

"Tatiana's in charge of the girls?" Amber said, surprise in her voice. "The last time I saw her, she was still recovering from her injuries. She must be doing a lot better."

Injuries? "So that's really her name? What injuries?"

"Yes, it is. Tatiana, like all the other girls, were lured and kidnapped from their hometowns. You know that, Reed. Some of the girls were"—Amber paused, looking for the right words—"not cooperative and thus suffered more."

In other words, they'd had to be "broken." Reed recalled all those girls he'd seen that night so many months ago and remembered how frightened they had seemed. Dilaver was dead, yet in a way, these scarred girls were still his prisoners. He wished he'd been the one to kill that bastard. If he were Lily, he'd be doing the same thing she'd planned on—getting the girls out of this place in any way possible.

"There's an article that just came out recently, written by reporters who had interviewed those girls face-to-face," Amber continued. "I'll give a copy to Nikki to pass on to you, so you can see what Lily and I were dealing with when we worked together."

"I would like that. They're still Lily's main concern, and she's trusted me to do this one favor for her," Reed told them. "From talking to her, I get the feeling that she's running away, not from you, Amber, or her handler, but from everyone."

"Is she really talking about herself to you?" Amber asked.

Not yet, but he intended to find out more. "I'm trying," he said. Lily responded to him emotionally, he wanted to say, but that would open himself up for a lot of speculation from these two very intelligent analysts. "I think she likes me enough to talk about other things besides the girls."

He managed to keep the tone of his voice businesslike, but he knew that there was very little that could be kept secret from field operatives who made a living inserting themselves into different lives. Inexperienced as he was at this type of covert work, even he would have drawn certain conclusions about the situation. At it was, he was grateful to the women for not bringing up the obvious. He didn't want to analyze his own feelings about what was happening.

"If you can find out whether she knows, really knows, what has happened to her, and if we can figure out what sets her off, then we have a way to save her. Otherwise, once we have the weapon in our hands and without any threat of her using it, we'll bring her in and work on her. If she doesn't put up a fight, that is. Sleeper cells usually have instructions for suicide, Reed. I'm sorry."

Reed definitely didn't like *that* idea. But he also knew he couldn't let Lily go. She was, whether she knew it or not, a dangerous weapon for someone to use.

"Why do you think Greta wanted Lily dead?" he asked.

"From talking to Johnny, we think Greta was led to believe that Lily was meeting you to sell the weapon. The shot in the club was meant for you.

They wanted to isolate Lily with what they thought was the device in her bag."

She had saved him. "But it doesn't make sense. Why did they try to run her over then? Because the car was definitely veering in her direction when we were apart."

Lily had pushed him out of the way, telling him to run, assuming correctly that she'd been the target. But he had been the first target. If he'd been killed, she would have drowned in the river. . . . Providence. It seemed that their lives were linked together.

"We can only conjecture about that, Reed," Nikki said. "Perhaps someone panicked when they saw that you were with Lily. Perhaps they'd thought you were the one who killed the man in the alley. Right now, not enough information. Hopefully T. will get some answers for us."

"How long will it take T. to find out more about Greta?" The faster they took down that double agent, the better. One less threat to Lily. "Greta sounds as if she's trying to get her hands on the device to use it again."

"Yes," Amber said, "I've been checking with my sources, and it doesn't look like she wants to sell it. There's only some market talk about a special weapon that was hidden in some cache in Dilaver's control. Not a beep about anyone selling it. That's good news too, because that means Lily's not doing that either. By the way, T. isn't back yet, but she did send a message to pass to you."

"What's that?" He wondered where the GEM chief was. How did one go about tracing a missing mole like Greta?

"She says that if you draw a sheep, remember to add a muzzle."

Reed went very still. A reference from his favorite book. The sheep in *The Little Prince* was meant to help, but it also posed a threat to the flower, since sheep ate plants. That woman had an uncanny knack of reading people's minds. She was trying to warn him against giving Lily too much help, especially when he didn't know how dangerous she could be. He tried to think of a smart rebuttal.

"I assume you know what she's talking about," Nikki said when he didn't reply immediately. "T. has a way of saying the most puzzling things."

"Yes. You don't sound puzzled. Does she always pop a bullet into you when you aren't looking?" he asked.

"You're the trained sniper, Reed," Nikki said. "T. does the same thing, except she shoots at invisible mental blocks. Use your own experience to understand her. She's just making you aware of something, that's all."

Maybe that was why she was the leader of GEM. He'd heard that she was very talented at maneuvering people. One would think those under her would resent a person like that. But he'd liked working with T. He found her outrageous flair for drama and her enjoyment of attention appealing.

"In that case," he said, "speaking from a sniper's point of view, please tell her when you talk to her again that her timing's excellent."

"Now that compliment will definitely please her," Nikki said with a small laugh. "T. loves it when she hits a bull's-eye. Tell me the weapons you think you're going to need. I'll see you soon."

11

Lily looked up. The faint sound of the cell phone's beeps called at her. She turned back to the open drawer, methodically lifting anything that could hide a few thin passports.

The phone stopped, then immediately started again. She gritted her teeth, then walked quickly back into the living room, where she'd left the stupid thing. She looked at it as it trilled merrily at her. It was a compact, weighing a few ounces, yet it'd felt like a hundred-pound albatross when she was holding it.

It's just Reed. Answer it. She couldn't. She hadn't been affected by wild mood swings since she'd stopped using one, so there must be some sort of connection. She hadn't been paranoid when she'd felt she was being followed. Someone *had* tried to kill her last night, so that was proof that she wasn't going mental.

The ringing stopped. Lily remained tense for a minute, expecting it to start again, to go through the whole process of arguing with herself. It stayed quiet.

She sighed. Never had she felt so cut off from the world. She'd thought she was a pretty fearless person, but this new . . . phobia . . . was destroying her freedom. She couldn't check up on the girls, for heaven's sake. Couldn't make the usual calls to get hold of her contacts. Couldn't make bank transfers or any number of chores that an ordinary person could do.

Sooner or later, she would have to face the demons, but she dared not chance it while the girls still depended on her. Once she'd gotten them to safety, she would sit down and deal with what was left of her life.

Lily snorted in self-disgust as she turned and walked back to the room where she'd been conducting a careful search. That shouldn't take too much time. There weren't that many options in her future. She couldn't live a normal life in the future if she couldn't pick up a phone.

"Not that I know what a normal life is!" she said out loud. She looked at the expensive furniture and equipment in the "media" room, as she called it, and waved her arm dramatically to declare, "*This* isn't normal."

In the space of twenty-four hours, she had danced the tango, been chased by a car, been shot at, jumped off a two-story bridge and almost drowned in icy water, been stripped naked after she'd passed out and been bathed by a stranger—a sexy, equally naked stranger—and sort of imprisoned in some kind of luxury suite. Not to mention—Lily could feel the wave of heat warming her cheeks—being treated as if she were a kept woman. She didn't even know the man! She touched her face. What had possessed her to let him do all those things to her?

Kept woman. He might as well have imprisoned her, even though he'd given her a cell phone and the codes to the elevator. She couldn't call anyone for help. She couldn't walk out of here without any clothes. Well, she could—but without even a vehicle, how long would she last in the cold weather? She laughed at the ludicrous image.

What would Amber say if she knew what had happened to her? She'd crack up at her right now, standing barefoot on thick carpet with nothing but a T-shirt on, with all her other clothes destroyed in a bathroom. Amber would be laughing her ass off at the idea of her relying on a man who might or might not come back with clothes, who seemed to be able to take them off her without any trouble, who had a way of kissing her and making her . . .

A half-hysterical chuckle caught in Lily's throat. "Oh, Amber," she muttered, "you'll be calling me a Wretched Wench."

The name was a mocking name, with an accompanying Wretched Wench List, which Amber and she had made up one night when they had gone out drinking during happier days. A Wretched Wench was a desperate woman who would let a man do anything to her because he could get her all horny. Oh, how they had giggled over that.

And then Amber had fallen hard for Hawk

McMillan, and Lily had teased her about becoming a Wretched Wench. It made Lily smile thinking about how totally in love her girlfriend had been.

She sighed again. They must be out of the country by now. Hopefully, they'd one day forgive her for her betrayal.

She opened the next drawer and looked listlessly at its contents. Loneliness was a strange thing. She had been lonely before but had never felt it so soul deep. It seemed that everything she'd built had fallen apart like a pack of cards.

"That's because you're a pack of lies, girl," she said as she pulled out another drawer. Empty. Just like now, she was trying to live a lie. She didn't want to do this to Reed, who seemed to want to help her, but . . . what was one more lie? She needed his passports more. "Where would he keep them?"

She hoped to find them in the few days that she'd be here. If she could locate the passports, there would be fewer she'd have to pay cash for. She had been mulling over the idea of an even bigger lie. Maybe she could use the stolen device she'd hidden to get more than just passports. With a good chunk of cash, she could pay off all the requisite bribes and expenses. That way, the CIA couldn't track her through her bank accounts. Nor could they try to force her hand by freezing up all her money. It was a tempting idea.

She wasn't planning on selling the weapon, of course, but if she could get Reed to set up a sale through Johnny Chic, all she needed was a big lie to carry off a fake device. She carefully pushed the last drawer closed. Once again she would be betraying a person helping her and her girls out.

"Sorry, Reed," she murmured. She wished there were some other way. He was a gunrunner; he'd sell the real device without care of the consequences. "I can't have this bomb thing in anyone's hands. I guess, when they programmed me, they forgot to take away my morals."

She heard the ping of the arriving elevator. Reed. The thought of his hands and lips on her body again made her shiver. She wondered whether he'd gotten any condoms this time. She forgot another line Amber had said. Wretched Wenches had no morals. Oh dear.

"Damn, why did I forget the gloves?"

Greta ran her thumb over the finger with the broken nail. She peeled the rest of the nail off and made a face at its shortened length. Her fault. She'd forgotten to bring the smaller pair of gloves that she was to use for rough work. Like climbing a stupid garden wall.

It was a cold morning, and she'd cocooned herself in her new fur coat before boarding the train. She had enjoyed a nice breakfast and read a good book. She'd wanted to be relaxed when she arrived.

She looked up at the brick wall, her rope hanging loosely, waiting for her. Damn it. She couldn't climb it without getting rope burns. She was very aware that her upper body strength wasn't what it used to be, even with working out regularly all these years. She hadn't actually practiced endurance and wall climbing. She could sacrifice her nails and do it, of course, but she'd wanted Gunther to look at his TV and see how effortlessly she was doing it.

She needed those gloves. They'd had a special sticky film sprayed on them to ease her climb. But after putting on her regular winter gloves, she had left them on the train.

"Stupid bitch," she muttered.

She wanted to make an entrance, to show Gunther what she was made of. The man didn't have enough respect for her capabilities, and she wanted to teach him a lesson. Killing was too easy. She'd always liked a little flair in her work. She still smiled at the memory of one of her best dramatic moments: She'd ordered one of her men to lob off the long hair of her CIA boss's wife, and she had hand-delivered the box to him herself before her escape. How she wished she'd been there to watch his face, but he would have done it in private, anyway, and her time had been running out. She'd had to disappear quickly or be caught.

But yes, that had been the highlight of her final days in the States. Too bad her man had fucked up. Somehow her final revenge hadn't finished with that woman's death. How that small little thing had managed to escape him was a mystery to Greta, but her sources had reported that the woman had escaped and that her kidnapper had somehow been killed and his body burned in a fire.

Greta shook her head. She had to stop gloating here. Gunther wasn't dumb. He was probably waiting for her to show up anyway.

She smiled. What could be a grander entrance than to ring the doorbell? He wouldn't kill her anyway, not yet. People were expecting her at home, and her death would point to him, since he'd been assigned to assist her. No, he just wanted to put her in a bad light so he could be the next big spy.

"Not of my stature, you won't," Greta murmured. He was incompetent at best. To jeopardize a whole mission just to get ahead in his standing was simply foolhardy. She was valued because she did her job to perfection. All her work was immaculate. If she said she was going to get a special explosive device, she would. If she was told to demonstrate how she could slip it undetected into a crowded, secured area with big political names in attendance, she would. She wouldn't have dreamed up a stupid scheme using some stupid unknown woman who had a few illegal things in her past to go there and blow herself up with all of them.

Greta went to the front gate and rang the door chime. She stood there calmly as the electronic camera zoomed in on her.

Granted, had Gunther succeeded, he would have gotten extra points for ridding them of a few powerful enemies. He'd have been rewarded for that, but Greta was very sure they wouldn't have approved of his brash disregard for the original orders. And that was why she would always be better than this new breed of operatives.

The wrought-iron gate opened just wide enough for one person to slip inside. It closed behind her as she walked up the path toward the front door. As she approached, it opened by itself, like in some ghost movie. She stepped onto the doormat and wiped her boots with deliberate care as she looked inside.

Hallway. Staircase. Two closed doors to the left.

She walked into the house.

"I'm in the back, Greta. Come on in," someone called out. "There are no traps, I promise."

Greta snorted. Like she was going to believe that.

How was it possible to be aware of so many details about a woman just by watching her walk into the room?

Reed gripped the shopping bags tightly. Lily's skin glistened with droplets of water, her long legs flashing every time the flap between the two ends of the towel opened up when she took a step. She dabbed the side of her face with a smaller one.

"Hey, it's you," she said.

"Were you expecting someone, wearing that?" he asked as he went toward her. "Why didn't you answer my call?"

Lily shrugged. "Shower. I didn't hear anything."

"I called the suite number, too," he said. "Surely you heard the ringing."

"I told you I was in the shower," she said, walking

back into the bedroom and tossing the small towel onto the bed. She picked up a bottle of lotion from the nearby dresser.

He watched her for a moment. He'd forgotten how much time a woman took to get ready. It always fascinated him to see all their rituals before they even put a piece of clothing on.

"There's a phone in the bathroom, Lily," he pointed out as he stepped closer.

She shrugged again as she poured some of the cream onto her palm. "I don't know, I didn't hear anything. What did you want?"

Reed placed the bags at the end of the bed. "I forgot to ask for your shoe size," he explained. "You should have everything else in these bags, though. We'll just get the shoes afterwards."

He watched her rub the white milky stuff up her forearms and shoulders. "Afterwards" had never sounded more erotic. He sat down on the bed.

"Oh." Lily turned, taking a few steps closer to the bed, where she placed the bottle of lotion. "You bought those for me?"

He didn't look at where she was pointing. "Yeah. They should fit."

"Okay." She bent and peered into one of the bags. "Thank you. I'll pay you back."

Reed reached for the end of the towel. "Okay," he said and tugged.

She turned toward him, surprise in her eyes. Her hand held on to the knot in the front of the towel.

"Don't you ever think of any other form of payment?" she demanded.

"I don't want your money. You need that for other things, anyway," he pointed out. "And for now, you need me."

He tugged again. She still resisted him. She had the most beautiful eyes, not totally black but a dark chocolate brown that reminded him of hot fudge on ice cream. Every time he looked into them, he wanted to lick her.

"I want to get ready to go," she said softly.

"I'll help you," he offered.

She shook her head. "Oh yeah, right. I don't think you have getting me dressed in mind."

He smiled. "Of course I do. I'm going to help you get ready. It's my clothes you're going to wear, so I should at least get to see you put them on."

He knew those words would rile her. He was beginning to enjoy seeing that glint of temper in her eyes. He liked it because that meant her focus was on him. He knew that running off wasn't far from her thoughts, and he didn't want her to think of him just as a way to get what she wanted. He pulled at the handful of towel in his grasp. She grabbed on to the knot tighter, at the same time lifting her leg to direct a kick.

"Uh-uh, no hurting your savior," he said, easily catching her leg and tilting her sideways. Unbalanced, she fell forward and had to grasp his shoulder with her free hand. The fruity scent of body lotion tempted him. "The first rule of kicking at your opponent is to not worry whether you're naked or not. Besides, I wouldn't mind the scenery."

He'd read in her file that although she wasn't trained in martial arts, she knew how to protect herself. As he steadied her, he ran a hand down her calf, feeling its slender strength. He'd like to take her swimming and watch those legs kicking underwater. She would enjoy surfing. He was sure of it.

The image of her on a surfboard took away a little of his enjoyment. If wishes were horses . . .

"So why didn't you pick up the phone?" he asked again instead. There was no way she couldn't have heard the ringing, even with the water running.

"It stopped ringing by the time I heard it," she said, her eyes not meeting his as she leaned down to kiss him.

"Liar." Reed reached up and pulled the knot out of her hand. The towel fell to the floor. He tried to ignore the parts he really wanted to touch. He wondered whether she had really been showering. The towel was dry.

"Did you get any condoms?" Lily asked, still landing soft kisses on his lips.

He was glad he was wearing clothes, because he wanted to pull her down into his arms and forget about protection. "No." He certainly wasn't going to get Petr to do that part of the shopping for him. She was trying to distract him. Trying to ignore her hand massaging the back of his neck, he ran a light finger over the bandaged gauze wrapped around her arm. It was barely wet. It should be soaked through if she had been showering. "I didn't see any down-stairs."

"So how are you going to dress me?" she teased. "Are you sure you have everything I need?"

"Everything is there but underwear," Reed told her. Her soft caress stilled as he reached for the bottle of lotion on the bed. "I like the idea of you not wearing any."

She straightened up. "You aren't going to do that to me again," she said. Her eyes were so dark they were black now. "Not when you aren't joining me."

"Call this foreplay."

She wanted to distract him. He would do the same to her.

Reed squeezed a generous amount onto her stomach. He smoothed the cream upwards, enjoying the silkiness of her skin. Her tummy went taut with anticipation as he ran his palms up her rib cage. If she wanted to play who could distract whom the most, she was going to lose. He cupped both her breasts. They filled his hands as she inhaled sharply.

"Why do I keep letting you do this to me?" she wondered softly, her eyes half-closing.

He kissed her stomach. "It's an honest response, sweetheart. Your body just likes me more than you think."

"What does that mean?"

Reed thought about all the secrets she was hiding from everyone. He gently teased the pink nipples into little hard nubs. "You won't answer my questions. Your body's response is more truthful than you are. You know what? I don't mind sitting here and doing this all day. Sooner or later, you'll have to give me some answers." He looked up. "Later is okay with me."

He reached for the lotion again. She looked at him, her breathing a little faster.

"What do you want to know?"

"Who's after you, for instance. I was shot at too, you know, so I'm more than a bit curious. And why do you need so many passports? What are they for? Tell me where you're going."

Where is the explosive device? Is someone still in control of you?

Her hands moved up to hold his face. "That's too naked for me," she whispered.

Reed had a feeling that her answer was very close to the truth. Llallana Noretski had hidden herself for so many years that talking about herself would be tantamount to being stripped naked emotionally. Except that, at this moment, she was trying to distract him physically.

"I know," he said in a low voice. He wanted her to capitulate emotionally. That was the only way to find the real Lily. Still holding her gaze, he squeezed out a blob of lotion. He rubbed his palms and smoothed the thick liquid onto her soft skin. He would gladly play her game, because he planned to win. "But that's the fun of foreplay. I get to strip you one layer at a time."

"Do I get to do the same thing?" she asked huskily. "And I don't mean rubbing skin lotion all over you."

"Ladies first," he told her with a small smile.

It was crazy. He wanted her to want him for more than just his help; he wanted her to want him enough to share all her secrets with him. In a way, not being able to have sex with her was good. He didn't want her to think that he just wanted to fuck her. He wanted more than that.

It was a crazy thought, but he was thinking of saving her for himself. Not possible, Vincenzio. The woman was wanted by a bunch of agencies. But he'd be lying to himself if he didn't admit that he was playing with alternative scenarios. He had, after all, been brought up a Vincenzio, and Vincenzios always found a way to buy and keep secrets.

Greta sipped on her coffee as she studied the man sitting across the table from her. She wasn't easily surprised, but Gunther Galbert had certainly done that this morning. She hadn't expected him to be breakfasting in his greenhouse, surrounded by tropical and semitropical plants and miniature fountains. Of course, he had a computer on a cart beside him, from which he could monitor anything he wished. But at the moment, he appeared to be immersed in his food.

"You sure you don't want some?" he asked in German.

She shook her head. "No, thank you."

He was probably a dozen years younger than her, but with the trimmed beard and professorial clothing, he looked older. She had dealt with him a number of times when she'd worked in D.C., passing information back and forth, and he'd always struck her as more of a courier, but here he had been playing her like a seasoned operative. She wondered what he had in store for her today.

"I like doing business on a full stomach," he said.

"I wasn't aware we were doing any business together," Greta said.

"You're still angry at the little trick I pulled on you, aren't you?" He wiped his mouth, then pushed his chair back. "You should've known you'd be tested now that you're back in the game."

She peered up at him as she took another sip from her cup. She licked her lips, savoring the strong taste of good coffee. "I'm not back in the game," she lied smoothly. "I'm retiring, remember?"

"Come, come. If you were, why did you choose to have the weapon hidden in one of your nephew's dropped CIA weapon caches?" Gunther lit a thin cheroot. He inhaled deeply, closing his eyes with enjoyment. After a moment, he added, "The old Greta I know would have found a better way of delivery, one that wasn't so risky."

She didn't like the way he used the word "old." "I was in a hurry to get out of the States," she said, then realized belatedly that she'd fallen into a trap. He was making her admit that she had been on the verge of being caught. She amended, "I wanted to be the one to handle the item myself, since this is my last job for the Agency."

His smile told her he wasn't fooled by her quick cover-up. She had to be more careful while sparring words with him. She had no intention of letting him know that her motivation was selfishness rather than concern over doing her job well. She had wanted to return home in triumph, to ensure that her record ended not with a hurried escape but with an operation befitting someone of her caliber.

"Why would you want to test an *old* lady?" she continued, trying not to choke on that word. "For ten years I've delivered, so my record speaks for itself. I don't have anything to prove."

"Forgive my curiosity then, but why did you want to be the one to demonstrate the device to headquarters? You were willing to take a big risk, sneaking in that device. My way was much better. I'd have sacrificed a stupid girl, instead of an experienced operative like you. There are people blowing themselves up all over the place these days. What's one more? Therefore, there's less suspicion that someone else planted a bomb." Gunther tapped his cheroot on the ashtray. "So, from my perspective, you wanted to show that you still have the skills. My question is, why, if you're retiring."

He really had a sharp and observant mind. It was a shame that she was planning to get rid of him.

"I like to do things personally because there's less chance of failure." She smiled nastily. "After all, if I'd been allowed to do my job, the device wouldn't have disappeared with the girl, would it? And we wouldn't be wasting all these months tracking after her and looking for the damn thing now, would we?"

He studied her as he smoked, seemingly unperturbed that he was the one who had failed. Greta wondered whether he was in trouble with headquarters, since he was the one who had deviated from the original orders. However, that still didn't explain why he was trying to stop her every time she got near Llallana Noretski. No, there was more to this than mere competition. He had mentioned doing business together.

"Actually," he said, as he exhaled another puff of smoke, "I was under orders to try something different. There are people up there who thought it would be too much work for someone who's just returned to action. So, they asked me to activate another one of our people in the CIA to see whether there was another alternative."

Greta looked at Gunther with as little expression on her face as possible. So she had been right. Some of them did think she wasn't capable anymore. That was what she was afraid of. Apparently, being ten years older meant she wasn't up to carrying a simple device into a summit of politicians and getting close enough to plant it on a target.

She patted her newly dyed hair. She had taken care of her face and body all these years, but of course, there were no pictures of the new look. All they saw was the dowdy old secretary she'd played so well. Too damn well, it appeared, because they had begun to believe that she really looked like that.

"Now you need me for some reason," she said. "What can an old lady like me do for you and the agency? I might as well pack up now and go home. I have many relatives I want to visit."

Maybe she should forget triumph and glory. She

could be just as happy at the dacha, enjoying meeting her family. She could finish knitting the shawl for her niece. And maybe even travel around.

"No need to be so dramatic, Greta. You were never this unreasonable when you were in D.C.," Gunther chided. "Why, you were always businesslike. I've enjoyed your professionalism whenever we communicated, but now, I'm seeing a different side of you. I must say you're looking very attractive."

"This is me," Greta said. She darted him a quick glance. Was he flirting with her? "That was Greta the secretary. I assure you, I'm a lot more capable than that woman."

"Oh, I know that. I've read your files. You're a legend," Gunther told her.

Why was he praising her now? "What is it you want?" she asked.

"I want you to contact your niece."

Greta looked up sharply and found him watching her closely. "Who?"

"I'm afraid your letting out the word in the market about a missing special weapon has caught a lot of interest. She's after the device. I want you to lure her out and make her a partner or something. She can't have the device. Or Lily. They are both important for our operations."

"My niece?" Greta frowned. "I haven't been in touch with any of my relatives for years. Security protocol, as you know. They're all kids still in school. Why do you think they're involved?"

"Ah, Greta, Greta. Ten years, my dear," Gunther

said, stroking his beard thoughtfully. "Your young nieces and nephews are all grown up. Don't tell me you still think they are teenagers? The niece I want you to contact was married to one of our generals, but you know how that is—poverty has turned her to more lucrative business. It seems female empowerment runs in your family genes."

"What are you talking about?" Her niece. Greta frowned again. Which one? There were three that she remembered, and they'd been the sweetest little kids when she'd left them. But . . . Gunther was right. They weren't kids anymore. "What's she doing now?"

"She's married to a general, I told you. That means she's been making money selling all the Russian weaponry that she could get her hands on. She's quite notorious back home, let me tell you. Our government indulges her because she does bring back some items for them, and she's promised them the device. We, of course, don't want certain parties in the government to have it. We are, after all, trying to rebuild the old system."

In many ways, her agency was just like the CIA, an entity with its own agenda apart from the government. "How do I contact this niece, then?"

"I've done it. I'm the handler, remember? She'll be here later today, because she's just as curious about meeting the legendary Aunty Greta, as she called you. We have plans for her, and we need your cooperation."

"My niece. What's her name?" She wasn't happy

about being caught by surprise again. It seemed Gunther had more advantage over her than she'd anticipated. "And how come I didn't know about this before?"

"How do the Americans put it—need-to-know basis?" Gunther put out his cheroot. "Do you remember Talia?"

Talia, dark hair and pink cheeks, with snow all over her hat when Greta had last seen her. Talia wouldn't be a gawky teenager any more.

"Of course," she said coolly.

Gunther tapped on his computer. "Here's our last photo of her. Except for the scar, a beautiful woman."

This would be the first time Greta had really looked at a member of her family. "Does she know why we want to talk to her?" she asked, pretending not to look too eagerly at the screen. From this distance, her niece looked absolutely beautiful. Dark hair and pretty smile, just as she remembered. "I don't see any scars."

"You're sitting too far away. It's not that noticeable, especially when she has makeup on. I'll print a hard copy for you after breakfast. She suffered some cuts on her face a few years ago from a homemade bomb. It didn't exactly disfigure her, but you know how it is with beautiful young women. She went for plastic surgery to repair the damage."

"She's gorgeous," Greta murmured. But then the women in her family had always turned heads.

"There's a thin scar from there to there," Gunther told her, moving his finger on the screen. "Other

than that, she's manage
more beautiful than ever,
found wealth, I'm sure she
here and there."

She took her eyes off the picture
operation details?"

"Talia's getting too close to what we're d
want you to eliminate her."

Greta swerved her gaze back to the man across t
table. "You want me to kill my own niece," she said
slowly.

Gunther smiled. "Not immediately, of course. You
can get to know her better first."

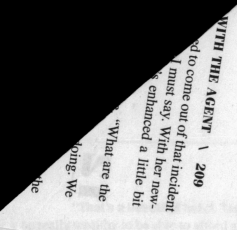

to come out of that incident . . . I must say. With her new-enhanced a little bit

"What are the

It wasn't just a regular hotel suite, not when there was a private elevator that led straight to the parking garage. Lily slanted Reed a sideways glance. She'd never met a gunrunner who had such highly placed friends. An art dealer, yes.

"Yes, he's very wealthy," Reed said as he backed the car out of its space.

"Maybe you should introduce him to me," Lily joked. "I need some of his money."

He glanced at her briefly. "I doubt he'd approve of how you'd spend his money."

"How could he say that?" Lily asked. "I'm helping girls get out of . . ."

She stopped, but not in time.

"I'm guessing that's what those passports are for." Reed drove the car out of the garage, turning into the side street. "It's still illegal."

Too late to deny it. It wasn't that difficult to put

two and two together. "He's friends with you," Lily pointed out, "and he lets you stay at his place. So he isn't as lily white as you make him sound."

Her comment obviously amused him. He had the most devastating smile when he used it. She barely knew the man, but she noticed little things about him—that he didn't smile much, that he knew exactly what to say to fluster her. He also knew how to arouse her.

She looked out the window, trying not to think about his hands and lips. Yes, she barely knew him, but somehow, in the short time they'd been together, she had gotten to know his touch too well. And unlike other times, when she'd been the one who'd left her partner satisfied, she was now on the receiving end.

She recognized it because she had done this to others. He had deliberately pleasured her intimately but had held himself back. Of course, it had been due to the fact that there hadn't been any available protection, but he was the first man she'd met who had let that stop his own pleasure. That told her a lot about Reed.

A few days with him. She shivered at the thought. Would she hold herself back like she always did when it came to intimacy?

"Cold? Do you want the heater higher?" Reed asked.

Lily shook her head. She didn't want to let him know that his foreplay in the suite had been a success. For months, all her thoughts had been focused on the girls and survival. How could one man's touch change all that? It was embarrassing.

She could trace it step by step. He'd seen her naked. He'd touched her. He'd kissed her intimately. And he'd dressed her. But it wasn't as simple as that. Seeing her nudity and touching her weren't the same as taking off her clothes and washing her body. She could still feel his hands on her nakedness. And then he'd managed to be even closer this morning when she'd woken up. She felt as if she'd given control of her body to him. He'd put on this sweater. He'd zipped up these pants. And he hadn't brought up underwear. She knew why. He wanted her to think of him all day.

Foreplay.

"Do you always get weapon supplies so easily?" she asked. "Make a call and then it's delivered, just like that?"

"I have good credit with my friends," Reed said.

"You have some good friends," she said, thinking of Amber. "Have you ever done anything to hurt them?"

"No."

"Keep it that way," she advised. "If not, you'll end up alone like me."

"What did you do?" he asked.

She listened to the quiet purring of the car for a few moments. "Betrayal." She hadn't said that word aloud to anyone. It was almost a relief. "The kind that's unforgivable. Have you done anything like that to someone you love?"

"No, but it's happened to me," Reed said. Stopping at a red light, he turned to her. "It isn't a nice feeling to be kicked in the teeth."

Lily laughed humorlessly. "Well, I kicked my friends in the teeth."

"Have you talked to them about it?"

"Of course not. I betrayed them, and then I ran." She shoved a hand through her hair. "Besides, it's not so simple. The light's green."

What would he say if she told him she had been programmed to do it? No one would believe her story.

Reed started the car again. "Nothing's simple when it comes to hurting those one loves."

"You sound like you've done it yourself."

"No, I told you, it's happened to me." He turned into what looked like a park. "Here we are."

She had to know. "So did you forgive whoever betrayed you?"

His gray eyes were very cool when he looked at her. "No."

Lily laughed again. "You're supposed to be tactful here and say, yes, Lily, I forgave them and now everything's okay."

"I have another friend who told me that," he said as he parked the car. He glanced around. "We're early."

She looked around too. There were several other cars parked there, but no one was in the vehicles. "Do we get out or stay in here? What are you looking at?"

"Making sure there isn't anyone targeting us."

She couldn't see anybody. She felt bad that she was putting him in danger. "I'm sorry to be so much trouble," she said.

He reached out for her hand and laced her fingers with his. "I've been in worse," he told her. His eyes warmed as his gaze traveled down the length of her. "And never with such lovely company by my side."

"Hah, flirt." She enjoyed the way he looked at her. "So what did you say to your friend who told you to forgive?"

He studied their entwined hands. "His name was Arch. He was sort of a father figure. Forgiveness is earned, Lily. I can't forgive when everything's not in the open, when no one talks about it." He shrugged. "It's a secret, so I can't talk about it."

"Oh, secrets. Well, I definitely can understand secrets." She had plenty of them. "Maybe the truth's just unbelievably hard to tell. Have you ever thought about it from my—I mean whoever did that awful thing's—perspective? Maybe we had to do it."

Reed kept quiet for a few seconds. "Maybe so," he said. "But if you want your friend to forgive you, don't let too much time pass by, sweetheart. Time doesn't heal if there's silence."

He was talking about himself, but his words resonated. Lily sighed. Even if she wanted to set things right, she didn't know where to start.

A black car drove up and parked alongside Reed's car. "Here we go," he said. He kissed the back of her hand before releasing it.

* * *

"This is Nikki Harden, a friend. Nikki, Lily."

Lily hadn't expected a woman. She studied the petite Asian smiling at her, noting the quick exchange of glances between Reed and her. How close a friend?

"Hi," Lily said, offering her hand.

Nikki shook it. "Reed's told me about you," she said.

Lily shot Reed a glance. "Really."

"Yes. When Reed called and asked for my help, I knew it had to be a woman, of course."

"I had to tell her because she's my connection to the news on the street," Reed explained. "If there's anything out there about you, Nikki will know."

Lily nodded as she looked around the van. She used to have a great source of information—Amber. She took off her gloves. It was strange to think that she would be news at all. She had been so careful. Yet someone had found out where she was anyway. Where was she going to go after all this?

"Here's the hardware you need," Nikki said to Reed, pulling up a bag sitting by her. "Is this enough?"

Lily watched Reed reach over and open the bag. He pulled out several weapons to examine. They looked new. He handled them with an easy expertise that showed his experience.

"Cool," he said approvingly, pulling two or three more out of the bag.

It seemed like a lot of weapons for just one man,

but Lily didn't say anything. She turned to Nikki. "You speak English like an American too," she noted.

"As do you," Nikki said. "Did you study in the States?"

"I spent some time there," Lily acknowledged noncommittally.

"I'm from D.C. and do quite a bit of freelancing there. What about you? What did you do in the States?"

Lily noticed that the other woman was just as vague with details as herself. She wondered briefly what they would say if she told the truth about recuperating and being trained at a CIA facility. At least, that was what she remembered. She knew now that somehow, during that time, the agency had placed her under hypnosis without her knowing it. Reed and Nikki would probably think her crazy.

"Nothing too exciting," she said blandly. "You seem like a boy with his Christmas toys, Reed."

Reed grinned. "How good are you with weapons?"

She wasn't a stranger to guns. Unlike many women, she wasn't afraid of touching them. The weight of the lethal metal made her feel safe, especially when she had to make the runs through the mountain passes. "I think I can handle a couple of them. If I'd had one of these last night, we'd have caught our guy and his friends in the alley."

"You look comfortable with weapons," Nikki observed.

"You sell them, so you should be too," Lily said.

Nikki shook her head. "I'm just a courier. Personally, I don't like them. Too violent."

"That's a strange thing to say in this business," Lily said with a smile. "Why don't you like them? They're just things, like everything else."

Nikki shrugged. "Things fall apart."

There was a short, drawn-out silence in the van. Lily wondered at the long look between Reed and Nikki again. So maybe they were that close. She curbed her disappointment. "Not that weapon," she said, pointing to the one Reed held in his hand. "I've had one of those forever, and it's never fallen apart. Good choice, Reed."

Reed handed it to her. She couldn't quite fathom the expression in his eyes. "You can keep this," he told her.

"What? I didn't mean—"

"You're going to need one for protection. Speaking of which—" Reed turned back to Nikki. "What information do you have on Lily?"

"She's Llallana Noretski," Nikki said. "Aren't you?"

Lily stiffened. Damn, she was good. "Yes," she replied.

"The description fits," Nikki said. "There's a high price for finding your whereabouts. It's been out there for two months."

The sum she named left Lily speechless for a second. She blinked several times, trying to digest the fact that she was on some kind of wanted poster, like a criminal. "Who would offer that?" she finally asked, hoping her shock wasn't too obvious.

It had to be the CIA, of course. She had something that they wanted.

"Anonymous through a reliable intermediary." Nikki cocked her head. "Why are you important to these people? Reed told me you're part of a human trafficking network."

Lily turned to Reed. "Who's she? You've told her too much about me. I mean, what would stop her from selling me out? That's a lot of money on my head."

She wasn't afraid for herself. She didn't matter. Sooner or later, they would catch up with her, anyway. But she preferred it to be at a time of her choosing.

Reed took her hand. "No, Nikki won't pass on this information."

"You trust people too easily," she said.

"Don't you trust Reed?" Nikki asked quietly. "You're here with him, though, aren't you?"

Lily had to, in her line of work. She'd bribed, bought information, and taken advice from—as well as handed over her girls to—complete strangers. One had to check one's wariness at the door when one was conducting shady transactions. The only thing Lily had to guide her was her gut instinct.

She looked at Reed, then at Nikki, and then back at him. They seemed to be waiting for some response from her. Strange how the issue of trusting Reed hadn't even surfaced in her thoughts.

"Point taken," Lily said. There was nothing much she could do, anyway. Her gut instinct was telling her that this was the best option. "Reed saved me from drowning. I'm grateful to be here and to have both your help. But, let's face it, that's a very generous sum of money on my head."

Reed turned her hand over and placed the gun in it. "Take this weapon and go then," he said. "Here's some ammunition. Here's the car keys. Go."

"Reed—"

"Go think it over," he said. "You know where to find me if you think you need my help any further."

"There's a warning that Llallana Noretski's armed and dangerous," Nikki said. "I don't think she should be out there alone."

"Get another blond wig," Reed said, ignoring Nikki's advice. "Stay out of clubs like The Beijing Bombshell. Use your cell phone to conduct business instead."

Lily pocketed the gun. "You're angry with me," she said. She didn't blame him. "I was just stating the facts."

"So am I," Reed retorted. "Hey, I'm just another stranger, right? You're right—all of us are in this for the money, but some of us also don't sell out people at the drop of a hat. It's a business, sweetheart, with advantages and disadvantages. I'm not a bounty hunter, by the way. I'm a gunrunner. I don't go around looking at wanted posters because that isn't my thing."

"Desperate people do a lot of things for money," Lily said. *Go.* Why was she trying to justify her actions to him?

"Have you noticed that I'm not the desperate one here? Nor is Nikki, by the way." Reed leaned over and pulled on the door handle. "Look, think this over and give me a call if you decide that you need me. You do, you know."

Lily pushed the door open. "Why do you want to help me?"

His gray eyes glinted with anger. "You're the one with all the answers. You figure it out."

She jumped out of the vehicle. The door slammed behind her. She cursed softly as she headed toward the blue car. Reed had put the decision solely in her hands. If she went back to him, it would be on his terms.

She started the car, tentatively looking back at the stationary black van.

"I can do this by myself," she said.

But she missed Reed already.

"That's a risk you took, saying the trigger line to her." Reed looked out the van's tinted window, watching Lily drive away in his car. When Nikki had said "Things fall apart," he'd found himself gripping the weapon in his hand tightly. "Why did you choose to do it now?"

During the weeks in training, they'd given him scenarios in which Lily might act, but he hadn't known her then. Right now, he didn't know what he'd have done if she'd become aggressive.

"No bigger than the risk you just took, letting her go. That wasn't in our plans."

"I wanted to give her a chance to make up her mind," Reed said. "Besides, there's a locator in my car."

"Which she could abandon," Nikki pointed out.

"I don't see you panicking," Reed countered. "You still haven't told me why you chose to try the neuro-trigger on her at this very moment. We don't know how she would react."

Nikki folded her hands in her lap. "Yes, we do. Do you remember the taped conversation we have, the one before Lily disappeared?"

"Sure, but when the trigger was used, it frightened her into running off."

Nikki shook her head. "No, it woke her up. I think, depending on the arrangements of the lines in that poem, it can either deepen the hypnotic state or give the individual full recollection. I was waiting to see whether Lily would give an automatic response, like an assigned line from the rest of the poem. That would signal a hypnotic state."

"Do you think she is under one?" Reed asked quietly.

"As you know, there are several levels of hypnotic states, and the deeper the individual is under control, the less likely she'd remember her past activities or real identity. The commands set by the trigger are embedded into the subconscious."

"Nikki, I've read all that mumbo jumbo. I understand it as much as reading an instruction manual on how to build a rocket ship. What exactly are we looking for?"

"I was trying to find out how much Llallana remembers. If she remembers everything, then it explains why she's running away from everybody, even her friends. The CIA, whom she'd thought saved her from a horrible life, had used her. She correctly believes that they're now after her to find out about the missing weapon. She might or might not know that Greta's after her too."

"And us," Reed said. In spite of all her problems, Lily was still concerned about her girls. It was a big responsibility for one on the run, and he couldn't help but feel admiration for her. "She didn't abandon her girls."

Nikki nodded. "I'm looking to save her, Reed." She looked at him perceptively. "Aren't you?"

He didn't want to appear as if his mind was already made up. "I don't know anything about psychological triggers," he said, "except for what you and the others have told me. I've said it before, I don't think Lily Noretski should be blamed for the things she's done."

"Remember, we have an agreement with Amber Hutchens to bring her friend in once we get the weapon out of her hands," Nikki said. "I came aboard this assignment because I know exactly what Lily has gone, and is going, through. It's part of my job to evaluate the weakness in a system, and in this case, it's the CIA 'Project Precious Gems.' The play in that name with our organization isn't accidental, Reed."

"You're . . ." Reed sat back in the seat as realization of who Nikki was came to him. With so many

new people to meet, he hadn't tied the obvious together. "That's how I've heard your name before.
You're the CIA operative who returned after being
missing for ten years. You were part of a congres-
sional hearing headed by my commander, Admiral
Madison. I know you said that you were captured
and subjected to psychological and physical torture.
Were you—"

He broke off to study the slight woman. She'd
never shared any of her experiences with him during
their talks together, although he'd always been very
attentive to her explanation of mental withdrawal
and identity replacement. With her belief in internal
balance and self-healing, she'd added an esoteric
bend to her workshop that had appealed to him. It
was hard to imagine that she had ever been a victim.

"I wasn't a sleeper cell, so I can't explain how it
feels to be under that kind of control, but my experiences as a prisoner for all those years give me insight
into how the mind can be injured in different ways."
Nikki took a deep breath, as if she preferred not to
think of her past. "The mind's a strange muscle. It
can heal its wounds by destroying parts of itself, or
hiding the events that caused the pain. In my case, it
was amnesia, and with the use of drugs by my cap-
tors, it induced a state similar to Level Four hypnosis. You could live quite normally without any desire
to remember, as I did for a while, but once the mind's
ready, the need to know burns inside."

She patted her chest. She smiled wryly and added,
"I know, you are wondering how that's connected

with Lily Noretski. You must already know her well enough to expect her to come back to you."

"No, I'm interested in what you're saying," Reed said. He had no explanation about his knowing Lily well enough, so he skipped that part of Nikki's observation. "It helps me understand what's going on in her head, what she's planning to do and, maybe, why. As a sharpshooter, I never have to do this, Nikki. I point the weapon, sight the target, and shoot. I did wonder why I was picked to do this particular operation."

"That's something you'll have to think about or ask Admiral Madison," Nikki said, her smile widening. The twinkle in her eye suggested that she had an idea but wasn't willing to share. "I believe that he picked you because you're the best one for this job. Isn't that what SEALs believe?"

"Yes."

"It's a state of mind, isn't it? To know you're the best and only you can do this one thing? To be trained to focus on one mission over all obstacles?"

Reed frowned. "Yes. Are you trying to tell me something?"

Nikki Harden was, after all, a GEM operative trained by T. And he had come to know about T. and her very odd ways of manipulating thoughts. Hawk had even told him the name for it—NOPAIN, short for nonphysical persuasion and innovative negotiation, some kind of interrogation program specialized by this agency.

Nikki tilted her head to one side. "I'm telling you

that Lily Noretski is on a mission. If you help her finish it, she'll be done with her journey and will be
ready to start anew. It doesn't have to take ten years,
not if you look for the right clues."

"Tell me," Reed said, knowing his answer was a
commitment of some kind. It was no longer point,
sight, and shoot.

"First you have to make her trust you. You'll have
to figure out how to do that yourself. But do it
quickly, Reed. Time's ticking."

13

It was a little over an hour and her contact still hadn't shown up. Lily finished her martini and signaled for another one. It had been a while since she'd bought herself any alcohol. She wouldn't mind a cigarette either, another luxury she'd given up. That hadn't been easy, since she tended to smoke one or two cigarettes when she was under stress. She could bum one off any of these men sitting at the bar, but she didn't feel like talking to anyone. Besides, she was getting paranoid again.

Funny, she hadn't had that looking-over-the-shoulder feeling when she had been with Reed. She'd actually slept through a whole night. Since then, the last two nights, in comparison, had brought back the same misery from the previous months—restlessness and weird dreams that she couldn't quite recall.

The bartender placed the new martini in front of her. She might get a good night's rest after finishing it. Her body was tired enough.

Maybe it was the nice, expensive, and comfortable bed at that hotel suite. Lily made a face as she swirled the liquid in her glass. Oh yeah. That and the man who'd come with it.

There was something about that man that made her feel safe. Ridiculous, of course. She didn't know him, and he was in a business that didn't include "safe" people. In fact, the way he'd deliberately kept her vulnerable showed how unsafe he really was. She shivered at the memory of how well he knew her body, of how she'd been so willing to give in to him.

She should be angry. At him. At herself. Something. Instead, she felt lonely and a little mad that he'd actually dared to let her go.

"Knight in shining armor," she murmured, taking a big sip from her glass.

She coughed and chuckled softly. Another no-no from the Wretched Wench List. Amber had written that one. A Wretched Wench needed her knight in shining armor to save her, she'd said. And then bed her, Lily had added, to which they'd both cackled like the tipsy idiots they'd been.

Lily sighed. She didn't want to go down that road tonight. Thinking about Amber would just lead to thoughts about what she'd done to her friend, and that certainly wouldn't give her the rest she was craving.

"No knight in shining armor for bad, wicked Lily," she murmured again, as she took another sip, then added, "Poor bad, wicked Lily."

She finished her drink. Two days of walking around the city trying to figure out her next move. Two days of wondering who to turn to next. She didn't have enough money to pay for another batch of passports. She'd gotten the hotel manager to call Tatiana for her again, passing on the message that she was all right. Then she'd bought a postcard and sent a longer note.

After that, she'd driven to an old address of one of her contacts. For once, luck had been on her side. Or so she'd thought. He'd told her he'd check around to see whether he could call in some favors.

Viktor was one of the few people who owed Lily a favor. She glanced over at the empty seat by her. Guess he wasn't going to pay her back this time.

She grimaced. Pity party over. She rose and jumped off the bar stool. There was no knight in shining armor coming to her rescue, so she would have to get off her ass and climb out of the hole into which she'd dug herself.

Outside, she wrapped her scarf around her neck to keep the chill away. There were a good number of people still out at this hour. She walked past the souvenir shops with their bright interior lights.

Someone was following.

How did that old song go? "Paranoia will destroy ya." The feeling persisted as she rounded the corner where she'd parked the car.

Lily slipped her hand into her jacket pocket. There were no milling people down this road. She thought she heard footsteps behind her.

"*Dobro govorite* engleski," a voice called behind her.

She turned around. A man was hurrying toward her, waving. She pulled her hand out of her pocket and waved back. "You're late, Viktor," she said. With his hat pulled low, she scarcely recognized him. That was probably why he'd used that greeting, so she'd know it was him.

Viktor dealt with stolen art and artifacts. They'd met when she'd saved him a bundle of money during a black market negotiation with an English art dealer and his associate. Viktor didn't speak English well enough, and the other two had used certain nuances in their conversation that had gone over his head. Lily had stepped in then.

Afterwards, Viktor had used that incident as a private joke whenever he introduced her to his business acquaintances. She "speaks good English," he'd say, "so you guys better quit talking about me like that."

"Sorry, sweet, couldn't be helped," he said as he came forward to hug her. "I'm glad I didn't miss you."

He suddenly grabbed the ends of her scarf and jerked her hard toward him. Lily's hands immediately went up defensively as she pulled back, but she'd wound the scarf around her neck snugly, and now it was choking the air out of her.

Viktor wrapped the long scarf around her wrists. Lily jerked her knee up and made contact with his groin.

"Fuck!" He tightened his hold on her scarf, twisting her hands painfully as he pulled the rest of it around her face.

With her hands imprisoned against her face, and blinded by the scarf, her only hope was to pull a surprise. Instead of continuing to resist, she lunged forward, head down. The top of her head smacked hard against his chest area.

Viktor yelled out again. Lily pulled back and repeated the move, this time aiming a little higher. The hold on the scarf loosened enough as Viktor struggled with her, and she managed to squeeze one of her hands free. She didn't have time for finesse. Reaching down, she grabbed hard at the obvious.

This time, Viktor's yelps of pain were piercing enough that she hoped they would bring her some help. Grabbing the scarf with her free hand, she desperately pulled and twisted to free the tangled mess. From the sound of it, Viktor was on his knees somewhere at her feet.

The sound of squealing tires. She had the feeling the car wasn't there to check out the commotion. She managed to pull the scarf from her head in time to see the car stop a few feet away. Two men came rushing out toward Viktor and her. She turned to run, only to fall over when Viktor tripped her with his leg.

She fell hard enough to have the wind knocked out of her. Hands grabbed at her, pulling her to her knees. She turned and bit a hand. Someone grabbed her hair and pulled her head back. Another hand covered her mouth. She was being dragged back toward the car.

Suddenly a shot rang out. The assailant holding her hair groaned, and the hold loosened.

Lily turned and swung a fist upwards, hitting the other man in the solar plexus. He crumpled but didn't let her go. From the corner of her eye, she saw Viktor pulling up unsteadily, stumbling forward to help.

"Hurry up! Get her in the car!" the driver yelled out from the waiting vehicle.

Another shot rang out. The other man holding her didn't even let out a scream as he slid lifelessly to the ground.

"Fuck!" Viktor dove into the open door. "Let's get out of here!"

A bullet hit the top of the car. The door slammed hard and the car drove off, leaving Lily and their friends.

This time she didn't wait to see who was coming to her aid as she staggered clumsily to her car. Not when there were two dead men at her feet. She didn't want to spend hours at some police station while they dug around for clues and reasons.

She sped off in the opposite direction, looking at her rearview mirror. No one was following her. After a few minutes, she slowed down to normal speed.

She massaged her neck wearily. Viktor must have gotten that information about her when he started asking around. She sighed. Even her contacts were seeing dollar signs when they saw her.

This is what happens when you betray your friends, girl. You get betrayed back. But someone had been watching her.

Lily thought about the whole incident. The shots had been from a high-powered weapon, probably with a zoom lens. Whoever it was, was a good shot. He had taken out two men standing in very close proximity to her. Maybe she did have a knight in shining armor after all.

"I'm sorry I was delayed, but I was in the middle of something and couldn't get away. I hope I didn't cause too much trouble."

"Not at all, Talia. Please come in."

Greta remained where she was. She cocked her head slightly, listening to the sounds and conversation going on in Gunther's foyer, which was directly outside the living room where she was sitting.

"Please, I hope you don't mind? Protocol," she heard Gunther say after a few seconds.

"An electronic wand? How . . . spy-ish, Gunther." Talia's voice was rich with amusement. "Ah well, as long as you don't zap me with that thing."

Greta frowned. Gunther hadn't used that on her. Either he trusted her—which she doubted—or he wasn't as afraid of her as he was of Talia. The thought didn't make her happy.

"Surely you've dealt with this type of security measure when you visit other agencies. Again, I apologize. We'll dispense with such formalities when we get to know each other better."

The husky laughter was very attractive. Cool as ice. Her niece knew how to handle tension. Either that, or she was totally foolish for walking in here unarmed. Yet she was supposed to be a smart woman.

"Do you say that to all the women you meet?" Talia asked teasingly. "As well as look through their handbags so thoroughly? It's fortunate I'm not embarrassed by a man playing with my tampons."

Cool as ice, Greta decided. After all, Talia was her niece. She would be able to run circles around men like Gunther.

"Only . . . the special ones," Gunther said. "Here you go. Please, do make yourself comfortable. You're going to enjoy meeting your aunt Greta."

"Yes, that was good bait. I wouldn't have come here if you hadn't dangled that, Gunther. I haven't seen my aunt in a long time."

Gunther needed her to get Talia's attention. That meant he'd been trying without any success. Greta smiled cynically. So that was why he hadn't gone beyond sabotaging her plans. He'd managed to infuriate her into coming here to see him and all this while, he'd been planning this meeting.

The door opened. Greta looked up expectantly. This would be the first time in a decade that she had seen any family. Talia, the snow princess. Talia, with whom she wasn't close because she was the older child, growing into womanhood when Greta had left. And it suddenly occurred to her that none of those nieces and nephews would be kids anymore. She'd missed their childhoods.

The woman walking in through the door had little resemblance to the dark-haired, chubby preteen with the rosy cheeks. Greta remembered the jet black hair and eyes. The woman stopped and studied her just as closely, her dark eyes piercing in their intensity.

Her niece had grown into a beautiful woman. Except for that long scar on the left side of her face, her skin was porcelain smooth, glowing with health. Her shapely lips curved into a knowing smile, as if she knew what Greta was looking at.

"Aunt Greta," she greeted, closing the space between them. Her next words were in Russian. "How marvelous to see you. I've heard that you were coming home."

Greta rose from her seat and let the other woman hug her. She didn't like hugs. She patted Talia's back awkwardly. She found she had nothing to say.

"When will you be officially back?" Talia continued. She sat down after Gunther indicated a seat for her. "I'm sure there'll be a celebration. We love our parties, as you know."

Oh, yes. That was the best part of Russian life, which she'd missed while in the States. No one celebrated like the Russians.

Greta smiled. "As soon as I'm finished with business," she replied, shooting Gunther a sly look. "Gunther thinks you and he can form an alliance."

Talia's eyebrows lifted a fraction. "That was a fast hello, Aunt. Did poor Dragan get the same treatment?"

Greta looked hard at her niece. "I barely know you, so I'm not sure exactly how you think I should react. If I'm too enthusiastic, you might be suspicious. As for Dragan, I'd been in contact with him on and off because of business, so when I finally saw him again, our meeting was warmer."

"Interesting," Talia murmured, turning to accept a drink from Gunther. "Thank you, Gunther. I came because I have these wonderful memories of Aunt Greta giving us treats and money, like an angel of mercy, really, since we were getting so damn near poverty from the job situation. You were always generous with Papa and Mama, Aunt Greta. I guess I let that color my views of you. Of course, I now know why you disappeared and left us, and understand you better for what you are."

It was true she'd given money to her relatives. Many of them had needed it after the cold war was over. There hadn't been many real jobs to begin with, and with the government shutting down, many government employees had gone without pay for a long time. Sometimes Greta had wondered how her relatives had fared after she'd gone off on her last operation.

"And what am I?" she asked. "I'm curious to see what you know . . . or don't."

"I'm sure Talia knows a lot, Greta, since she married a general and had access to a lot of powerful people," Gunther chimed in. His eyes were admiring as he glanced at Talia. "You were rather low profile till recently, of course," he said to Greta's niece, "but you've grown into quite a legend yourself, especially with that last escape from the explosion."

Talia touched the left side of her face, then shrugged. "Everyone brings that up," she said in a bored voice. "It's just a part of my life now. I'm good at what I do and am glad that there are people jealous enough of my success to kill me. It's a good sign."

Gunther laughed. "A very positive outlook on life," he said. "Most women would have been destroyed by the whole experience. And yes, I also meant the injury to your face. The plastic surgeon did a fantastic job, by the way, and if nothing else, the disfigurement is superficial at most and adds to the mystique of The Baroness."

Greta watched as Talia laughed that smoky laugh again. She couldn't quite decide whether she liked her chubby little niece growing up into this sophisticated adult. She could kill this woman.

"A new face, Gunther, is easy to get these days," Talia said. "I'm blessed with great bone structure, so the doctor said, and he just corrected minor problems. I'm glad you approve."

Her smile was too perfect. Everything was very practiced. "You're very well trained," Greta said.

Talia turned back to her. "Of course," she said. "After you left and after my marriage, I found out where you went and what your real job was. I applied and went through the same training you did, Auntie. Can't you tell?"

"Training doesn't make one good, niece."

"And practice makes perfect, Auntie," Talia countered. "But I'm not here to argue about that. You obviously need something from me or you wouldn't have gone to so much trouble contacting me."

"I don't need anything," Greta briskly said. "That was Gunther's idea. However, he invited me here so I could meet my niece. It's been . . . enlightening."

"In a good way, I hope? You're my role model, Auntie. An independent woman who makes lots of money. That's very hard to do back home, you know. I'm enjoying it very much, thanks to you." Talia toasted her silently and drank from her glass. "Life has certainly been a lot better now that I'm in the business of moving government items about, I must say."

"I didn't do it to make life better," Greta lied. It *had* made life better, but it hadn't been her first reason for being an assassin for the government, and then a double agent. "I did it for love."

Talia looked surprised. "Love? You view killing for money as a quest for love?"

"I mean, you must love your job," Greta said. So young and so cynical already. No wonder these kids would never rise to her status. "You can't do what I do without deep love, Talia."

"Oh, indeed. Ten years in the bowels of the CIA as a dowdy secretary." Talia shuddered. "I don't think even I can do that, but of course, who knows? In ten years . . . no, no, I don't even think I can do that in ten years. I don't have your love, Auntie, for sure. I'm in it for the money, pure and simple."

"And that's why I like you, Talia," Gunther interrupted smoothly. "The Baroness has a reputation for delivering, and you've promised to deliver a certain item to the government for a large sum of money. I have information that might be of help, but I need some of that money too."

Talia looked at them both consideringly, a small, secretive smile on her face. "I'm greedy enough to listen but not dumb enough to believe you, Gunther. Now that you've trapped my aunt somehow to be used as bait to bring me here, let me really hear what's on your clever little mind, hmm? And then maybe, maybe, I'll think about this alliance."

Greta couldn't help smiling back at her niece, feeling just a tinge of pride. The girl had inherited her genes. Ambitious and beautiful. She would go places. But only if she didn't get in Greta's way. After all, glory could only belong to one woman. And it was her time, after all her sacrifice.

Reed snapped the GPS unit shut. She was heading toward the hotel. He released a sigh of frustration. Finally. He put his car into gear and took the shortcut back. That woman had the hardest head. He'd been following her the last few days as she'd driven around the city. Yesterday, it had appeared that she'd found an old friend.

Reed hadn't liked the way that guy had hugged her. And then later, she'd gone to the bar. He was still mad about that. Didn't she remember that the last time she was in one, she'd ended up being shot at? He'd thought about it and had finally concluded that she must have been meeting her friend. Still, it was a risk he wished she hadn't taken. . . .

The fact that he'd been right didn't make him feel any better either. The woman was in grave danger, and she was wandering around alone.

Reed shook his head. It couldn't be helped. She had to decide on her own to come to him. If she'd really found someone to help her, he'd have stayed in the shadows to watch what she was planning. After all, she didn't have much money left. There was only one way she could raise quick money.

In the planning stages, one of the scenarios had pictured Lily handing over the weapon to another dealer. This had actually been the ideal stage, with a cut-and-dried scenario. Target sighted, target shot. Weapon retrieved.

However, Amber's stipulation—that GEM had to try to save Lily—made things a little more complicated. Reed liked the fact that GEM was keeping its side of the bargain. Some agencies, he realized, would just have agreed and done it their way. Llallana Noretski would have ended up another statistic, an accident.

But they had picked a sharpshooter as the foil, just in case. Reed parked, pocketed the GPS unit, checked the area to make sure it was secure, then went to the elevator. He'd followed Lily long enough to make sure he was the only one tailing her, and then he'd veered off into a side street. It should take her an extra seven or eight minutes to reach here.

It wasn't long before his blue car pulled into the garage. She didn't stop in front of him, driving by as if she hadn't seen him. He waited as he watched her park.

She locked the car, taking her time, then turned and approached him slowly. Reed slipped his hands into his jacket pockets. Damn it, didn't the woman eat? She looked like a wind could blow her away.

"I'm back," she said, uncertainty in her eyes.

"You should have called me. I might not have been here," Reed said.

A small smile appeared. "Where would you be? Besides following a woman around and shooting at people?" She cocked her head. "Why did you do it, Reed?"

Reed reached out and pulled her against him. She tilted her head back, anticipating his descending mouth. He kissed her roughly, threading his fingers in her hair. He'd thought about doing just that the last few days. How could one woman get into his system so quickly?

She kissed him back ardently. Her response had always been explosive, but this time he sensed a desperate edge, as if she was very close to falling apart. He gentled his hold, slowing his own raging need.

"You're exhausted," he said, his gaze taking in the dark circles under her eyes. "You don't take care of yourself, do you know that?"

"Well, I got spoiled, you see," she replied. "The cheap hotel bed just won't do after that decadent luxury up there."

Reed turned, inserted the key card, and punched in the code. "Then you should have called earlier. It would have saved me some sleep too."

She touched his arm. "You still haven't told me why you followed me around."

"To make sure you're okay."

"Why?"

The elevator door opened. She hesitated a second before following him in. "Because I like to think of you in one piece," he told her as he pushed the button. "Because I was worried you might end up in a river somewhere in the middle of the night. Because I didn't think you knew what the hell you were doing out there."

Her chin tilted up defensively. "I've been taking care of myself for a long time, Reed. I don't need a babysitter." The look in her eyes softened. "Not that I'm not grateful for what you did."

The door opened. She hesitated again, peering into the semidarkness of the suite.

He didn't want to make it easy for her. Why should he, when she'd prefer dealing with that scumbag who'd mugged her? "Afraid?" he asked softly.

Her chin tilted higher. "No," she said. She took a deep breath, then stepped out of the elevator. "I came here because I need your help. Just like you said."

That made him unreasonably irritated. He didn't want her to need his help. He wanted her to need him. "I know that," he said. "We can talk afterwards."

She stilled. "Afterwards?"

He strode toward the bedroom without turning on any lights. "It's late, Lily. I can't help you right now, anyway."

"You're doing this on purpose," she said, her tone of voice accusing as she stood there in the dark foyer.

He turned on the bedroom light. "Yes," he said. "You look about dead on your feet. Eat, then talk. Then sleep. In that order."

"Eat?"

"Lily, I've been following you around. You haven't eaten all day. You had two, maybe three, drinks at the bar." He pulled out a T-shirt from the drawer. "Like I said, you don't know how to take care of yourself."

"I have things on my mind, if you haven't noticed," Lily said wryly.

"Come here," he said.

She finally came into the room, her fingers unbuttoning her jacket. She paused when she caught sight of the T-shirt. "Was the hotel mad about the way the bathroom was left? There was dirt all over the shower." She pursed her lips. "I guess I should have brought my stuff from my room."

"The hotel hasn't kicked me out yet. And you would have your things here if you hadn't decided to go off the other day," Reed pointed out. "As it is, those three days you promised to give me were wasted."

And nights, he added. He'd spent all of those following around instead of having her here, safely out of the way, while things were being arranged. But her persistence was a remarkable thing to watch. She simply refused to give up.

He picked up the phone and ordered food, his

gaze following her around the room as she put away the jacket, smoothed her hair in front of the dresser table, sat on the bed to pull off her boots, then went off to check the bathroom. How could a woman's presence make such a spacious room so small?

She reappeared. "I want you to contact Nikki Harden," she blurted out.

Reed frowned. He hadn't expected that. "Why?"

She sighed. "She said someone has a price on my head. I know who it is. It's the CIA." She walked toward him with a serious expression. "I want you to go through Nikki and send a message that you want to collect the reward. Tell them if they want me, they'll guarantee me safe passages for a group of girls, that they will give you these passports. As soon as my girls are out of the country, you hand me over to them. The money's yours, Reed, and you, too, can get out of this place."

Reed listened in stunned silence. This was one scenario that hadn't been brought up during discussions. Lily was going to sacrifice herself.

14

Reed was a trained sharpshooter, able to sit for hours, if necessary, waiting for his target to appear. His job had always required very little more than patience and absolute control of his weapon. He could aim and shoot at a Ping-Pong ball dangling from the end of a dummy positioned hundreds of meters away. He could pick out moving targets among moving objects with a scope and hit them in rapid succession from a distance.

Some of his targets had shot back. It was part of being in a firefight—when one was shooting at something, be prepared to be shot back at.

He stared hard at the woman standing in front of him. When had she become his blind spot?

Part of the reason was that he didn't view her as a target anymore. Instead of sitting quietly and watching, focusing only on that one job of pulling the trigger, he'd let his mind wander off. He'd become emotionally involved. And somehow, in so short a period of time, he'd convinced himself that he needed to save this woman, instead of letting that be only one option open to him.

Matters of consequence. Of course, the stupid book that had been haunting him lately had to choose this moment to taunt him. Someone up there was messing with his mind, all right.

Arch was in heaven having a belly laugh over this. Because it was he who'd taught Reed that life wasn't just waves and sun with a hot Betty in his arms. There were matters of consequence, things that were important to people.

Dude, life's sweet not because of the things in it, but because of the things that keep you going. Everyone's got to find what matters to his heart, or everything's just going to wash away like the sand. And boy, are you going to miss it when it's gone. I ain't talking about hot sex either, although that's one very important thing that keeps life going!

Reed could remember the belly-roll of a laugh Arch had given as he'd slapped him on the back. He'd assumed Arch had been talking about surfing. Everything had revolved around the sea for the older man, all the way back when he'd been the surfing champ in the area, to the travels to the best beaches in the world, to his own untraditional nuptials, standing with his bride in a humongous sand castle he'd built. He'd carried that photo with him wherever he'd gone, and Reed had looked at it hundreds of times, though the significance of it had been lost on him until Arch's last journey into the ocean.

"You're quiet. Are you going to help me?" Lily interrupted his reverie. She rubbed her bare arms, worry in her eyes.

The thing was, he knew the worry wasn't for herself. She was afraid he was going to refuse.

It humbled Reed. Lily was someone who knew what mattered to her heart, and, like Arch, she would do anything to protect what was important.

He understood the importance of his mission, that he couldn't allow the weapon she had in her possession to fall into the wrong hands. At the same time, the lofty ideal of protecting the world and fending off the forces of evil was nebulous, childish even, when compared to the simple human level of Lily's goal, which was something he should be doing—protecting the lives of innocent kids. In spite of all that psychological mumbo jumbo about embedded hypnotic commands, in spite of what she'd done to her friends, Lily was intrinsically a good person, someone who understood she had to right a wrong.

Hadn't that always been something that was missing in his life? Someone who would admit to a wrong and correct it?

"You're angry," Lily said.

Reed shook his head. "I'm just thinking. You've left a lot of your background out. That part about the CIA being the one behind this reward explains why people might be after you left and right, but it doesn't tell the reason that they're so eager to get you."

"I told you I betrayed a bunch of people. Well, the CIA is some of them," she said dismissively. "Now they're after me."

She wasn't going to tell him. He had to get her to admit about the weapon. "Did you work for them, then? Is that why you said you betrayed them? Most of us on the outside prefer to put that another way, sweetheart. Like, our side won one against them, for instance. Betraying . . . how're you involved with them?"

"I wasn't willing." Lily turned away. "It's a long and complicated story."

"I have time. Are they also after these girls you're helping out?"

She swerved back, her expression fierce and protective. "No, they're my girls," she said angrily, "and if they offer any help to take them in, you can tell them the deal's off."

He wanted to take away the pain she was desperately hiding. Betrayal. It was Lily who'd been betrayed first.

But first, he needed the truth. "Why? The CIA has plenty of resources to help those girls out. They have easier ways to move them than what you or I could do with fake passports."

"I know them and you don't. Are you going to help me or not?" She looked away again, blinking hard. He suddenly realized she didn't want him to see the tears filling her eyes. "Trust me, Reed, they're going to use them like they used me."

Trust. That was what stood between him and this woman. More than anything else right now, he wished he could tell her the truth about who he was, to make it clear that he didn't want to hurt her or those girls. But in the end, wasn't that what he was going to do? He suddenly felt a deep loss inside, like helplessly watching a precious keepsake fall to the ground and break into irreparable pieces.

"If I let them have you, what do you think they'll do once they get whatever it is you have taken from them? Set you free?" The double meaning of his words mocked him. Even though GEM wanted to have her extracted in the least painful way, it was as an agreement to Amber Hutchens. What about afterwards? He put a finger under her chin and tilted it back to him. "I'll have to think about this."

Her dark, expressive eyes were sad. "There's no other way. Don't you think I haven't thought about every possible way out? Tonight, you saw how it was with someone who knew me—he wanted the reward money for himself." She smiled. "I figure I'll give the money to someone I like, which, lucky person, happens to be you."

"You can come away with me," Reed said, surprising himself. Where had that come from?

Lily shook her head. "And leave the girls? No way. I've betrayed enough people as it is, and they are what matters right now. Besides, it's time I get a little comeuppance for what I've done in the past." Her voice turned into a husky whisper. "This way I know a bunch of young girls will have new lives ahead of them. I'm going to give them a chance to turn out differently from the way I did."

He wanted to shake her. Those bastards had really done a good job at giving her low self-esteem. With her usual resources gone, she was as alone as one could get, with not even a friend to whom she could turn.

But she turned to you.

Suddenly it was important to make sure he didn't fail her with what mattered to her heart. He wanted her happy. And safe. He wanted to take her away from this and make it better.

The intercom buzzed. That was dinner on the way up. "Let's eat first," Reed said. He kissed her softly, wanting to reassure her that everything would be all right. But he couldn't say that. He had to find another way. It mattered to him that Lily complete this thing that was so important to her heart.

He glanced at her as he turned on the lights in the dining room. She was beginning to matter a lot.

"I can tell you don't like your niece."

Greta looked at the weapon in the display case in Gunther's study. The man, it appeared, collected everything. Last night she'd checked out his tropical and semitropical flowers, which he'd specially ordered or imported from overseas. The night before, she'd seen a whole shelf full of his movie video collection.

She moved to the next display case. "Why do you say that?" she asked, tracing the glass top with her finger. The whole wall in front of her was a cornucopia of a thug's dream, but she doubted Gunther actually knew how to operate half the weapons here. But she'd underestimated him already; she wouldn't make that mistake again.

Gunther reminded her of that movie that constantly irritated her in the States because it was always on—*Revenge of the Nerds*. He was a geek who wanted to be a bad boy. And like all geeks, he went overboard with the security stuff and the weaponry collection.

"I have a feeling that you were disappointed after your meeting, like you expected your niece to be less beautiful and more normal."

Greta rolled her eyes. "Please. You're making me out to be a very shallow woman, Gunth. Beautiful women don't make me jealous. As for normalcy, I haven't been around normal people enough to know what that is."

Which was a lie, of course. She'd the best neighbors where she'd lived in the States, even though she'd mostly kept to herself. They'd been typical Americans, with their two-car garage and three kids in school, their little backyard barbeques and the family dog, their family reunions during Easter and Thanksgiving that had filled the street with cars. They'd even invited her because they'd felt sorry for a lonely old woman.

She had, at first, scoffed at their stupidity, that they couldn't see who she really was. Then she'd congratulated herself for her excellent disguise, that she'd wormed herself into their hearts. Her dacha, when she went home, would be so much better than these little cookie cutter houses and their Ken and Barbie lives. She would own more interesting things than—she glanced around Gunther's study—the latest electronic gadget.

But she'd grown to like her neighbors after some years. They were her source of entertainment when she was bored. Sometimes, the kids had reminded her of her nieces and nephews.

One of whom was dead now, killed by a damn SEAL. Another who was using her husband's privileges to steal weapons to sell to the highest bidder. That irked Greta. She would never steal from her country. Talia didn't seem particularly bothered by that fact.

"Everyone's doing it, Auntie," she'd drawled. "Look, I'm not a scientist pimping my brain out to the highest bidder from other nations. I'm not even one of those who are selling our Russian girls to European and Asian bordellos. I'm sorry I didn't aspire to be like Dragan, whom you approved of so much."

Greta pursed her lips. Of course she'd known about Dragan's big moneymakers—sex slaves and drugs. These had been the things that had financed the illegal arms business.

Ah well, maybe Talia had a point. She was young and independently wealthy. Greta should feel proud. So why did she feel vaguely irritated at the fact that her niece didn't seem to need her help?

"So do you think you can get along with her long enough for us to get possession of the item?" Gunther interrupted her reverie. He lifted a pearl-handled pistol that was cradled on a stand and handed it to her. "She still has value."

"And how much value do I still have to you?" Greta mused. *And vice versa,* she wondered silently.

Gunther smiled, his lips disappearing under his mustache. "You have tremendous value, Greta, what with your excellent knowledge of the U.S. Intel system. I've always been a bit envious about that fact. There you were, in that place, the CIA shrine, surrounded by all that juicy information. I would have given anything to be able to hack into their system from the inside."

A geek who wanted to be a bad boy. Greta had met one or two before, even at the CIA. They were malleable as long as one fed them what they wanted, which was high-tech wizardry with which to play. An idea started forming. She rubbed a loving finger across the antique pearl handle of the pistol, admiring its luster.

"I do like parts of your plan, but there are some parts that I think are absolutely horrendous."

Gunther's smile widened. "Be my guest. I'd love to hear your opinions."

"I think it's a mistake that you veered from the original plan, which was for me to be the one to handle the explosive device. After all, I sent it out to my nephew. All I had to do when I left the States was to find the exact cache of weapons with which it was dropped. By involving Llallana Noretski, you've gotten yourself into trouble as well as lost the weapon, too." She paused to gauge his reaction. With his arms folded, one hip leaning against his study desk, he looked curiously amiable, as if he were enjoying a class lecture. "Second, I thought your trying to undermine my operation extremely narrow-minded and unwise. I am, as you've kept insinuating, an old lady just wanting to have a bit of fun before retiring. Yet you wanted me to look bad to HQ. That was disrespectful, and frankly, after all these years of dealing with you, a bit immature. Why did you prevent me from getting Llallana Noretski the other night at the club? It'd taken me months to locate the damn woman, even with the offer of a reward, and now she's disappeared again."

Gunther straightened up and pulled out his cigarette case from his pocket. "It's a nice long story, so you'd better sit down at the desk and be comfortable."

After she'd done so, he leaned over her shoulder—a little too close, she thought—to move the keyboard toward him. She didn't say anything as she watched him punch in some commands.

She hadn't typed in a while. God, how she'd hated being a secretary, slave to the keyboard. Sure, most of the information she'd procured had been very important, but she'd had to handle hundreds of boring and mundane things in between. She kind of missed it, she supposed. After all, that office had been efficiently run by one of the best assassins-turned-double-agent. She smiled at the thought.

Gunther tapped the cursor to open a file. "Some time ago, I was advised to look at a classified file out of a bunch of folders given to me from one of our network operatives. The person who called wanted me to read about an old CIA experimental program called Project Precious Gems. It was a fascinating read. On the surface, it was an operation that extracted a group of young women and children who had been kidnapped from various parts of the world, you know, the ones that your nephew used to buy up for his business."

Greta gave him a sideways look. Was he poking fun at her or being sarcastic? He pointed at the screen, so she returned her attention to it. There were thumbnails of photos and a very familiar red Classified on the heading. During the past ten years, she had seen and handled hundreds of documents that had looked like that.

"These are the subjects they extracted," Gunther continued. "Like I said, the extraction was just the surface story. The CIA, while rehabilitating them, decided to use them as test candidates for their new sleeper cell project. It seemed that these young girls, who had undergone tremendous mistreatment by the sex traders, were prime candidates because of their emotional damage. The CIA, in essence, was looking for people with strong hatred and a need to channel that emotion. With brainwashing methods and, later, hypnotic implantation with certain commands—*voilà!*" He snapped his fingers.

Greta frowned. "Human elements planted in the midst of normal society where they live quietly till they're activated for a special assignment. We've seen

plenty of that, even in Russia, where Chechnyan"—
she stopped, then continued slowly—"women appeared to be detonating themselves in high-profile
places. Llallana Noretski—"

Gunther clicked on one of the thumbnails, and the
photo enlarged. The face of a very young girl with
dark hair and eyes stared back solemnly at Greta.

"Llallana Noretski," Gunther said. "She's one of
the sleeper cells. Can you imagine, Greta, a collection of young girls who could take out hordes of UN
soldiers while they caroused in Europe? And the
wonderful chaos and scandal it would cause when
it's traced back to a CIA sleeper project gone awry?"

15

At least I have one answer, Lily mused as she stared at the ceiling. It wasn't the luxurious bed that had given her that wonderful sleep the other night. If it was, she should be happily in la-la land, floating in that place far away from her present problems.

Instead, she was tossing and turning, trying to get comfortable, as if the bed were filled with marbles instead of feathers. All the while, her internal radar was focused on the man in the media room. He had been in there an hour already. Had to think, he'd said . . . couldn't he think in here?

She sniffed. Maybe not. She knew she wouldn't be able to think if she had him beside her in bed. Every time he came within a few feet of her, her whole body lit up like Christmas lights on a tree.

Lily grimaced grimly. Christmas. She probably wouldn't be celebrating Christmas this year.

"Hey, no last-minute rushing to buy presents," she said humorlessly. Not that anyone would be buying her any. By then, if everything went according to plan, the girls would be gone, and she would be . . .

She turned over and punched the pillow. Morbid thoughts at night. That ought to put her to sleep so much easier.

What was Reed thinking about? She'd offered him all that reward money; wasn't that incentive enough? He could be far, far away from here by Christmas, too, whooping it up with his new life.

Lily rubbed her eyes wearily. A new life. How ironic. They'd given her a new life and new identity, and look where she was now.

But I didn't know! She smiled wryly at the fierce denial. No one would believe her—not Amber, not Hawk, and especially not Brad, who'd been attracted to her. There had been something between them, something that had called to the Lily inside her to free herself, yet in the end, she hadn't been able to. She hadn't liked the things the voice had been telling her, that her friends were—

Lily frowned. Something just clicked that she hadn't remembered before. A voice. Cell phone calls. She jolted up suddenly.

She remembered a phone call! No, she remembered two. Was it two?

"What's the matter?"

She looked up, startled. She hadn't heard Reed coming in. She shook her head distractedly as her mind chased after the snatches of conversation in her head.

Reed turned on the table light and sat on the side of the bed. "Lily?" he prompted, frowning.

She shook her head again, waving a finger to him to give her a moment.

Everything in the room became blurry as she fought to concentrate.

Things fall apart. A male voice had said that. Wait, hadn't she heard that line recently? She frowned, raking her hair carelessly.

All relationships must be severed. Only the girls. You know what will happen to the girls. What will happen if you don't do this and save the girls, Llallana? Answer me.

"Things fall apart," Lily muttered, then pounded the bed with excitement, repeating it louder, "Things fall apart! That's it!"

She looked up to find Reed watching her like a hawk. He must think she'd gone mad.

"What about things falling apart?" he asked calmly, his eyes probing her face. His hands reached for her. She suddenly realized that she was trembling so hard he had to steady her.

Lily started to explain, then closed her mouth. She couldn't tell him: where would she start? And what would she say? Something like, "Well, Reed, I was programmed by the CIA as a sleeper cell, you see, with these embedded commands in my brain. Anyway, for some reason, they wanted to steal a weapon that could hide a bomb from this bad guy, Dilaver, and so they activated this subconscious trigger that makes me listen to them.

"Then, they had me betray a few friends of mine to Dilaver so I could make a grand escape to finish my job, which was to go to this big political summit and detonate a bomb and kill everyone at that meeting. Only one of my friends somehow got hold of me and did something to stop me—I can't tell for sure—but this big explosion never happened. And now everyone's mad at me—my friends who also wanted this weapon, my enemies who had this weapon, and the CIA who had—"

She started to laugh hysterically. "—who had this device in the first place and lost it," she gasped out, then realized she'd said the last part aloud. Falling back against the pillows, she laughed so hard her sides hurt. All the while, Reed sat there, his face strangely expressionless as he watched her.

"It doesn't make sense," she told him in between chuckles.

"What doesn't?"

She shook her head again. "If I tell you, you'll be just as confused as I am now and tell me I'm certifiably insane. Then you'll probably refuse to do what I asked of you earlier."

"Lily, you aren't making sense either way. But I like the way you laugh."

She sniffed and wiped her cheeks with the back of her hand. They were damp. "That wasn't laughter. That was hysteria." She accepted the tissues he handed her and blew her nose hard. "Oh God, Reed, my life's a mess. But you know what? I suddenly feel a lot better."

"Good." He tilted her chin. His lips were gentle against hers. "I'm glad."

It didn't matter that she could be angry, sad, or even freaked out. All he had to do was touch her and everything immediately became less important. One look. One touch. And dark, long-suppressed desire would surface. This time, she would reach out for it.

She wanted the kiss to be longer. She was so tired of running away, fearing that she was a danger to people she cared about. She probably still was, but she'd had no contact with any phone all these months. She was very sure now that it was through the phone and not by person. She had proof.

Nikki Harden had said that same line the other day . . . "Things fall apart," she'd said, when they'd been talking about weapons. And nothing had happened. Lily had even said the line aloud, and it hadn't invoked that dreaded feeling of doom she remembered experiencing during those days. She hadn't gone off the deep end and rushed off to get the weapon.

Those damn men playing with her brain had made sure she wasn't triggered off by random sentences that might contain the line from the poem. They must have set it so that she could only be triggered through electronic means. Something easy, like a phone call.

She slid her hands up Reed's arms. "Kiss me again," she said. There were no embedded orders to kiss this man and make love to him. "I like the way you kiss, besides other things."

His lips quirked. "I'm glad to know that."

"Reed," she said, pulling on his arm. "Come to bed. I need you here, tonight."

She was tired of lies and lying to him. She would like one night in which she could remember her emotions as being real, that it was Lily Noretski the woman who wanted this man, and not Lily, the savior of all female victims, seeking vengeance for her kidnapped sister. There had never been any sister; the missing sister was actually herself. Those damn assholes who had raped her mind had channeled her anger and hatred through lies, making her forever look for someone who didn't even exist.

They'd taken away her past and tainted her future. She wasn't going to let them control her any more. One way or another, she would find what was real and what was programmed.

Lily smiled up at Reed, her hands caressing his shoulders as she urged him closer. All these feelings she had for this man were real. That was why she'd found so much pleasure in his touch, why she wanted him to touch her all the time. Before, she'd always had to be the one in control, and she had never been able to find real joy in intimacy. If her emotions got too involved, some warning signal always sounded, ordering her to push away.

But not with Reed. She couldn't get enough of his touch. And she hadn't wanted to be in control.

Tonight, she wanted to experience lovemaking with no thought of her past and future. "Are you going to refuse me this as well?" she asked, and it felt so good to know she could tease and mean it. "One night with me might change your mind."

Reed leaned forward and trapped her against the pillows, his strong arms on either side of her. "That'd never happen," he said. "I wanted you the first time I saw you, but there were too many things happening that got in the way."

"Not tonight, Reed," she told him. She slid lower down the pillows, her hands pulling at his T-shirt. "Let's have nothing between us tonight. We'll let things happen tomorrow, but right now I'd like to make love."

"Make love," he echoed.

"Well, we'll fuck afterwards," she said, grinning. "Do you know I haven't seen you naked since you bathed me in the bathroom?"

"I thought you only saw me naked when I dropped you on the bed."

She blinked, then bit her lower lip, trying to look chagrined. "Oh." Oops, she had said she was tired of lying. "Well, I peeked earlier. Do you always call out the parts of your body when you're washing?"

The intensity in his gray eyes curled her toes. He had a way of looking at her that made her heart zing around inside her like a balloon losing air.

"It's so I don't miss anything," he said, climbing onto the bed now, straddling her body. He pulled his T-shirt over his head and threw it onto the floor. Her eyes were drawn to his wide shoulders and muscular chest. The man was . . . hot. "Now that you're fully awake, I think I'll have to do it all over again, just to make sure. No, I'll take care of the shirt myself, just like before. You must lie here quietly while I concentrate."

He slipped his knee between hers, nudging her thighs apart. She gasped at the intimate contact.

"I really love your penchant for not wearing underwear," he said approvingly.

He pushed the T-shirt higher. She lifted her arms over her head, helping him. Even before the shirt was off, his head dipped, and his mouth covered her right nipple.

The position of her arms pushed her breast higher, and she gasped again when he cupped her other breast and gently squeezed. His weight trapped one of her legs, while his knee pushed her other one. It was a vulnerable position, similar to when he'd had her in the shower. But he didn't touch her as he paid attention to her breasts, then kissed his way up her neck, moving his knee as he did so, pushing her legs still further apart.

"Wrap your leg around me like you did when we tangoed," he said. "That's it."

He gave her that devastating smile, telling her he'd known even then how much she'd wanted him too. How appropriate. The tango—the mating dance, where the woman opened herself sexually to the man.

"What now?" she asked softly, pulling her arms out of the sleeves.

"Now I get you very wet," he told her, his hand moving lower, his finger unerringly finding the most sensitive spot. Her head rolled back. Her body was melting with a slow, burning pleasure as his finger glided slowly, taking his time.

She grabbed his arm, digging her fingers into his muscles. "No, I want you in me, Reed."

She closed her eyes, her body already looking for release. She moved her leg restlessly, arching her back. Easing his weight off a little, he slipped his other arm under her and raised her higher. His finger continued its intimate caress, building her desire like the incessant beat of a song.

"The moment a man dips a woman in a tango, she falls back passionately, the release literally taking over. Let go for me. I'll catch you, Lily." His lips brushed her jawline, the corner of her lips, her closed eyes. "Imagine my mouth doing that to you next."

The erotic knowledge of how clever his mouth was pushed Lily over the edge. She heard herself calling out Reed's name as waves of pleasure washed over her body.

There was such a happy brightness in her eyes that Reed couldn't refuse her. There wasn't any sign of the shadowy pain that always lurked in those dark eyes. She told him he'd think her crazy if she told him what was on her mind. Actually, he was already crazy. The woman had just shouted the very line he'd been warned was her embedded trigger, and then her whole personality had changed from worried and unhappy to temptingly sexy.

He should be backing away, looking for a weapon she might have hidden in the bed. She was talking about making love. There was a teasing light in her eyes he'd never seen before when she brought up their shower together.

The minx had been aware of his difficulty that night and had pretended to still be unconscious as he'd struggled, trying not to think about her nudity sexually. She was laughing at him now, challenging him.

He couldn't help himself. The woman must deliberately not wear anything underneath that T-shirt. Knowing that drove him nuts while they ate dinner.

And now, as she came in his arms, he realized he was crazy all right, crazy for this woman. He'd broken all kinds of professional rules where she was concerned.

At first he'd chalked it up to attraction, but he'd been fascinated with her since that first glimpse of her through his nightscope. It was the strength of the woman, he realized, that had pulled him to her. And despite her being in danger, that strength had persisted and stubbornly pushed her on, putting those she loved first, and his admiration had grown as he'd watched her.

He'd grown up pretty much a loner, and he recognized the same in Lily. He understood her in the intrinsic way that a soul recognizes its mate. He knew his aloofness came from the fact that he felt he didn't belong, even among his teammates, who were like brothers to him. Lily, with her manipulated memories, must have felt something missing too, just enough to always put space between her and others. And added to that was the pain of betrayal and being betrayed and the sense of loss that followed. He had an idea how devastating it must have been for her when the truth—the fact that her perception of reality wasn't accurate—had come crashing down.

Stimoceiver, hypnotic manipulation, subconscious trigger—he went through all the terms that had been floating in his brain ever since he had gone through training with GEM. He'd argued all night with himself, but a few facts had actually emerged while he'd tried to find a way to handle the situation.

It was clear that Lily wasn't being controlled consciously or subconsciously right now, or why would there be a reward for finding her? Obviously, whoever her handler was couldn't reactivate her. Finally, Lily's decision to turn herself in was proof that she knew why someone was after her and that she was actually running *from* them.

"You're beautiful when you come," he told her. Inside and out.

He lowered her back onto the bed, watching her as she stretched lethargically. She traced his face with her fingers, slowly circling his eyes, outlining the shape of his lips. He turned and caught one finger between his teeth, nipping her gently.

"And you're shy," she said, tugging her finger free and tapping his cheek playfully.

He arched his eyebrows at her. "Shy?"

"Like I said, I haven't seen you naked since the first night." She peered down. "It's disconcerting how often my clothes come off whenever you're around and yours don't! So you must be shy."

He chuckled. He had his reasons. He took hold of her hand and guided it to his fly. "Feel how shy I am." He was in a constant state of discomfort because of her. "Definitely not shy."

"Ummm," she said, squeezing him lightly through the fabric. He sucked in his breath when she caressed the length of him. "I'm afraid to ask—did you go shopping while I was gone? Please say yes."

"Yes," he said. He'd come this close to deciding that he shouldn't buy any protection, because that would mean he was planning to sleep with her. Fortunately, he'd ignored his own advice.

"Thank God. I was going to say let's do it anyway if you didn't. Does that sound desperate?"

He had been desperate for her too. He had wanted her to touch him like he had her, but he'd known that he wouldn't just stop at touching if he had let her do that. He would have gone all the way, and that was one rule he wouldn't break.

"No, not desperate, baby," he assured her.

"Good." She pushed him with her other hand, and he went on his back obediently. "Where are the condoms?"

He pointed to the drawer, and she leaned over to open it and rummage inside. He watched her break the seal off while he unbuttoned his pants. With some tugging on her part and kicking on his, the pants came off. Freed from its confines, his erection stood at attention, waiting impatiently.

"You're the beautiful one," she breathed as she circled his engorged flesh.

He almost came at her touch. It had been torture ignoring the painful need to climb on top of her and have his way.

"Give me the packet," he said.

"No, I want to taste you first."

All his blood seemed to rush straight to his eager erection, and the pleasure was almost painful. He watched her head lowering toward him. Electric shots of pure white heat zapped through his body at the sensation of her wet, sweet mouth. She sucked, and he almost lost it. He closed his eyes, carried away by the sensation of the insistent pressure that was building inside him.

Her tongue flicked and teased the sensitive spot on the underside of the head, over and over, until he thought he couldn't stand it any longer. She angled her head. He held his breath, watching his whole length disappear inside her mouth, stretching his control to the breaking point.

She peered up at him, her languorous, dark eyes knowing. She was enjoying being in control, punishing him for the same tortuous pleasure he'd given her. Her mouth slowly and erotically released him inch by inch.

He reared up then, reversing their positions. She lay there, her dark eyes knowing, as she watched him fumbling with the packet. He positioned over her and pushed.

Reed grunted from the sheer pleasure of tight, heated flesh resisting his entry, squeezing his pleasure the way only a woman could, taking and giving at the same time. Her thighs grabbed his waist, urging him to go deeper. He stroked in and out, pushing a little harder each time, and she moaned as his strokes became longer and harder, her channel eagerly milking his whole length.

There was no finesse, just a need to take, his focus on where they were joined together. Every slippery glide increased the pressure, and he wanted to both stop and push at the same time. Her first internal spasms massaged him, adding fuel, taking him higher and higher, like one of those big waves that promised a spectacular ride. She groaned under him, her nails digging into his back.

Release was so close. One more stroke. He pulled out, the sensual sensation curling the tension in his stomach into a ball. One more stroke. One more . . . he grunted, lost somewhere between pleasure and need. Reed rose over the crest, on top of the world, and rode that wave home.

16

She was right. Lily turned over sleepily. It was the man and not the bed. She smiled as an arm slid over her tummy and gathered her back closer to him. The man was a furnace. No wonder every time he came close to her, her body temperature rose up several degrees.

She felt his lips on her shoulder, his hand wandering leisurely. She'd never known such joy at exploring another's body. She smiled again, this time with satisfaction. It wasn't she who had been unable to stand sharing herself with a man; it had been those programming bastards. All these years, she'd thought something had been wrong with her because she just hadn't been able to finish with a man; her need had always driven her to run away, afraid that giving in meant humiliation and loss. But last night proved that she wasn't like that at all. Despite what she'd gone through, she wasn't a clichéd, man-hating frigid bitch; she was a normal woman, with normal needs.

"Awake?"

Even the sleepy drawl of his voice turned her on. "Mmm," she replied.

She really didn't want this to end. She sighed. Unfortunately, this normal woman with normal needs didn't lead a normal life. Last night was just a reprieve. Her problem remained very real.

"Your shoulders are all tensed again," he noted from behind her. "After all the hard work I put into relaxing you, too."

She chuckled. "Hard indeed," she agreed. The empty packets scattered somewhere on the floor were testament of his hardness. She pushed her ass against him suggestively. The satisfaction that filled her was purely feminine.

"It's my morning alarm clock," he told her. His hand slid down between her legs. "And only one thing can turn it off."

"How very like a man to think of using his dick to wake up," Lily said wryly. "What else would they think of next . . . using it as a way to relax and fall asleep too?"

She felt his amusement even though his tone of voice was serious. "It's a multipurpose tool. It could even tell time if you wind it up properly."

She shook her head. Men. "And how do you wind the thing up?"

"I can show you," he suggested. She reached behind her. After a few seconds of silence, he said huskily, "I guess I don't have to show you after all."

She turned around, and this time the loving was slow and tender. She savored each kiss and caress, taking in his scent, delighting in the shape and taste of him. She knew this could be the last time, and every moment was precious.

Reed seemed to sense it too. He gave her everything she wanted and more, making every moment special, whispering words that lovers shared. She needed to hear them; she'd never taken the time, never wanted to share herself.

He kissed away the tears in her eyes afterwards. "I know," he said simply.

She'd never met a person who could shut away his thoughts so completely. She was quick-tempered, often to the point of being rude. It was something she wasn't especially proud of; it was her temperamental nature that clouded her judgment when it came to issues that were personal to her. Like the girls and their plight. The last few months, she had been very careful not to do that.

Thank God for Tatiana. Without her, Lily wouldn't have been able to function. The girl had gone through the worst, with physical and emotional scars to show for it. Lily had turned to her out of instinct. Maybe it was because they both shared that hatred that had killed a part of them. Maybe it was because they had both wanted to strike back at their kidnappers, be it a few months earlier for Tatiana, or years for Lily.

"You've spoken to Tatiana," she said softly. "She's one of the group of girls who had been kidnapped from their countries by thugs. They were sold and some of them abused. All of them are very young, way too young to be on their own. Tatiana was one of the unlucky ones. I didn't get her till after she had been sold to a *kafena,* those horrible brothels in Macedonia. She doesn't want to go back to her hometown. She wants to start a new life, she said."

There was a bond between her and Tatiana. After leaving Velesta, the younger girl had come out of her shell and become Lily's aide, taking care of the girls when Lily had to go off somewhere, and calling on the phone to make appointments because Lily couldn't. She had accepted Lily's story without question, fiercely protecting her in the same way Lily had protected her those months when she had been so broken she hadn't wanted to talk or see anyone.

Tatiana and the girls deserved new lives. No matter what the future brought, Lily wanted to accomplish this one thing.

"These girls mean that much to you," Reed said.

"Yes. They are the last group, and I don't want to fail them."

"The CIA—"

She put a hand over his lips. "Don't trust them," she said.

He took her hand in his, kissing the tips gently. "What did they do to you?" he asked. "And why would they want a bunch of young girls?"

"If I tell you—"

"I might believe you," Reed said. "Why wouldn't I?"

Lily hesitated as she thought it over. A few months ago, she herself wouldn't have believed the story of experimental programs using young girls as sleeper cells. She could use less fantastic terms and try to explain it to Reed. He was a gunrunner, so he would be able to deal with certain realities. But not about implanted poem-codes and mind triggers.

She searched for a term that was close to the truth. "Brainwashing," she said. "The CIA will take my girls and brainwash them."

To her relief, he didn't laugh or react negatively. He studied her with those calm eyes as his hand massaged her neck. "Did they do that to you? Is that what you mean when you talked about being betrayed?" When she nodded, he asked, "How did they brainwash you? What did they have you do?"

"I'm not sure." That was the truth, at least. She had no idea how they'd managed to do that to her. "But I know I betrayed my friends because of their brainwashing."

"Were you like these girls once?" He angled her chin up so that she couldn't escape his penetrating gaze. "Lily, were you . . . kidnapped?"

She didn't want to tell him about her past, not when she herself had trouble dealing with the memories. She still felt as if all those awful things—events that she could now remember—had happened to someone else, and not her. To that imaginary sister, actually. In that sense, the CIA manipulation was still working. It was kind of a relief, in a way. She wasn't sure how she would handle it if the real emotions were transferred back to her. Probably end up like Tatiana when she first came into Lily's care.

"I . . ." She sighed, trying to find the words to explain. "Yes. Then they came and rescued me, and I spent a long time at one of their facilities getting rehabilitated. I suppose I was not in the best of shape, you know? Reed, I'm not worried about me. I just don't want my girls to be used by these people."

"I'm trying to understand your story, sweetheart. They're offering a lot of money for you, so I know you have something they want, besides your being brainwashed. You did something for them but didn't deliver. Yes or no?"

He was too darn smart to allow her to gloss over the details. She tried to look away, but he held her chin gently but firmly.

"Why don't you just give it to them? Maybe you can negotiate that, instead of giving yourself to them."

"No!" She knew, through Amber, that the weapon device was American made, that it had been stolen from the CIA. Somehow or other, it had ended up in Dilaver's hands. When she had gone for it, it hadn't been to return it to anyone. At that time, she'd believed the right thing to do was to use the weapon device at an international summit where certain Eastern European leaders were attending. So that meant the CIA had somehow ordered her to do that. She had been activated to sacrifice herself, that part she understood. But there was a puzzling fact that had been niggling at her consciousness. She said slowly, thinking aloud, "I think someone in there is a . . ." She waved her hand, looking for the word, "you know, a bad CIA agent."

"A mole?" Reed suggested. "And this mole is the one putting up the money on the street?"

She frowned. "I don't know. You don't believe me, do you? I told you, the whole thing is complicated." At least he wasn't laughing. Or backing away carefully. "Reed, at this moment, I don't really care. I have nothing to lose once I can get the girls away."

"What about you?" he countered quietly. He rose from the bed, propping his head on his hand. "You didn't answer my other question. Why are you against negotiating your freedom with what they actually want from you?"

She turned her back to him. She didn't want to tell him how dangerous the weapon was. He was a gunrunner, after all, and . . . she bit her lower lip. Trust. But if he knew, he might be tempted to get hold of the weapon too. It was too soon to trust.

He saved your life twice. She sighed. She would trust him with her girls but not with the knowledge of a device that many different people would kill for. She had to keep it a secret; it was her final ace up her sleeve.

"I won't give it to them because they betrayed my trust once and I hate them for it," she finally said. Contempt filled her. "Whether it's a mole or not, it doesn't matter. They aren't going to use me again, and giving it to them will mean that they've succeeded in doing just that. Can you understand that?"

It felt right to finally be able to say it out loud. She had no one with whom to share her innermost thoughts about what had happened. Tatiana was too young, really, to be that kind of a confidante. It was good that she didn't ask any questions, but at the same time, it also made it difficult for Lily to see clearly.

She hadn't told Reed the whole story, but laying it out in that simple way clarified a few things. She wouldn't give the device to those bastards. She would rather die.

Reed's hand ran up her spine, a soft, reassuring caress. "Yes, I understand what you're saying. Turn around and look at me."

Lily did so, trying not to look too hopeful. He studied her face quietly, as if the truth was written there for him to see.

"I'll help you, but it has to be done my way," he told her.

She gave him a puzzled look. "My plan is the simplest, Reed. You deliver me and take the money. All I ask is that you spend some of it and get my girls out, with written instructions from me. The girls will follow my instructions and won't cause you any trouble, if that's what you're afraid of. You'll be set and . . . mmmmph—"

He pushed her back against the pillows and kissed her hard, cutting off her words. "You think too much about others, you know that?" he muttered against her lips. "Full of plans, all about everyone and everything, but nothing about you. Hell, you even have my cash flow all planned out. Now listen to me for once, hmm? I don't want that kind of money, paid for by your blood. I don't need you to take care of my travel plans. And I definitely don't want you to give yourself up to them. I have a thing against traitors, anyway, so I'd rather they don't have anything that's dear to me."

"Dear to you," she echoed, eyes widening.

His smile was tender. "Yes," he said.

Her heart swelled with emotion. "I don't think . . . there's any hope for us," she said. It was too much to hope for, and much too late. "If there weren't the girls, I might do things differently, but this is the only way to make sure they're free to go wherever they want."

She had no home to go back to, no friends that would welcome her, and no love who would miss her. And once the girls were taken care of, she would have no one at all. She looked up at Reed. It was too damn ironic. She'd finally found herself a man she wanted to share herself with, and it was too late.

"So let's get the passports and get the girls off your hands. Then that's one of your biggest worries gone, right? After that, we'll deal with these CIA people who are sending thugs to kill you off."

"But—"

"I'll take care of the passports, Lily. I don't need the money. I've told you this over and over. I didn't save your life to let you throw it away either, so you'd better stop thinking about doing this alone. Here's your other option—me. You place your trust in me and let me handle this."

She stared at him, not really sure what he was saying. "But how are you going to come up with all that money so quickly?"

"You leave that to me. But you must agree to do something back for me."

For the kids to be free? For the hope to be with him? "Anything," she said.

"You promise?" he asked, a quizzical expression on his face. "Can I trust you?"

"I betrayed my friends," she said carefully.

"I know that already," he said. "I want your promise to do something back for me. I think the Serbs and Croats call it *veza*."

She remembered telling him a little about it. She owed him her life. And if he could accomplish this one thing for her, she owed him a lot more. She didn't think he would ask her to do anything that would endanger her. "Yes," she said.

"Good. Let's get started."

Greta looked around her. Talia, she had to admit, had great taste. Of course, with her new wealth, she could probably afford an interior decorator, but she had a feeling her niece was a control freak. Confident people tended to be like that, and Talia was a supremely confident woman.

She could tell by the way her niece had entered Gunther's house unarmed. She hadn't been insulted by his searching her. Instead, she had been amused, as if she'd expected it and the joke was on Gunther.

In that respect, Greta was in agreement with her niece. They both knew Gunther was weak, because he didn't like to dirty his hands. He preferred others to put his plans into motion and finish for him, and then he would take the glory as his. Greta thought that despicable. He had a brilliant plan, true, but he needed partners to get it done. A man like that was a weak link.

"He's very smart, Auntie. Be careful."

Greta turned back to Talia, her gaze sharp and assessing as she watched her stretch into a yoga position. "You're very good at reading minds," she commented.

"I've been told that. It's a talent."

Talia folded into an awkward-looking position. Again, her confidence rubbed Greta the wrong way. If it were Greta, she'd be sitting in that chair at that side of the room, keeping an eye on the other person, watching her every move.

But I'm her aunt. Maybe Talia was more relaxed because of that.

She wanted to put her theory to the test. Without warning, she kicked out at Talia, aiming for the arm. Just a little bruise would teach her a lesson.

She kicked air. Her niece had rolled out of the way with such speed that Greta hadn't even seen her unfold from her position.

Greta swerved and kicked out with her other leg, this time going for the torso. Her foot jabbed air. She looked back to find her niece on her back. Talia's hand shot up, neatly catching Greta's calf. She jerked it sharply. Unable to balance, Greta fell on her knee so she could use her weight better. She kicked again, freeing her leg, then she rolled toward her opponent, this time viciously aiming for the throat.

Her elbow hit the floor hard enough to jar her funny bone. She ignored the reverberating pain, trying to move out of the way of her opponent's legs. They scissored her throat area, and she found herself staring up in a very humiliating way between her niece's legs.

"I'm very smart and very quick, Auntie," Talia said softly. "Yoga really loosens the muscles. You should try it sometime."

A moment later and Greta was freed, lying on her back on the Persian carpet. She stared up at Talia, who was adjusting her clothing. She had underestimated how well trained her niece was.

Talia offered her hand, and after a moment, Greta took it, letting her help her up. She was angry at herself. It was a huge mistake she'd just made—a huge mistake. She had thought she would show Talia a thing about being careful, and she'd ended up being the one who had learned something.

"I have to learn to anticipate a lot of things because I'm a woman in this business," Talia said. She released Greta's hand and turned away. "You've taught me that, you know."

"I did?" Greta asked, surprised.

"Do you remember when you would come visit us and brought us all those beautiful toys? I asked you how to get to be like you and go about as I like. You told me that I have to remember that I was a woman in a man's world and not let them take advantage of me."

Greta didn't remember that particular conversation, but it sounded like something she would say. Talia had always been the inquisitive one. "I'm glad you followed my advice, then," she said stiffly.

"I'm sorry you're mad at me now," Talia said, walking to the table and pouring some tea into two cups. "I was excited to finally see you again, Auntie. I forgot that you might still need to adjust to me. Forgive me."

Greta joined her at the table, accepting the cup of tea. "No, my fault," she said a bit gruffly. "I've been out of this for so long that I want to try out everything, even though I know better. Even though I kept up with my defensive skills, I didn't have a live person with whom to practice."

"Yes, it's not quite the same without a partner," Talia agreed. She sat down on a love seat with an intricate brocade cover. "Which brings us back to the reason you're here alone. I know Gunther sent you here to sweeten me up and get me to agree to the alliance. Of course, I don't think he asked you to try to fight me."

Gunther wouldn't have liked it. Greta shrugged. "I do as I please." She opted not to tell her niece that she'd just met Gunther in person herself. Again, dealing with a voice all these years and finally meeting him in person wasn't quite the same. "I've thought over what he offered and decided that his plan suited mine."

She would get hold of the weapon device without tracking down Lily Noretski. That had proven to be too troublesome. She would also save some more money, which was always good. She didn't want her account to dwindle too much without a contract that would replenish her funds. She wasn't—she looked around surreptitiously again—that wealthy a woman. Damn it, but she should have gone into the sales business.

"It's an intriguing proposal. He's thought it out very carefully." Talia played with the tiny porcelain teacup, her eyes thoughtful. "He has a contact within the CIA who's willing to set up a program like he's talking about. He needs you to cover for him at your end, in case HQ sees what he's up to. He needs me to provide the start-up cash and later, the contracts with the agencies, *and* to cover his ass in case something goes wrong. Our man has a big ass."

That made Greta laugh. "Yes, that's a good way of putting it." She looked down at her cup for a moment. "It's a lot of money involved," she said.

"Definitely a good business plan, if you want to look at it that way," Talia said. "Each girl could potentially bring in a huge contract, depending on who or what the buyer wanted to destroy. Girls that young won't be the prime suspects for a while. And if this experiment fails, and I guess there are always bad scientific experiments, we'll still make a pretty bundle from the duplicates of the device. I think my buyers will definitely be interested in looking at one of those. We just need to get someone to reverse the technology and test a few with these girls."

It dawned on Greta that that was exactly what Gunther had been trying to do when he'd ordered Llallana to bomb the center opening ceremony with all those attending leaders. He'd wanted to make a sales pitch, so to speak. Fortunately for her, he hadn't quite succeeded. "So are you interested?"

Talia's eyes gleamed with amusement. "Do you think, after all this time, I'd let a man call the shots?"

Greta smiled back. She really was beginning to like her niece just a little. "Having been a secretary, I do have an excellent memory about files on computers. He showed me the facilities where he's going to house the girls. I've seen the map. If we could get the inside layout, we could locate the weapon device once he has it."

"We could even use the facility for ourselves," Talia said.

"Of course," Greta agreed smoothly. She set down the cup on the marble table. "I do want one other thing, though. I want the original device as soon as it's been copied. That way I can finish my assignment."

That was important. She wanted her reputation intact. Money was great, but glory was everything.

"Not a problem. So how did Gunther finally track down the girls? I understand they're very well hidden in a small town."

"Yes. Llallana, for some reason, had her hotel manager call them several times. It was easy to procure the number from him and track it, of course."

"Again, I give credit to Gunther. He does cover all the details," Talia said. Her dark eyes looked at Greta thoughtfully. "He's very quick, isn't he?"

Greta nodded. It still irked her that he'd had his people following Llallana when the girl had finally been spotted in town, and hadn't told her. He'd said he hadn't been sure, since she'd been wearing a blond wig, but it had sounded like one of his half-lies. No, he'd wanted Llallana for himself.

When he'd realized that Greta wasn't going to give up like the old woman he'd thought she was, he'd decided he could use her. She looked across at her niece. Oh yes, he needed her so he could convince Talia to come aboard. Talia with all that wealth.

Once this was accomplished, wouldn't he start to think he could get rid of her? She had to play this very carefully. Let them do the hard work, get Llallana and the device for her. Then she would turn the tables and get rid of Gunther. She hadn't decided what to do with her niece yet. Maybe, if things worked out nicely, she'd invite her to tea at her beautiful house, something a little grander than this.

"Do you like shawls?" Greta asked.

Talia tilted her head, looking a little surprised. "Shawls? I haven't worn one in ages. Why?"

"I made one for you. But if you don't like shawls . . ."

"How . . . sweet," Talia said, smiling. "You loved us so much, didn't you, Aunt Greta?"

Love? Not really. But she'd missed them because they represented home. "Knitting was a good way to deal with stress. Besides, you learn patience too," she replied.

"I'll have to pick up the hobby sometime then."

Greta glanced down at the beautifully manicured hands. She didn't think Talia would really take up knitting, but they were both being polite now that they'd tacitly agreed to work together.

"I'll draw you the map I saw," Greta said briskly, coming to a decision. "Good. We can start planning on how to distract Gunther too as soon as we know he has the weapon."

Talia stood up. "That would be easy. Once that girl reveals the weapon's location, there'll be no need for Gunther."

Greta smiled back unpleasantly at Talia. Killing Gunther would be a pleasure. He'd delayed her retirement present long enough.

"Reed, we have another name you have to be aware of. His name is Gunther Galbert. His profile shows extensive contact with different CIA operatives who used him as a contact or courier between them and double agents working overseas. His contact name is The Walrus," Nikki told him the moment he called in and call conferencing was engaged. "He's now in league with Greta, and they're both after Llallana Noretski."

"That offer Greta put on the street has gotten quite a number of other people after Lily too," Reed said coldly. He thought of the bruises he'd seen on Lily's body this morning. He hadn't said anything about them to her. "There was another attempt at getting her into a vehicle last night."

"That's why we wanted you to keep her close," Nikki reminded him quietly.

"Is she all right?" Amber asked.

"Yes. This time it was one of her own contacts who wanted to collect the reward. Some guy named Viktor."

"Viktor? He's done business with her for years," Amber said. "Damn it, we should have thought of a better way of protecting her."

"She doesn't trust anything CIA, but I do have an update on her condition," Reed said. "The most important thing is that she came back of her own free will, looking for my help. She's upstairs in the suite now, so at least she's safe from bounty hunters. By the way, last night she said the trigger line twice to me. Nothing happened. She also attempted to tell me about her past this morning, except that she called what happened to her brainwashing."

"She said the line out loud?" Nikki asked. "That could mean that the trigger's beginning its effect on her. Depending on how deep the hypnotic treatment was, neuro-triggers act as timers."

"No, wait," Amber chimed in. "You said she talked about her past to you. Did she mention her sister?"

"No," Reed said. "I specifically asked whether she was the one who was abused. She never brought up her kidnapped sister story that she told you about. Also, her main concern is to not let the CIA take the girls under their care because they abused her trust when they did the same to her."

"Nikki, did you hear that?" Amber asked, excitement in her voice. "She would never say anything like that to me. During all the years I've known her, she was very secretive whenever I brought up her past. That final couple of months, she gave me the kidnapped sister background. She didn't lie to Reed this time."

"Yes, that part of it is very encouraging. It's also clear now that she isn't going on any mission to return the device to any group or person. Those girls are her number-one priority."

Reed was glad to hear Amber's views. He'd had to curb his own exhilaration when Lily had started to talk about her past. The questions he'd asked her were very important, not just for him but also for how GEM would deal with her.

"Yes, I agree," he said. "She's shown no interest in selling anything. In spite of being pushed to the point where she didn't have any single option left but me as a gunrunner, she didn't do what we'd anticipated. Instead, she proposed an alternative."

He told them about Lily asking him to help her by posing as a person who could deliver her up for the reward money. He found it tougher than he'd thought to talk about the previous night with as little emotion as possible, for he was still reeling from his own discovery about how much he'd grown to care for Lily. Before, it had been a duty to protect her; now, it was personal. But he didn't want that to come through in his debriefings. He wanted those working in his team to come to the conclusion about Lily as objectively as possible.

"That's the Lily I've always known," Amber said. "She has always put those girls first."

"We do know that they used her strong emotions as a way of controlling her," Nikki noted. She sighed and added softly, "Rape can break a person physically and mentally. The victim might push the memory away, or she might choose to channel her fear or her hatred toward a goal. In Lily's case, they made sure it was the latter. Activating the mind trigger meant a higher emotional level toward topics that generated hatred and fear. Those emotions are the driving force of sleeper cells."

"Yes, and so in the last couple of months, she was almost incoherently fanatic to Hawk, Brad, and me," Amber said. "She started accusing us of not acting fast enough, not caring about the girls' safety enough . . . nothing satisfied her, not even when Tatiana started talking again. Hawk was the one who got through that wall of silence, yet Lily went off on him as if what he'd done had damaged the girl even more. I should have wondered about that more."

Reed wanted to go after those bastards. There must be a place in hell for people who would abuse victims a second time. And the thought of Lily . . . he clenched his jaw in anger.

"Amber, there was no way you could have guessed what was happening to Lily," Nikki said gently. "Reed, did you notice any of the same hostility when it came to discussing the girls' present problems?"

"No." Thank God, no. He'd kept an ear open for unusual outbursts or even the accusations that Amber had brought up. Lily hadn't shown any sign of that behavior. She was upset and afraid, but so damn brave about it that he felt like a cad for doing his job. "I made a suggestion, and she's agreed to let me do it my way."

"What's that?"

"As you know, she wanted me to basically be the one to take her in for the reward money. I told her that since those girls were her number-one reason that she would consider taking such a risk, we should take care of that problem first." He paused, knowing that his own proposal was going to be controversial. He looked at the portrait of his father. "I'm getting the passports and transporting the girls out. This way, she would see that I could be trusted. Also, with them out of the way, she has nothing to lose. GEM can make a deal with her—the weapon device for . . . whatever she wants."

He wanted to say *freedom,* but that would clue the others in on how personal this had become for him. He needed permission to do this and didn't want his motives—that it was important to ease Lily's worries—to be questioned. To him, it was a matter of priorities—take care of what was important to Lily first, then go from there.

"And after that?" Nikki prompted.

Of course, to GEM and to his commander, Admiral Madison, their number-one priority would be to get the device out of anyone's hands. However, Reed didn't see any point in forcing Lily to tell. It would destroy the fragile thing growing between them, and he didn't want that to happen. Now it was up to him to strike up a delicate balance between his duty and his heart. He would accomplish what he'd set out to do—get that device and deliver it to GEM. He also knew he would have to bring in Lily as well, for her sake. GEM had promised Amber Hutchens they would help her friend.

"I'm hoping that she won't put up a fight when I tell her the truth." To Reed, Lily was fine the way she was, but he knew that if she even half-understood what the CIA had done to her, she was probably living in constant fear, wondering whether she would be reactivated. Hell, he would go crazy if it had happened to him. He added, "Trust is important to her."

"She trusts you enough to believe you won't dump the girls and run off with the money," Nikki pointed out.

That had been on his mind too. "She's very close to giving up," he warned. "I think she's hoping that everything will turn out fine after she's gone."

"Like I said before, you're her last hope, Reed," Nikki said, "but she hadn't thought things through. What's going to happen when she gives herself up to these people?"

"I think she knows," Reed said grimly. It wouldn't

be hard to get her to tell where the weapon was hidden. Gunther Galbert was probably the one who had activated her in the first place. He would know how to put Lily under his control again. "I'm not going to allow that to happen."

Not a snowball's chance in hell.

17

Over the next few days, Reed quietly retrieved files from his accounts and portfolio, something he'd not done in years. It felt natural to help Lily as much as he could. He had never transferred such a large amount of money before. As a Vincenzio, he had a sizable bank account open in his name, but for years he hadn't checked how much was in there. He'd known it was substantial. His father had given his brothers and him a small percentage of Vincenzio holdings when each of them had turned twelve.

When he was a kid, he had dipped in and had had more than most teenagers. He'd been able to afford almost anything without asking his parents to buy it for him. He'd never known how privileged he was till he started surfing and met the kids on the beach. Most of them had worked so they could buy the cool surfing and body boards they'd cherished. Reed still had the first board he'd actually worked for when he'd applied for a job at Arch's surf shop.

Reed looked at the numbers on the computer screen. He'd always known he was wealthy, or at least well-to-do. His father's hotel empire was very successful; the stocks Reed owned brought in good dividends without any of his input. But he'd never thought of it as his own money.

Since leaving home, he'd started his own savings, his own life. He returned home for visits, that was all, and participated less and less in the family affairs. Much to his father's disappointment, he supposed. After all, his two older brothers had settled into the hotel business and branched out from there after their wild days.

Of course, his own savings wouldn't cover a portion of the expense of purchasing illegal passports and the cash it was going to need to cover transportation of a bunch of girls. He had to smile wryly. Hadn't Arch told him that he would need all that money some day?

Hey, he gave it to you, didn't he? So it's yours. Keep it, dude. You're gonna use it for something special one day.

"Right again, old man." Lily was special. He couldn't let pride stand in the way. He would deal with the repercussions later. GEM had wanted to take the girls in and move them legally, but that wasn't what Lily would want. He knew that she'd become suspicious and worried. No, this way she would see the girls off with her own eyes. He'd said there were people who would take in these girls once they were out of the country; he would have her contact them and start arranging things the way she'd always had. This way she would be hands-on and in control of the process. Perhaps then she would see that he had no intention of hurting her.

He let himself out of the office. One more errand and he would go back up to the suite. He wondered what Lily was doing. Perhaps she'd called Tatiana with the news that they would all be going back to their respective countries soon. He wondered what she would say if she knew about his background. They had only been enjoying each other the last few days, and he hadn't given her much chance to question him.

"Sir, your father called about three hours ago. He told me that the moment you're out of conference you are to call him immediately," Petr said, looking up from his paperwork. "Shall I connect for you?"

Reed had left specific instructions not to be disturbed while he was in the office. "All right." He'd put it off long enough. "Call him."

"Here you go, sir."

Reed took the receiver from Petr. "Hello, Father," he said. "How are you?"

As always, his father got straight to the point. "Mylos, I have a suspicion that your mother has gone there to see you. She heard that you're staying at the suite, and she's disappeared this morning. She's been waiting impatiently for your call this past week."

Shit. "When?" Reed asked.

"She should be waiting for you in the suite. You really should have called. She's off her medication again. I found some pills this morning, hidden in a wad of tissues."

Double shit. "I have to go, Father. I'll talk to you later." Reed hung up without waiting for a reply.

His mother. Up there with Lily. Not a good thing.

Lily felt like screaming. How could she have missed all the clues? If she'd stayed there, she would have bloodied him. And that would have made his mother even more hysterical than she was already. An American. A swimmer. A sharpshooter. That tan on that beautifully sculptured body. She accelerated onto the freeway, stepping hard on the gas pedal.

A Navy SEAL.

She'd known it was his mother the moment the petite woman had walked into the suite. The dark blond hair, high cheekbones, clear gray eyes that darted around the room before resting on hers—they were the same as Reed's.

Then she'd started questioning Lily nonstop about where "Mylos" was, why hadn't he called, who she was, before Lily realized that "Mylos" must be Reed himself. The woman had never stopped to give Lily a chance to reply, though.

Reed's mother had sounded and acted over-wrought, to the point that she'd broken down in tears when she'd found out that Reed—Mylos—hadn't been hiding from her, that he really hadn't been in the suite. It was then, when she'd gone into a long, rambling speech about his having joined the SEALs to get away from her, that he could have a nice job at any of the hotels his father owned, that she missed him so much, that everything had clicked into place.

The hotel . . . the suite. The "friend" who owned the penthouse was Reed's own family, probably his father. When they'd walked through the hotel lobby a couple of times, she'd noticed a few speculative glances from the staff, but she'd assumed it had been curiosity about guests staying on one of their luxury floors.

She'd had to get away. There had been something clearly wrong with Reed's mother, though. The woman hadn't even noticed when Lily had gone into the bedroom to change back into her clothes.

Lily gripped the steering wheel tightly. Stupid, stupid, stupid. There was only one conclusion she could come to now that she knew Reed was also a Navy SEAL. He was, no doubt, working with Hawk McMillan, the only other SEAL she'd met. Hawk had been looking for a certain weapon a few months ago in Macedonia, and since she was the one who had stolen the item, she now knew exactly what Reed—Mylos Vincenzio, she corrected herself dourly—was after.

"He and quite a number of other people," she said aloud grimly, checking the rearview mirror. "Let's face it, Lily Noretski, you're a very popular chick."

There were cars behind her, but when she slowed down, they went around her, speeding past. She didn't see any vehicles following closely.

Disgusted, she smacked her hand against the steering wheel. She'd really fallen for his cock-and-bull story about being a gunrunner wanting a new life. He'd probably been following some script to slowly gain her trust so he could get his hands on the weapon.

"And then I'm off to jail." Or worse. Much, much worse.

But her alternative was the same. She knew that Reed didn't work for the people who had put out a reward for her, or he wouldn't have saved her all those times. Nor did it make sense that he would take her to that hotel when she'd almost drowned. No, he and Hawk were part of some other agency. Either way, everyone was after her, and she was running out of time and places to hide.

She swerved the car down the exit ramp and came to a stop at a shopping center close by. She rubbed her eyes wearily. She needed to think this out.

Was everything a lie then? He had been so tender these past few days . . . her hands fisted at the memory of him touching her, kissing . . . *no stop! The bastard is a lying son-of-a-bitch!*

But you were lying too, another voice in her head reasoned. *He also saved your life, remember? He's like Hawk, a SEAL. You've seen how good Hawk was to Amber.*

"Amber," Lily muttered. She was really slow today. If Reed was part of Hawk's outfit, then Amber would be in this too. She drummed her fingers on the car seat. Amber and Hawk probably viewed her as a traitor, but Amber and she had been partners for four years, moving the girls they'd helped to safe locations. One thing she was sure of: Amber would never hurt the girls.

She started the car again. She was tired of running. She wanted to look her old friends in the eye and tell them her side of the story. Maybe they would forgive her a little for what she had done to them.

Then there was Mr. Mylos Vincenzio. She wondered what he was thinking right now. No doubt he would be upset. He'd taken a big chance taking her to that hotel. She wanted to ask him why he'd done that. She frowned. The more she thought about it, many of the decisions he'd made had been really risky. He could have taken her anywhere that first night, but he hadn't. He'd let her drive off on her own. Well, not really . . . he'd followed her everywhere. But what had he been doing that for? It just didn't make sense.

She wanted to hear his reasons. Most of all, she wanted to hear from his lips that everything that had happened was just a lie. She was so tired of all the deception—her own, especially. Then she would clear everything up all at once.

After that, she would cut him up in tiny pieces, the lying bastard. Her lips twisted wryly. She hadn't felt this "normal" in months. If nothing else, Reed had given her back herself for a while. Being with him had made her realize that her sense of self-worth was almost nil, that she hadn't been able to commit herself to anyone because she hadn't been able to trust them.

Lily frowned. She'd trusted Reed. And she had felt so safe when she'd been in his arms. How could this man do all that when so many had failed?

* * *

It took forty-five minutes for Reed to calm his mother down and get Petr to call his father to pick her up. He knew he could follow Lily with the locator unit, but he didn't want her to be too far ahead. It took another ten minutes to have someone sent up to sit with his mother while she waited for her ride.

He felt like hell for doing that to her. He hated to see his mother cry, always had, but she'd cried so damn much that it had taken years before he'd realized that it had just been another way for her to manipulate the people around her. Everyone felt sorry for her, and that was what she wanted.

He took his pack with him. From the unit, he could see Lily was on the freeway, meaning that she was heading out of town. Probably running from him as fast as she could. He didn't blame her.

He slammed the car door. It was strange how events had piled up to be against him lately. His parents always spent winter, especially near the Christmas season, at their Manhattan penthouse. They liked the holiday season there, with the usual social rounds of seasonal parties that his mother adored. So why the hell were they over here?

He turned on the engine. Snafu—situation normal all fucked up, as they said in the Navy. His teammates would joke and warn him that he was getting too damn complacent in civilian clothes.

Anger wouldn't solve anything right now. He had to get to Lily and somehow make her listen to him.

That was, if she would even let him near her. He flipped the locator open, then pressed on the GPS button to get a visual.

He frowned. Lily was heading the other way, back toward the city. Had she forgotten something? The woman was always doing the unexpected. Was she coming back to him after all?

Yeah right, back to you.

He ignored the dig at himself as he concentrated on the locator for a few more seconds. He could sit here and wait till she reached the closest exit and turned back into town.

His cell rang. It was Nikki's secured number, not the one he'd hoped for.

"Reed here," he answered.

"Reed, code red."

That meant that things had changed and he needed to bring Lily in. "What's the problem?" he asked. Snafu.

"Gunther Galbert's people have found Lily's hideout," Nikki told him. "The girls are being transported right now to another facility."

Reed stilled. "Is this confirmed?"

"It's reliable information. You have to get Lily before they get her."

He looked at the unit in his lap. Lily was about ten minutes away from the hotel. "Where are we to meet you?" he asked quietly. "It might be difficult to convince Lily how I got this information. I think my cover's been compromised."

There was a pause. "Is she with you?"

"Not at this moment," he said, "but very soon. Let me talk to her first, and then I'll get back to you."

"ASAP, Reed."

Lily was going to have questions, and he didn't have a lot of time to convince her to trust him. He especially hated the fact that he had to tug on her emotional strings to get her to do what he wanted; everybody had been doing that, taking advantage of her. He didn't want to do that.

He got out of the car and waited where she would see him the moment her vehicle turned into the garage. He wondered why she'd turned back around.

The sound of a car entering echoed through the garage, and he straightened from his stance. His blue vehicle came around the corner, its headlights turned off as it slowed down to a stop nearby.

He stayed where he was as Lily climbed out. She came up to him, her face set, her dark eyes searching. He could see the anger and hurt, yet there was something else there. Without saying a word, he reached out, threading his fingers through her short dark tresses, holding her face still for his kiss.

Her mouth opened, giving him access. It reassured him somehow, knowing that that part hadn't changed, at least. She still wanted him.

"There's nowhere to go, really," she said simply.

He was part of the reason why she was being left with fewer and fewer options. It was what had to be done to make her come out in the open, to force her to make a move. Yet, he didn't want her to feel that way. He wanted her to know she could always come to him, but this wasn't the time or place to tell her that. He kissed her again and reluctantly let her go.

"I owe you an explanation, I know," Reed said, "but we need to go now. I just got word that those after you have gotten to Tatiana and the others."

"What? But you said you talked to her just two days ago." Her voice was a shocked whisper. "How . . ."

He would have done anything to take away the fear in her eyes. "They traced it from a call you made. That's all I know. Right now, we know where the girls are. We're sending in an extraction team."

"A call I made . . ." She frowned. "Oh no, the hotel manager . . . they must have gone to the hotel and questioned him. Who told you this information, Reed? How do we know it's the truth?"

"Simple. Call Tatiana yourself. Here." He pulled out his cell phone and handed it to her. "If she answers, ask her where she is."

Lily stared at the phone for a long moment, not taking it. He frowned. Her face had turned chalky white. She reached for it, then snatched her hand back as if the phone were a snake. "I . . . can't," she finally said.

"Lily?" Something was definitely wrong. He suddenly recalled the calls he'd made to her and how she'd lied, saying she hadn't heard the ringing. *She had him call Tatiana for her.* He cursed softly. "That's how it works on you, isn't it? Through the phone. We've thought it was just the phrase itself, but saying that didn't get any reaction from you at all."

She looked up, startled. "You know?"

Reed nodded brusquely. "About your . . . condition, yes."

Her eyes searched his. "How much?" she asked. "How much do you know?"

His answer seemed important to her. "Enough to believe that what you did wasn't entirely your fault, Lily," Reed said. "The only thing we were all unsure about was whether you knew that you were stopped from following through with your orders, and whether you were deactivated."

"Deactivated," Lily murmured bitterly. "So that was the word I've been trying to come up with for my condition. Like a damn computer program."

He'd tried to imagine what it would be like, to know that part of his mind was in someone's control. It was an impossible subject to grasp, much less explain to someone. Lily had somehow figured out how it had been used on her, and she had sought to avoid being trapped that way again. What was astounding was the fact that she'd had to resort to doing things in a roundabout way these last few months and hadn't lost her focus one bit.

The phone, after all, was the easiest way to contact the people who would have helped her get the girls out of their dilemma. He was astonished at her resourcefulness, at her taking care of so many details without the one thing that seemed to be running the world these days.

Another person might have given up and told the girls to fend for themselves. Not Lily. He felt a fierce pride and admiration for her. The woman had a core of steel.

"Lily . . ."

She turned away, but not before he saw the frustration on her face. "Everything I've done has hurt somebody. I thought if I got the girls out, that'd be one thing I did right. Instead, I've endangered them even more. They want me so badly, they've taken my girls. How am I ever going to get them back, Reed? I don't even know you . . . you're some guy named Mylos. . . . I don't know anyone in this stupid tangle I'm in."

He took her by the shoulders, pulling her into his arms. She leaned back, a sigh escaping her lips.

"You do know me. I'm Reed," he told her. "It's my middle name and that's what my friends call me. You're not alone in this, Lily. There's Amber Hutchens and Hawk McMillan."

She stiffened in his arms. "Yeah, two people I'm sure love me to death," she said sarcastically.

"We all have one goal and that's to stop the weapon device from getting into the wrong hands."

"So you guys came after me," Lily said. She cocked her head, a stubborn expression forming that he was beginning to recognize. "You understand I can't give it to you till I see my girls rescued."

He'd expected as much. "Everything's being arranged. We'll talk more about this later, after we get the girls back. I'll make the calls, get the logistics and get everyone on the same page. Is that okay with you?"

"Do I have a choice?" she asked bleakly.

He turned her around. She looked defeated, and he didn't like it. He wanted to see some of the feistiness back. He shook her lightly. "Not for this one," he told her. "They went after the girls because they knew they would get you through them. If you want to have the girls rescued, you have to trust me on this, Lily. But . . . you do have a choice about one thing."

"What?"

"About us. About what you want to do with us when this is over."

She stared at him as if he were out of his mind. "You're Mylos Vincenzio, you know—wealthy heir to some huge fortune," she said evenly. "I'm Llallana Noretski, someone with nothing, not even a future to look forward to."

He shook her harder. "If I had time, I'd take you back upstairs right now and show you all the things you can expect to look forward to, but we have to be on our way right now. Come on, let's go."

"Aren't you going to tie me up or something?" she asked. "After all, I have something you want."

She was thinking about the weapon she'd stolen, but her words conjured up images that had nothing to do with the present emergency. He ran a possessive hand down the side of her arm, then cupped her breast. She jerked at his touch.

"Later," he told her and knew from the look in her eyes that she'd gotten the message.

* * *

Lily listened quietly as Reed discussed the situation over the cell phone. It was interesting to hear things from his perspective. She realized, for the first time, that he was actually concerned about her. The first thing he brought up was how she didn't use phones any more.

She bit back her frustration. It didn't matter now, she wanted to shout. She was going to be using one really soon. Reed confirmed her own suspicions.

"Galbert will be waiting for Lily to call up Tatiana. If he's the one who activated her trigger, I'm going to say that he'll do it again, and this time get her to bring him the device."

Galbert. She now had a name. That voice had a name.

"Right. I second the idea." Reed turned to Lily and gave Tatiana's number. He then put the phone next to her mouth. His gray eyes looked intently into hers. "Say something in Croatian or Serbian into the phone, Lily."

"Why?" she asked, frowning.

"Nikki wants to modulate the pitch of her voice to fit yours, so that when she calls Gunther, he won't suspect anything."

"You're kidding me, right?" When Reed didn't say anything, Lily said, in Croatian, "I would like the opportunity to kill this Gunther Galbert myself, please, before your agency locks me up. Please bring the girls back safely."

"Why do you think you're going to be locked up?" Reed asked.

"You don't think they're going to let someone like me walk around free, do you?" she asked. "Don't think there'll be much of a future, Mr. Vincenzio."

"We'll see," he said and got back on the phone. "Is that enough to work on, Nikki? Yes, will stand by for further instructions."

"What's going on?" Lily asked when he hung up.

"We're going stay put and wait for Nikki to call back. Why do you think Gunther's waiting to check in on the girls?"

What was that word he'd used? "To . . . activate me," Lily said, tapping her head. "Then he'll tell me to bring him the missing weapon."

Reed nodded. "That's right. He'll pick you up, and by that time we'll set a trap to get him."

"What about the girls?" It all seemed too easy.

"Nikki says we have an extraction plan ready and are waiting for the interior layout to be forwarded to us."

"Who is Nikki?" Lily asked. "Is she your boss or something?"

She recalled those looks they'd given to each other in the big van. Had she imagined it, or had they been warning looks? Maybe they were lovers too and Nikki was worried how intimate Lily and Reed were. Of course, if the situation had been reversed, Reed would have been a dead man already. Lily wasn't that sharing a person.

"Nikki works for an agency called GEM. I'm on a SEAL team that's part of a joint venture with it.

We've been targeting this weapon you have for months now."

"Hawk McMillan's on your team," she said.

"He's my commander," Reed acknowledged. "He was too injured to continue with the mission."

Lily bent her head. Hawk must have been more injured than she'd thought when he had gone off to save Amber. Another person she'd inadvertently caused pain.

"What do I do?" she asked resignedly. She had to make things right somehow. These people had a mission, and she had been in the way. Now they were taking over her problems without even making sure she really had the weapon. "I'll give you the device now. It's safer out of my hands, anyway."

His hand caressed her face, and she resisted the urge to turn to seek comfort. When had she gotten to need him so much?

"There are people over my head who will be reading debriefings and reports after this," Reed said softly. "An act of faith on your part will show them that you weren't against them."

"Just misguided?" she countered.

"Hey, look at me."

She didn't want to. Looking at him directly weakened her resolve not to feel anything, especially about him.

"Are you afraid?" he asked.

She pursed her lips, then met his eyes determinedly. He saw too damn much. She knew he could see all the feelings she was trying so hard to hide, and there was nothing she could do about it.

"I don't hold you responsible for what you did," he said. "A group of people inside the CIA took advantage of you. You weren't given a choice in this, so don't beat yourself up because of it. I know what it's like to wake up and have the whole world as you know it taken away from you, but at the end of the day, it doesn't matter. It's still you inside."

He tapped his forehead, mimicking the way she'd done it to herself earlier. There was a hint of emotion in his gray eyes, which were usually so unfathomable. He spoke with the sincerity of someone who had gone through a similar pain. She cocked her head.

"I want to know one thing. Who betrayed you?" she asked quietly.

For one heart-stopping moment she thought he would refuse to answer her. He put a hand on her shoulder.

"My mother," he said quietly. "You've seen how she is. When she's without her medication, her behavior becomes more erratic, to the point where she has disappeared for weeks. Before she was diagnosed as a manic depressive, she did exactly that. When she returned, she was pregnant. With me."

She didn't know what to say. She hadn't expected that. "You mean, your mother was . . . raped?"

He shook his head. "Nothing that melodramatic. My guess is that she met somebody who made her forget whatever it was she was trying to run from.

It's hard to explain, Lily. She just did it and then she came home. I was born and didn't know about this till I hurt myself surfing one day and needed a blood transfusion." He fell silent for a second, then continued. "Things became clearer after that incident. I never understood why my father always seemed to avoid looking at or talking to me. It was always 'your mother' or 'your son' in the conversations."

"I'm sorry, Reed," Lily said. "I didn't mean to pry. You don't have to tell me your family secrets."

He shook his head. "It's okay, I want you to know. It's not as devastating as being implanted with subconscious triggers, but I want you to see that I understand about deception, and how it can hurt when you know you're the cause of it. Father took care of me like I'm his, but there was always something missing. He loves my mother very much, and I think he's forgiven her for what she did, but I was a physical reminder of it every day, so he avoided me. I made it easier for him after I found out the truth. I drifted away. I joined the Navy and seldom returned home. I haven't gone into the family business. My two other brothers—half brothers, I should say—are probably relieved I haven't."

He shrugged and scratched the back of his head, as if he was a little embarrassed at how much he'd revealed. This was probably the most she'd ever heard him talk. A lot of things made sense now. His adamance about protection. His aloneness.

Lily slipped her hand in his and squeezed. He smiled that rare smile that always left her a bit breathless.

"Feeling sorry for me now, aren't you?" he teased.

She nodded. "Poor little lost boy," she said and tiptoed to meet his descending mouth.

"Poor little lost girl," he murmured against her lips.

It seemed so right, at that moment, that they'd found each other.

18

Time seemed to speed up when one was no longer alone. Lily looked around her, feeling a little bewildered. Reed had gotten the call to meet up, and they'd driven to a location just outside the city. It had looked like a factory from the outside, but once they'd driven through the fenced yard and into a warehouse, the door had slammed behind the car and everything had gone black.

She heard a loud humming, and everything vibrated as the bottom of the car moved. It was, she realized, some kind of lift. They were going underground.

"You okay?" Reed asked.

"I think so," she said. "I thought we were going to the place where Gunther Galbert wanted me to meet him."

"Not yet. We have a team here, and everyone needs to be on the same page, including you." The lights came on. "Come on, everything's going to be all right."

Lily got out of the car and followed Reed. There were armed men, dressed in black, none of whom were paying attention to her as they moved things around the meeting room. Nikki came in from the other door, also dressed in black. She was talking to someone using a wireless mic. She waved at Reed.

Reed set his weapon bag on the floor by the table and went to pull up some chairs. Lily looked at the charts stuck on a board. Maps. A picture of the car in which she was last seen. There was one of it now—a total wreck.

Lily scowled. She had released the brakes and let the car roll off the cliff that night. She hadn't gone very far, had she? All these months—these people had been following her moves, anticipating her decisions, trying to figure her out, and she'd thought she'd been all alone.

She turned away from a photo of herself and froze. Amber was walking toward her. Her former friend didn't look angry, like Lily had thought she would. She should be. If it had been the other way around, and it had been Amber who'd betrayed their friendship like Lily had, Lily would have taken a gun right now and shot Amber. She took a deep breath. Released it.

They stood several feet apart. The commotion in the room seemed to recede into the background. Lily didn't know what to say. She hadn't thought she'd ever meet Amber again. *She'd drugged and given her friend to an enemy.* Saying sorry was quite inadequate.

"Nothing I say can ever erase what I did. You can do whatever you want to me after this," Lily finally said, "but only after the girls are safe. They don't know what happened, so please—"

She stopped. Please . . . what? Please don't tell them? She deserved every bit of hatred from everyone for what she'd done. She wouldn't plead for herself.

"They're my girls too, Lily," Amber said. Her eyes always turned an intense blue when she was emotional about something, and Lily could see the tears she was holding back. "We don't have time to talk now, but I want you to know I'm still your friend."

Lily stared at Amber. "Don't say you forgive me," she whispered. "It'll make me feel worse. I much, much prefer hatred. Do something. Hit me."

"Too bad. I'm a missionary's daughter, remember?" Amber gave her a small smile. "I know what's on your mind. I'm okay. Hawk came in time."

Lily closed her eyes. Night after night, she'd imagined the worst to punish herself, that Hawk had rescued Amber after she'd been tortured and used by Dilaver and his men. She'd turned back to the city to get the girls that night and had heard the huge firefight going on. Later, she'd gotten news about people being flown to another base because of injuries. And she'd known it had to be Hawk and Amber.

"It doesn't hurt any less," she said. She opened her eyes. "You were my best friend, and I loved you like a sister. I can't explain how I could just suddenly forget that and let someone order me around. I can't forgive myself for not having put up a fight. I keep thinking that a part of me would recognize that I was hurting you, but—"

She stared down at her clenched fists. Sometimes she still couldn't believe that she'd done what she did.

"I've done a lot of research on what they did to you, Lily. I had to because I couldn't believe that you could have done that to me willingly. And you did put up a fight. You drugged me, remember? You told me you didn't want me to go through the whole thing conscious. Part of you didn't want to hurt me."

Lily glared at her friend. "Don't give me the easy way out, please," she exclaimed. "You're supposed to yell and call me names. Kick the shit out of me. Tell me not to ever come near you again."

"First you're going to have to endure a hug," Amber told her.

Lily shook her head and backed away. "Don't," she said.

Amber calmly came to her and put her arms around her. The hug turned fierce. Lily swallowed back the tears stuck in her throat. "I've known the real Lily for four years, and she was the most generous woman I knew. She did everything for a bunch of girls who had nowhere and no one to turn to. You don't think, when she has no one now, that I would abandon her, would you?"

Lily could only hold on, her heart in her throat. She looked over Amber's shoulder. Reed stood by the table, quietly taking in the whole scene. His eyes were just as intense as he studied her reaction to meeting Amber.

She realized now that he must know about Amber and her friendship. He'd asked her many questions about her past. It must have been part of his assignment, to find out how much she remembered. But he'd never pressed her about Amber or her betrayal in any way. He'd understood her pain and had respected it.

"You ready to go get our girls?" Amber asked, letting her go.

Lily took a deep breath. "Yes." There would be time later to talk.

Reed straightened and came to join them. "Lily's given me the location where she's hidden the device," he said, his eyes never leaving Lily's. "We have to pick it up before the meeting with Gunther."

Amber nodded. "Agreed. Let's get started."

Lily tugged on Reed's sleeve. "Thank you," she mouthed.

"For what?"

"For being a friend." She wanted to kiss him. She was beginning to realize that it mattered to her that he saw her in a good light, that he didn't think she was a traitor. "For taking care of me."

His serious expression softened. "It's becoming a habit. I think I deserve a hug too."

In spite of the tension of the moment, Lily found herself smiling back at Reed. "Later," she promised.

* * *

Greta inserted the decoder into the USB port on the laptop and clicked the Run command. Gunther had told her that tonight would be the big one, when they would get their hands on both the weapons device and Llallana Noretski.

She didn't care about the girl so much. That was Gunther's thing, even though the project sounded intriguing. But after giving it some thought, she'd rejected the notion of a true alliance. No, this would be her little revenge for the problems he'd caused her. The most satisfying part was getting rid of the guards he had put in his house. As if they could stop her!

First, and most important of all, she was going to deliver the weapon to Headquarters. That was her original order, and she was going to stick to it. Deviating from it seemed wrong, especially when she was so close to finally being home. Why throw it all away because of ambition?

Gunther would have those girls. That ought to placate him. Or she could get Talia to do that. She seemed to get along with him so well.

A part of her was a little jealous. If she were ten years younger, Gunther would be paying her the same attention. She wasn't beautiful like her niece, but she had her ways with men. She'd always been able to get any man she'd wanted. She touched her face.

Maybe a little face-lift by the surgeon that had redone Talia's face. Why not? It'd be a great second celebratory present for her retirement. Her first one would be getting the device, of course.

Greta picked up her cell phone and called Talia. She inspected one chipped finger nail.

"There's no problem at my end. I found the tampon in the wastebasket. Ingenious. Gunth didn't check your handbag thoroughly enough," Greta said. There was half a micro-drive hidden in the cotton. It fit into another part that was in another tampon Talia had handed to her. Together, once inserted into the USB port of a computer, it would upload and download information like a flash drive. Quite an amazing gadget. "I'm downloading what I've taken from his house to your network now."

"Good. With the layout, we won't have any problems going straight in and getting what we want," Talia said.

"Yes." Greta was still mulling over what to do with her niece when this was over. She didn't think she needed to kill her. It irked her, though, whenever Gunther smiled at her, as if he had been having second thoughts about getting rid of her. Once she'd given him some funds, would he still smile at her that way? "What has Gunther said to you about the plans tonight?"

"He's getting everything secured and moving immediately to the facility. He wants to show me how it's done with that girl, so I'll be going there, of course. That leaves you to call in late. Give a simple excuse. A flat tire would suffice, Auntie Greta, nothing elaborate or he'll know something's going down. Secure the rest of the information he has on his hard drive and leave. We'll analyze it later together. Do

you need me to run through with you how to activate
the decoder to get his passwords?"

"No, I know how, don't worry." She had been doing that for ten years. Decoding. Encryption. Blah
blah blah. She wanted action. "I'll download everything to your network and join you all. If Gunther
gets too suspicious, Talia, make your move before he
does. He's a lot quicker than you think."

"I'll be surrounded by all his men, Auntie. I can't
make any move unless I want to get killed. I'm depending on you to get this done right. Be sure you
load the file that he'd mentioned, the one the KGB
had left in the archive. He said that's the program he
wants to study. If we want to take over this whole
thing, we want to have everything he's got."

"I'll see you soon." It felt good to be finally getting the best of Gunther. Greta might not be able to
climb walls like she used to, but she could still out-
smart someone like him. He had no field experience.
Tonight she would show him what a counter-mission
was all about.

19

So far so good. Gunther Galbert had fallen for the trap, thinking that he'd reactivated "Lily" when Nikki had called.

Reed looked through the binoculars, easily picking out Lily sitting on the bench. Gunther Galbert had instructed her to meet him with the device at a children's playground. At this time of the night and in this weather, there wouldn't be many people around.

He didn't want Lily out there alone, but he had no choice. Galbert would be looking for her. He knew what she looked like, so using a decoy wouldn't work.

The idea was to keep it as simple as possible so that Lily didn't have to talk to the man. The moment he pulled up, she was to pretend to turn and get the box, then run like hell as an element of surprise. This would give Reed and the team enough time to shoot. Game over for Galbert.

"I can do this," Lily had assured Reed. "Promise me, if anything goes wrong, just shoot. Don't let him use me again."

"I won't let him take you," Reed promised.

Nikki had said that Greta, the other person looking for Lily, would be picked up later. Reed assumed that she was guarding the girls somewhere while she waited for Galbert's return. He'd been told that Hawk and his SEAL brothers were running that particular mission. He missed being with them, but—he sighted the scope again—he'd rather be here to protect Lily. The men who were with him here were good professionals, but he didn't know them well.

A car's headlights cut into the darkness. He watched Lily adjust her jacket, touching her mic briefly, to make sure it was still there.

"Everyone on alert," Reed said over his mic. "Stand by for signal."

"Ten-four."

"Ten-four and ready to shoot at target."

The vehicle slowed down as it approached Lily. The door opened.

"Run," Reed ordered softly, willing her to move.

His heart sank as Lily remained where she was, staring into the vehicle. Why wasn't she running? She was standing too close for them to shoot.

"Hold your fire," Nikki's voice came on the mic. "I repeat, hold your fire."

Reed couldn't breathe as they all waited.

"Good evening, Llallana. As you can see, I have your friend here with me."

A man's voice came over Lily's mic, and Reed trained his eyes on the scene below him. Lily still hadn't moved. That had to be Galbert talking to her now.

"Let Tatiana go," she said, sounding tense and angry.

Damn it. Galbert had prepared for a setup. "He's got one of the girls with him," Reed said, knowing the men around him would need an explanation. "Lily isn't going anywhere. Not if she sees Tatiana in danger. Let's hope our guy doesn't realize he's surrounded by a team."

From the recorded conversation with Nikki, Galbert appeared to be under the impression that Lily was still alone, except for the man she'd been seen around town with. That was Reed, of course. Galbert had ordered "Lily" to be alone. Obviously, he hadn't trusted that his orders would be followed.

Reed laid down his weapon. He needed to get a lot closer.

"You don't think I'd come here without some sort of protective measure, do you?" he heard the man continue. *"Just in case it wasn't you on the phone, you know. Now, in case that boyfriend of yours is around, the one you met at the club, he won't shoot just yet, not if you come with me quietly, right? Talia, go on out and tie her up. The girl can fight, so be careful."*

Reed paused to use his scope again. Was that Greta? No, he'd heard Galbert call her Talia. Another woman exited the car, pointing her weapon at Lily. Damn it, by the time he got down there, she'd already be in the car. He could shoot the woman, but Lily would still be in danger as long as she didn't get out of the way. He watched helplessly as the woman tied Lily up.

"Do we have a vehicle ready to follow them?" Reed said into the mic, trying to keep the fear from showing in his voice. Once Galbert had Lily and realized there was nothing in that box, he'd make her tell him the truth, that Hawk was on the way to pick up the device. Reed's jaw clenched at the thought of what might happen to Lily then.

"Yes, it's taken care of," Nikki replied. Reed had to give it to her. The whole plan had just gone to hell, and she sounded as if there was nothing wrong. "We'll have to see what Galbert does next before we move."

"He's going to open the box." He couldn't keep that calm. "I'm going down there, just in case."

"Reed, hold your fire till I say so," Nikki warned. "Trust me on this."

Not replying, Reed jumped off the ledge onto another. He didn't want to confirm that order, not when he couldn't see for sure what was happening. Listening in only magnified the danger. He'd found that there was no way to be an objective sharpshooter when his emotions were engaged in Lily's and Gunther Galbert's conversation.

"Now, I suspect there's nothing in this box, Llallana, and that you've once again disobeyed me. Am I right?"

"If you know already, why are you here?" Lily asked. *"And stop jamming that gun against Tatiana. You have me now. Let her go. In fact, why don't you give up? I called the authorities, and they have this place surrounded."*

"Good girl," Reed mouthed. Sound desperate. Make the bastard think you're trying to deceive him.

"I've had that man of yours checked out. He's an MIA UN soldier. He's been working on his own for a while now. I don't think he wants the authorities to be in on this. No, he's out there right now wondering what the hell to do next. Choices, you know? Money or love? Device or Llallana?" There was a gasp of pain. *"This little one reminds me of you. Full of hate, the powerful emotion. She's going to be an excellent candidate for a sleeper cell, don't you think?"*

"You bastard!" Lily's voice shook with rage. *"I'll kill you before I let you do that to her."*

"We'll see who gets killed tonight. Talia, put those headphones on her."

"What are you doing?" Lily asked.

Reed could hear struggling as he slithered down a rope, using his legs to push off the wall. He was almost down on the ground. What the hell was Galbert doing to her? Then everything quieted down. His heart thundered in his chest as he kept going.

"Look at her, Talia. She's under already. She's been programmed to respond to that signal, you see."

"Amazing, it's like she's waiting for something."

"My instructions. It's only been a few months, so she'll go under easier. The first time I found her, it took me several tries before I realized that there were different levels. She had a pretty strong mind and fought the urge to obey for a good while. Look at her now, though, totally under my control. Just to be

sure, I'll leave the headphones on till we get back. I'm going to get her to lure that boyfriend of hers out. After we've dealt with him, she should be ready to lead us to the weapon. Start the car. I'm sure he'll follow."

There was one last ledge onto the ground below, very close to the edge of a small wall that enclosed the playpen for young kids. Once he got down there, he would be close enough to see the details of the vehicle. The window was cracked open slightly. He wanted to rush over there and take out Galbert immediately. Reed couldn't let her leave with that bastard. He wouldn't let her be used again. It would devastate her.

"Reed! Did you copy my orders?" Nikki asked sharply over the mic.

"Copy," Reed said reluctantly. His attention was focused on what was happening inside the vehicle as he moved to the edge of the ledge.

"Llallana, can you hear me? Do you know that things fall apart?" Gunther asked.

"No!" Reed said aloud, jumping and rolling on the ledge.

"Things fall apart and what's the next line, Llallana?"

"She's quiet. Is she resisting?" the woman in the car asked.

"She can't resist. Continue driving, Ivan."

Reed pulled up his weapon, aimed at the speeding vehicle, and fired. The car swerved to the right, corrected itself, and kept going at high speed.

"Stop shooting, Reed! You'll injure Lily and the other girl if the car overturns or smashes into one of the walls," Nikki ordered.

Reed cursed as he glared at the taillights. So near, yet so far. He was not going to fail Lily.

"Reed, there's a vehicle on the way to the south end of the playpen. Get there now."

He stared at the car taking Lily away for a second, then rushed to the location, all the while listening in on the conversation in the car that was getting away.

"He's good," Galbert was saying. *"Like I suspected, nothing in the damn box. Let that bastard follow, just in case he has the device. That would save us a trip back."*

Reed jumped into the waiting car. He nodded curtly at the commando who was driving. If he had his way, he would be the one driving. Damn it, if he had his way, he would have shot out both tires by now. But Nikki was right; that could have caused an accident.

Why wasn't Lily saying anything? Reed clenched his jaw in frustration to keep the flow of cuss words from tumbling out. Nikki was still on the other end of the intercom.

"Are we going to get our reinforcements behind us?" he asked instead.

"No, your team's already headed that way, Reed."

It was the first piece of welcomed news he had. "My SEAL team?" he asked, just to make sure.

"Yes, it's the STAR SEALs, with Hawk McMillan and Jazz Zeringue at the helm," Nikki said. "They're awaiting inside information of the layout as of now, but not all of it has been delivered."

"We can't afford to wait any more," Reed said impatiently. "With Lily as prisoner, Gunther will have access to the weapon's location. His facility will be well armed, so saving her before he enters his building is top priority."

"I'm radioing your team commander now and getting his opinion. Stand by, Reed."

As Reed looked on the vehicle in the distance, an unsettling thought occurred to him. What if Hawk didn't care whether he saved Lily or not? After all, she had almost gotten Amber Hutchens, Hawk's girlfriend, killed.

"Reed?"

"Yeah."

"Here's Hawk's message, and I'm reading it word for word. He said, 'Tell Joker we'll make a direct hit when the vehicle goes through the electronic gate. Once the vehicle isn't functioning, the target would call in for help and it'll give Joker a few minutes to approach the vehicle. The target would probably be using Lily as a hostage situation. Joker has five minutes to get her out of danger. We don't know how many hostiles would be coming out to help Galbert so if he doesn't get her away by then, we have no other option but to do a direct strike with Lily as captive.' Did you copy that, Reed?"

"Copy. Ten-four," Reed replied.

Hawk was telling him that he had only one small window of opportunity to save Lily. Reed gripped his high-powered rifle tightly. Please God. Don't let him fail Lily.

*   *   *

Reed wound down the car window. Gunther Galbert didn't seem to care that he was being followed. Through the mic, Reed heard him chatting amiably to his female companion, telling her how he'd gotten hold of the secret CIA files and tracked down Llallana Noretski.

He listened with a quiet, building rage. This was the man responsible for what had happened to Lily. She'd carried the guilt all these months, but he was the one who had played on her paranoia, using it to feed the emotional trigger that he had used, slowly moving her as a pawn in his endgame. And now he had plans to use these other kids the same way, too.

"Nikki, if you're listening in to this piece of shit, you of all people should understand why I'm going to take him out," he said, unable to keep the anger out of his voice.

There was a short pause. "I heard it all, Reed. There are just too many scum in this world to worry about, aren't there?"

These GEM operatives. They never liked to speak directly, did they? "One less scum won't be missed," he agreed. Galbert's car disappeared down a small country trail. Reed turned to the commando driving the car to warn him. "Possible ambush."

"We're getting close to the old converted factory. It has an underground tunnel used during World War Two. Once Galbert gets inside the grounds, he'll use the tunnel to confuse us." The man glanced at him. "Of course, he thinks that it's just you against his men. He wants you alive still, just to make sure you don't have the isotope explosive device."

Reed looked sharply at the other man. In the dark, he had only been able to make out the blond hair under the pulled-up hood. The black body suit did its job of giving anonymity. "You know it's an IED?" GEM had been very careful to only use generic terms when referring to the stolen weapon. Only a handful of people knew what the isotope explosive device looked like, including its compounds and materials. GEMs . . . Hawk . . . the admiral . . . COS commandos. "What's your name?"

The man looked at him again, and this time his eyes gleamed with what Reed thought was amusement. "A little late for introductions, don't you think?" He turned his attention back to the dirt path. "Watch for your team. They're about to move in on Galbert."

The old building reared up in the darkness like some haunted house. The car lights lit up just enough for Reed to see the electronic door opening. The vehicle ahead of theirs slowed down.

"Nikki, he's speaking in German," Reed said. "I don't understand what he's saying."

"He's telling his men to allow the vehicle behind him to drive into the compound. He ordered them not to shoot you until his say-so."

"Glad to know that," Reed said wryly.

A flare flew into the air, landing right in front of Galbert's vehicle as it passed through the gates. A second flare bounced off its hood. The car jerked as the driver reacted by braking hard.

Reed heard Galbert curse and order the driver to move on. At that very moment Reed's companion stepped on the gas and rammed into Galbert's vehicle.

Reed leaned out the window and shot out the tire. He shot again, taking out the other back tire. He remained in the car, his weapon trained on the vehicle. He knew it would be difficult for Galbert to spot him or the man next to him just yet. He had the advantage of listening to the hushed conversation inside that vehicle. All he needed was to find the exact spot his target was sitting at and which door would open first . . .

"My team's heading down closer. No one else but Galbert, Reed."

That he could agree to. "Ten-four," Reed said, wondering for a split second how Nikki could be behind him so quickly.

"I think you're seriously underestimating your enemy, Gunther," Reed heard the woman say. *"There's more than one! Tell the guys inside to shoot!"*

"They're watching," Gunther said calmly. *"You don't think I would let this young man in here and let him just shoot me, do you? Llallana should be ready for our use by now."*

"You think of everything. Now what? I fear if we go out, they're going to start shooting at us."

"We're going to take Llallana with us, of course. Obviously, she means a lot, or he'd have started shooting already. Something isn't right. Where are the others? We only know he followed us with that

one car. Let's get him to follow us into the tunnel. Come on. You take the other girl. I'll handle Llallana. You go out first."

Nice guy, asking the lady to go first so she'd be the first to get shot. Reed waited. He pulled out his earpiece as he opened his car door and stepped out. No distraction. He was going to need his entire focus.

He saw the woman emerge with another girl. That must be Tatiana. The other door opened and Lily came out first, with Galbert behind, holding her like a shield. Reed was close enough to hear bits and pieces of what he was telling Lily.

"Stand in front of me. Call out for your friend. We need him where we can see him."

"Reed!" Lily called out obediently.

"That's right. Talia, move toward the tunnel. Reed!" Gunther Galbert yelled out. "If you shoot, I'll kill Llallana."

Reed stepped out where he could be seen, gambling on the fact that Galbert had ordered that he wasn't to be shot. "What do you want? Why did you bring me here?" he asked. Lily didn't react to his presence at all. "Lily?"

Galbert kept Lily in front of him, backing up, moving toward a corner of the building. The lights were dim and Reed couldn't see his target's body behind Lily. He moved forward slowly, following them.

"Don't pay attention to him," Galbert said to Lily. "You, where's the device? That's all I want. Llallana stole it for me first."

"I'm there. I'm going inside," Talia said, a little ways ahead of them.

Reed ignored her. She wasn't important to him right now. Nikki would handle everyone else. All he wanted was that one shot.

"Give me Lily and I'll give you what you want," he said.

Galbert laughed. "I think I have a better advantage with her as my prisoner." He took a few steps back and turned the corner of the building.

Reed charged forward, dashing round the corner. He cursed out loud. Galbert and Lily had disappeared.

Suddenly dark figures jumped out of the shadows from different directions. Reed turned, anticipating his teammates; he was sure they had been watching the whole incident.

"Joker, follow me." The voice was barely a whisper, but Reed recognized the figure easily. It was Hawk, his commander.

"Yes, sir," Reed said, moving into team position as if he hadn't been out of the team the last few months.

His teammates seemed to have the location of the tunnel already. Hawk hand-signaled the order to move in single file, then slipped into the open hatch.

As Reed passed Jazz, who always guarded the rear, he was handed gear, as well as a pair of glasses. He put them on and recognized them as gifts from GEM in the recent Joint Mission operation in Asia. They were infrared glasses, enabling the wearer to look for laser alarms and body heat.

"Gunther Galbert is an electronics and computer expert. We have to watch out for laser traps. He probably knows you aren't alone by now. We're separating into three groups once inside, and we'll do a search and destroy, except for hostages."

"Copy, sir," Reed said grimly. His mind was on Lily. She was the main hostage as far as he was concerned.

They moved off in three directions, with Hawk leading his group. The infrared allowed them to move quickly, efficiently taking care of the "blobs" of heat that revealed hidden positions.

Rat-tat-tat of gunfire in the other direction. Discovery.

Reed followed instructions and shot out the first door. Hawk was inside before him. The room looked bare, like a holding room. Hawk cocked his head, listening.

"Ten-four," he said. He turned and gestured. "Three hostiles in the hallway. Then up the stairway to the right. Hostiles in that room, and they can see us with their video there."

Reed realized Hawk had been listening for instructions. He remembered Nikki telling him that they had been waiting to download hacked files of the floor plans of the target location. Someone at GEM must have finally broken the code.

He dodged behind what looked like pipes. Bullets ricocheted against the steel. They must be under the building. A short exchange of gunfire. He counted two hostiles down. The third one had run off.

Reed rushed up the stairs. He heard a door opening and ducked as something sailed over his head. In that split second he shot blindly, hearing a yell when he got his target, but he didn't like the feeling of suspicion about the thrown object flying through the air at that moment.

"Hawk!" he yelled down. "Up, man, up!"

He hung on to the railing as the bottom of the stairway blew up where the small explosive landed. The flare lit up the darkness, and relief and adrenaline moved through him when he caught sight of Hawk's heat blob clinging on to something a few feet away.

Grimly he reached out and pulled at his commander's arm as he scrabbled away from the hole below. The stairway was gone.

Reed pulled a small Uzi from his gear. Hawk had lost his main weapon when he'd grabbed the railing. Reloaded, they mowed down the entrance, each of them on either side. They moved in, firing.

"TV room, hostiles down," Hawk reported. "Next? Reed, the others have found the girls, no sign of Galbert."

Reed nodded grimly. "Where's the next set of hostiles?"

"I'll take care of it. They're reporting two figures moving rapidly up onto the roof and a helicopter heading toward the area. That means some government agency is getting involved. You have to get Galbert before the helicopter shows up. We don't

know how much Lily has told him. We aren't author-
ized to interfere with agency maneuvers."

"Yes, sir." Reed listened as Hawk gave directions.

Reed's mind raced with decisions as he made his
way up. Galbert had called for help in his own
agency. It was clear now that the agency for which he
was working had government connections or was
part of the government itself. Neither GEM nor his
admiral would want an international incident.

He pulled open the door at the top of the stairs.
The cold night air contrasted with the heat inside the
building. He could still hear fighting below him as
his team mates continued the search and destroy.

Reed didn't care at the moment. Someone had
turned on a spotlight, probably using it to signal the
incoming craft. He breathed in sharply. His target
was in sight.

Gunther Galbert stood against the wall edging the
building, a gun to Lily's temple. He gave Reed a
mocking smile, then nuzzled Lily's ear, crooning
softly like a lover. "She'll do anything I tell her to do
right now. Llallana, do you know why he was at The
Beijing Bombshell? He's one of those people who
use girls. I'm protecting your girls from him. That's
right, you know how things fall apart if you don't
take care of the girls, don't you?"

"Things fall apart," Lily echoed softly. "I remember."

Galbert looked up at Reed triumphantly. "Why
don't you tell your boyfriend you don't love him and

that you're coming with me? Tell him you're going to keep the girls safe from people like him."

Reed stared at Lily. She couldn't have forgotten everything they'd shared so quickly. He told himself that she didn't mean it, that whatever she was going to say, she didn't have a choice.

He heard the unmistakable *chop-chop-chop* of a helicopter approaching from far off. Reed didn't take his eyes away as dark figures popped up from the side of the building. Galbert backed away even more. For the first time, he appeared nervous.

"What's the matter, Galbert?" Reed mocked. "Feeling a bit surrounded?"

"My government's on the way. You don't want to start any incident you can't explain."

"You'll be dead, Galbert." Nikki's voice surprised Reed from behind. "I don't think your government will care once they see your dead body lying here. They want you as long as you're alive."

That was direct permission to Reed to get his target. His finger rested on the trigger of his weapon, trying to get a clear shot, but Gunther had cleverly put Lily in his way.

Reed made himself look at her. If he failed, he would kill both her and the bastard behind her. She looked so calm as she stood there. The sound of the copter was getting louder. He didn't have much time left.

Her gaze was intent on him, as if she wanted him to look at her. He needed her to move eight inches one way or the other. That would be just enough to . . .

"I love you," she said. At the same time she bent forward and slammed her body weight hard against Galbert, pushing him into the wall behind them. The impact surprised her captive. There was a shot from the weapon Galbert was holding.

Instinct and training took over. Without thinking, Reed pulled the trigger. He got Gunther Galbert's face with one shot. The man slowly slid down to the ground, his hand still holding his gun.

"Lily!"

He ran to her, flooded with an unfamiliar fear that Galbert's shot had hit her. There was no blood. She was moving. Thank God. Thank God.

He knelt down, his breathing unnaturally harsh as he turned her into his arms. That had been too damn close, even for a good shooter. Her hands were tied behind her back, so she couldn't get up. He pulled the damn earphones off her, his hands tangling in her hair. He was surprised to find them trembling hard. He pulled away from the open, using the vehicle for cover. "Lily, can you hear me?"

He ignored the rush of people moving behind him. The helicopter was here and it hovered over the building, stirring the air. He looked up to see Nikki talking into a radio, her attention on the helicopter. It appeared as if she was conversing with their visitors, pointing in Reed's direction.

He pulled Lily out of the way so that any interested party could see Galbert's dead body. A spotlight appeared from the helicopter, and, after a second's confirmation, it turned off and the craft flew off. No one was interested in a dead spy.

"God, Reed, it took every bit of my nerves to do that. I kept thinking there was no way you could not hit me, too. Can you untie me?"

Reed looked down at Lily. Was it safer to leave her tied up till someone took a look at her? She sounded so normal. What did an activated sleeper cell sound like anyway? But if she was still under the influence of some trigger, she would still be under that bastard's control. He turned to glare at Galbert's body.

"Reed!"

He turned back to Lily. "I can't free you just yet."

She blinked at him, then smiled. "Don't you trust me? Didn't you hear what I told you and everyone just now?"

Reed frowned. He had been so focused on Galbert that he hadn't really paid attention. Galbert had been mocking him at the last moment and . . . "You said you loved me. Yelled it out, actually. And Galbert wanted you to tell me you didn't!" He pulled her into his arms. "Did you mean it?"

"I can't hear you that well. Can you pull the things out of my ears?"

"Your earphones are off," he told her.

"No, dearest heart. There's something else stuck in there. If you would just freaking untie me, I'd get them out myself." She shook her head wildly. "Will you pull them out?"

"Is she okay?" Nikki asked, coming down on her knees.

"Yes, I think so," Reed answered. He examined Lily's ears and felt around. He felt something. He gently pulled it out, then shone his flashlight on his palm. "What the hell?"

"That other woman . . . she put them into my ears while I was fighting her," Lily explained. "I couldn't hear very well after that. She winked at me."

Reed squeezed the small foam bits in his hand. "Earplugs?" he asked, puzzled. "She plugged your ears first so you couldn't hear the signal."

"Good idea," Nikki said. "Can't hear signal, can't get hypnotized."

"Now will you free my arms?"

"Did you mean it then?" Reed demanded. "That last part, when you yelled out for everyone to hear."

Lily sighed. "Nikki, can you please tell this man what I said at the top of my voice? It seems he had earplugs in, too."

"She said she loved you, Reed," Nikki said with a smile, then got up. "I think the whole team heard it. Did you hear it, Hawk?"

Reed looked up. His commander regarded Lily for a long moment. Reed felt her stiffen in his arms.

"Everyone's accounted for," Hawk said, then turned and walked away.

Lily sighed. "He hates me," she said.

Reed hugged Lily fiercely. Other problems could be dealt with later. Right now, all he cared about was the woman in his arms. "I couldn't lose you," he told her. "Not this time. I was so damn afraid he'd got to you. When you didn't run—"

"I couldn't. He had Tatiana. Tatiana!" Lily sat up. "I need to make sure she's all right. Poor thing was white as a ghost."

"Nikki will go to her. My team's here and everyone's safe." He slowly untied her, then kissed her. Long and slow. "We belong together, Lily. Don't think of leaving me now."

Providence, he thought. Arch had said there were worlds to explore, and he'd become a SEAL, traveling everywhere, looking for that missing thing in his life. Getting away from it all had only made him feel even more alone. He'd seen and done a lot, but nothing had satisfied him.

He slid an arm around Lily. Until he met an unexpected flower with fierce thorns. He looked up at the cold, wintry sky. Damn it, Arch, you old fox, you were right, man. *I caught myself a big wave, dude.*

Greta glanced at her watch. They should have the device by now and be heading back. The house hadn't been unguarded, like Talia and she had thought, and she had wasted some time. She thought of the three dead bodies in Gunther's house. Satisfaction bloomed in her.

"Old lady against three big guys. Old lady three points. Three big guys, three big zeros," she murmured. It felt good to prove Gunther wrong. She dismissed the thought of having to explain the bodies. She'd think of something.

There was just enough time to look over these files quickly. She didn't want Talia to be the first to see them.

There was something about her niece, which she couldn't quite put her finger on, that made her just a little wary. It was difficult to explain. Greta enjoyed Talia's company, though, especially when she showed her the old photos from her family album. It made Greta even more determined to finish this assignment. A nice holiday at the dacha, catching up with family and news.

The beep from the computer disturbed her reverie. A little window appeared on the screen, asking for a new password.

Greta frowned. Talia had said the decoder would handle the passwords and all she had to do was follow the instructions on the screen before inserting the micro flash-drive. Now what?

She was stumped. She pressed the ESC key. The screen went blank. *Scheiss! Please, please don't erase any files that I'd downloaded!* These damn computers were so unreliable. One moment one held the world in the palm of one's hand. The next, with a stupid beep and a blank screen, it held one's balls with its stupid cursor.

She didn't have time to restart. Tentatively, she reached out and hit the ESC key again. The screen blinked, and a list of files appeared. Greta breathed a sigh of relief. At least there seemed to be something in the drive.

Her eyes ran down the rows of files. Names . . . familiar names, some American, some Russian. Gunther the Geek had collected quite a bit of information. Her name was there too.

Van Duren. What did the man have on her? Impulsively, she moved the cursor over her name and clicked.

Photos of her. Famous cases tied to her with question marks that Gunther had noted down. Greta smiled. Of course, no one would ever know which of those had been her doing; that was the sign of a great operative. Gunther had been trying to figure out what was truth and what was legend.

She read on. Disappearance? Possible death?

"Reassignment, you stupid man," she said. These must be notes he'd made before he'd found out she had been moved from assassin duty to undercover as a secretary in the CIA.

A picture of her after she'd gone through training, just before she'd relocated to the States. Damn, she didn't remember the plastic surgery to change her eyes. No wonder she'd always hated the way her eyes looked. She had—

Greta's hand went to her mouth. She had . . . screamed and fought against having her face changed. *She was an assassin. How dare they want her to undergo training to learn how to fucking type! She was* not *getting too old to seduce and kill! She certainly was* not *growing old in some stupid behind the desk job moving information! That wasn't her at all! She—*

Her hand shook as she reached out and clicked on another date. That was the day she'd officially been taken off duty. She recalled how she'd screamed at the deputy in charge—

The needle—

Ich will dies nicht! Ich will dies nicht!

The file took a moment to open up. Gunther's notes on top: *What are these?* Greta stared at the graphics that followed. Rows and rows of familiar patterns.

"Reading something interesting?"

Greta looked up, startled. She hadn't heard anything. Talia stood at the doorway, looking at her casually. Way too casually.

"Did you know about my file here?" Greta asked calmly. I don't want this! The screams rang in her head over and over. She covered the weapon on her lap with one hand.

Talia walked toward her. "Really? A file about you?"

Greta moved the weapon beside her. "Yes," she said. Her attention went back to the screen. She needed time to digest this. Talia must never know. . . .

"Does it show strange images that remind you of those knitting patterns you're so fond of? Maybe the afghan and shawls you've knitted over and over?" Talia asked, her voice strangely serene, her dark eyes watchful.

"You . . . know?" Greta had to force herself to stop looking at the pattern. It was so beautiful to look at.

"Level Five hypnotic state is the hardest to come

out of, Greta. Years and years of hypnotizing your own self with the same message. The Russian way has always been a little crueler than the American way, don't you agree? They programmed you to program yourself and you spent ten years being what you'd vowed to them you'd never be. That pattern you're looking at is the release, just like Llallana Noretski has her own release."

"You're lying!" Greta returned her gaze to the screen. She moved the cursor down. "You're lying!"

"You didn't like family, Greta, never had. You left your German family to go to the Soviet Union way back then, don't you remember? You don't remember your nieces and relatives. That's why you accepted anything I said about your past with me—you can't remember."

"Gunther—"

"He wasn't sure. He hadn't quite figured it out yet, but he would have, eventually. But too late for him, he can't do anything about it now," Talia said. She took a few steps closer. Her voice was gentle. "They've prepared you to go home in the grandest manner, a final big assignment for one of their best. Wasn't that what you kept telling yourself? Do you really think there is a dacha waiting for you? Or are they going to take you away, give you another face, reprogram you, and stick you behind a desk for the rest of your life?"

"No!" Greta realized she had to destroy all evidence, as well as Talia. No one must know this. No one! Her eyes were drawn back unwillingly to the screen, and she had to move the cursor further. She needed to see that pattern . . . so beautiful . . . it'd be perfect for a rainbow afghan, one to decorate the living room in the dac . . . no!

She was seeing scenes in her head that made no sense and explained too well. A screaming, fighting session. The needle. *I hate typing! Ich will dies nicht!* She heard herself yelling. There was a fleeting second when she caught an image of herself being distracted by someone screaming. . . .

"Look at the screen! Zahlen Sie Aufmerksamkeit!" a voice had reprimanded sharply.

She'd returned to her knitting, following a pattern on a huge screen. Then they'd put some earphones over her ears. . . .

Greta screamed, pushing the computer off the table, pulling up her weapon. Talia lunged forward and locked her arm, directing it upwards, and Greta's shot went harmlessly into the ceiling.

She was an assassin. She knew how to kill . . . she turned sideways and viciously elbowed into Talia's stomach. Talia released her hand that was still holding the weapon.

Triumph went through Greta. She pointed her gun. Talia kicked, and Greta lost her grasp. The weapon fell to the floor.

"I'll go back and show you it's a lie!" Greta screamed, shaking her hand in pain.

She fought like she hadn't fought for years now, countering moves like she used to. She swung at her opponent, connecting hard. She gasped when she received a painful fist in her stomach. She staggered back and grabbed the chair. She cursed when her niece dodged and the chair hit a corner of the table. She smashed the remaining broken leg against Talia's defending arm, and it broke into half. She threw it away in disgust.

Talia was fast, but Greta was Greta Van Duren. She'd once been the best assassin and her muscle memory was still there, even though she was older. . . . She cried out in anguish at her lost skills as Talia found an opening and made contact, a merciless uppercut against her jaw. She fell hard on her back, rolled, got up a second too slow, and received another kick that sent her flying backward. Nausea and dizziness. She lay there, panting.

"We can work to give you back your past if you'll answer some questions," Talia said. "We want to know what you've done at the CIA, that's all."

That's all? Greta laughed. She'd given ten years of her life and they'd reduced her to this . . . she saw the weapon on the floor. Rolled. Grabbed. She would *not* be bested. She was Greta Van . . .

A shot rang out.

"Duren," Greta finished as she crumpled to the carpet. Her hand went to her chest. Blood, lots of blood. She coughed and tasted blood.

Someone kicked the weapon away. Greta looked up at Talia. Their eyes met for a long second. Then Talia turned away.

Voices . . . far away.

"You've killed her."

"She would have shot you."

Greta strained her ears. That wasn't Gunth talking. She was dying. She could feel her heartbeat slowing. She must . . . see . . . who . . . had finally gotten . . . her. She angled her head.

"What are you doing here, Alex?" she heard Talia ask.

She watched, her eyesight dimming, as a tall blond man in a black body suit came into view to stand in front of Talia. Not Gunther at all. Gunth was not this good looking. Greta coughed out a laugh, and choked on her blood, her breath rattling as she tried to escape the encroaching darkness. How dare they pay her scant attention! She reached out, her fingers curling inches from the weapon.

"You and I have unfinished business, Tess," the man said, reaching for Talia.

The world went black.

20

Six weeks later

    Lily would be lying if she said the past month and a half had been easy. There was nothing easy about being put into seclusion and treated like a lab animal. That was how she felt, being led from room to room by people wearing crisply ironed lab coats, and being subjected to tests and questions, and then, more tests.

It was necessary. She didn't like being prodded and tested, but she'd found out a lot more about her "condition." To her relief, there was nothing implanted in her brain, like some of the manuals had suggested. She didn't know if she could live with the knowledge of a chip in her head.

Her anchor was Reed. The only reassurance she got that she wasn't going to be kept this way forever were his visits. He came to her twice a week, giving her strength, making sure she was all right. Without him, she would have been lost. Without him, she would have run off from these people.

Among these new people, she had become friends with Nikki Harden, who had privately shared with her her own horrific experiences. Lily suspected she was one of a privileged few who knew all the details. The woman had gone through so much, and yet, here she was, a happily married woman.

"Almost normal," Nikki had told her, with a wry smile, "although my husband's still learning new things about me."

Husband. That word had never been in Lily's thoughts before, never been considered part of her vocabulary. It signified a normalcy that she couldn't imagine for herself. She told Nikki so.

"Baby steps," Nikki advised. "I rejected the idea of a husband, or someone who would actually want me, for ten years. You know what I've learned?"

Lily watched curiously as Nikki opened her powder compact and handed it to her. At Nikki's prompting, Lily peered into the mirror.

"Check my makeup every day?" she suggested dryly, arching her eyebrows in mockery. She made a face at herself.

Nikki laughed. "No. What you see in the mirror isn't what people see. I've learned to look at myself through other people's eyes," she said. Lily looked at her, noting the darkening emotions in the other woman's eyes. "Especially my husband's. There's nothing like a man's true love reflecting your image in his eyes, Lily."

How beautiful to know that. Lily closed the compact and gave it back to Nikki. "You've obviously never been a Wretched Wench," she said, grinning. She always felt relaxed enough around Nikki to joke with her. "Ask Amber what that is."

"A Wretched Wench?" Nikki repeated, amused. "You're going to keep me hanging till I see her? Can't you tell me now?"

Lily nodded to Reed standing at the door. "Not when he's around. Some things we women have to keep from them."

"Damn, and I'm interested in the subject of wretched wenches," Reed said, walking into the room. He had a pleased look on his face. "This is the first time I've shown up and not seen both of you in deep discussion. It's good to see you laughing, sweet."

Lily shrugged, a small smile on her face. She still didn't trust this place, Command Center, or Command, as they called it. Even when the doctors explained to her the exact procedure of the test they would be conducting, she didn't trust them. After all, she'd learned a lot about hypnotic levels in those manuals they'd given her to read in her spare time. She was a Level Three—they thought. That meant she could go under two more levels and not even know it.

She looked at Reed. She'd learned that his sharp gray eyes never missed anything. Even though he didn't often tell her everything he saw, she knew that he was the one who'd suggested bringing in people she'd once trusted. Talking with them, she could reconnect with her "old" self, as well as know that she wasn't being manipulated.

Or, at least, that was the theory. She was still afraid, sometimes, that everything around her would go *poof*. Good things never lasted, right?

"I'll see you both at the wedding," Nikki said, taking her leave. "Good luck, Lily."

Lily thought of her visitors. Talking with Amber had been easier than she'd imagined. They had even brought in Tatiana. Knowing she was all right had released a lot of tension inside Lily. She had wondered what had happened to her girls. Tatiana was adjusting easier than she herself was, which was pretty amazing, when she remembered how the girl had been so broken that she'd sat in her room staring silently at a closed window for weeks.

Lily couldn't believe that Reed had used his own money to help most of the girls who hadn't wanted any help from GEM or any authorities. After their experiences with UN peacekeepers, they weren't going to trust any agency that easily. Lily was glad. Selfishly, she didn't want them to be dependent on any group of people. Again, Reed had understood her better than anyone else. His generosity and quiet strength calmed her worries. He was as solid as a rock. For the life of her, she couldn't understand what he saw in her.

Talking to Tatiana gave Lily hope. She pursed her lips. Today would be a little harder.

"Ready?" Reed asked.

"Yes." No. She didn't want to do this. It was going to be one of the most difficult things she would ever do.

"Are you sure?" he asked, his eyes calm and assessing.

"Standing and ready, sir!" she mocked, covering her fears.

His smile lit up his usually serious face. "I see you've taken a liking to that line, ma'am."

"Oh, yes, indeed, Joker." Ever since she'd found out that was what his teammates called him, she'd had fun teasing him about it. She enjoyed secretly knowing that the real Reed had his own sense of humor that he shared only with her.

He offered her his hand. "I'll be on the other side of the door," he told her.

"I'll be okay," she assured him.

"Nevertheless, I'll be there," he said firmly.

The walk to the solarium was quiet. One hand on the heavy door, she gave Reed a quick smile, knowing that he wanted to be with her, that he didn't want her to do this without him. But it wouldn't be the right thing to do.

"I can do this," she told him. She took a deep breath and entered.

Bradford Sun turned around from the artificial waterfall by the rock pool and studied Lily silently as she made her way to him. He carried his jacket in front of him. It was warm in the solarium, very different from the rainy weather outside, and one of the few places in the Center that she actually liked. Her heart sank at the sight of his drawn face. He was looking thinner, and there was a hardness about him that she hadn't seen before.

"Hello, Lily." His voice was still that soothing diplomatic tone that had always irritated and attracted her. It seemed like a lifetime ago.

She stopped a few feet in front of him. "Hello, Brad."

A heavy silence fell between them as they stared at each other. The last time she had seen him, he'd been unconscious. They had been lovers, and afterwards, she had received one of those phone calls that had turned her head inside out. It had made her believe everyone was using her and her girls, that everyone would betray her if she didn't follow instructions. She had taken a hypodermic needle out of her purse and . . .

She swallowed. "I didn't mean to hurt you. Not in that way."

His smile was slightly bitter. "You did call emergency just in time. As you can see, I survived."

"And you saved me in the end too," she said, her gaze direct, even though she felt like a heel. "You called me and provided the release code. Why? I wouldn't have done it if it had been the other way round."

"You were going to decimate a whole summit with some kind of explosive device, remember? I couldn't allow that to happen." He released a sigh. "It's been difficult letting you go, Lily. I know, from my own sources, that you've started a new life, that you're with someone else now."

She looked away for a second, then glanced back. "I'm sorry, I'm really sorry. I was an angry woman who only acted on emotions. I don't know how to explain it, not even now, but yes, I was attracted to you and yes, I acted on that attraction. But I never fell in love with you. Never loved you." Her voice softened at the haunted look in his eyes. "Brad, nothing I say will ever, ever earn me forgiveness. I'm not here to ask it, but I do want to look you in the eye and tell you I'm ashamed of what I've done and that I'll always carry the cross of what I did to you and Amber."

Brad kept quiet for a few seconds. "Still the same Lily, though," he finally murmured. "Still charging ahead as if it's you against the world. No one is after you now, Lily. Not even me. I came here for closure because I had to see this woman that I fell for, to see whether I really was that stupid and blind."

Lily winced. "You weren't stupid or blind."

"I feel it. And even more stupidly, I still want you." Moving closer, he shifted the jacket, freeing a hand from under the folds. He reached behind her, pulling her to him.

He didn't hold her, but Lily didn't turn away from his kiss. She realized she didn't want to touch him because she was afraid that she might still feel something. His touch was firm but gentle, not angry, like she'd expected.

And she felt nothing but compassion.

He stepped away, his expression unreadable. "Was any of it real?" he asked. "Was it all manipulated?"

"No, it wasn't all manipulated," she said. "But—"

"But it's too late for both of us."

"Yes." They could never go back to those days. Besides, she wouldn't fit into his world. She would still have avoided him after their time together, she was sure of it. She hadn't wanted any kind of relationship with a diplomat. "I wish you only the best, Brad. Thank you for saving me."

He laughed, a rough sound devoid of amusement. "Good-bye, Lily," he said quietly. "Go."

Her eyes met his for another long moment. She didn't think she would see Bradford Sun again, but she refused to say good-bye. Someday, she would make amends, even if she had to do it without his knowing it.

She turned and the door opened. Reed stood there, waiting for her. His gaze was intense as he ignored the man behind her. She walked steadily toward him, knowing Brad was watching, understanding that this was the closure he wanted. Her walking away from him meant something to him.

When she reached Reed, she turned and looked back. Brad had already turned to face the fountain. His stance was rigid, his head bowed. The waterfall was oddly loud as it echoed through the solarium. Guiding her out, Reed shut the door.

"You okay?"

"Yes," she said. She glanced at the glass windows at the far end of the wall. "You were watching."

"Yes," he said.

She cocked her head. "And?"

"That kiss lasted too long." He paused, his gaze searching. "But I'm okay with it, if it made you sure about what you want."

She smiled. That explained why he'd opened the door after the kiss. He wanted to make sure she was walking back to him. He'd understood her need to find out, yet he hadn't been willing to stand outside passively. He was, after all, a SEAL, and not likely to want to be second to anyone.

"I'm very sure," she said. She squeezed his hand. She didn't want the subject of Brad to be between them. "Seeing him doesn't change how I feel about you. It was important to do the right thing."

"I know. And he saved your life. For that the man deserved a thank you kiss, at least," Reed said, as they made their way to the front of the building.

She cocked her head. "Did you really think that I wanted to go back to him? Would you have let me go?"

He shook his head. "Not a chance, babe. I'd never have let you near him if there had been any doubt in my mind." He draped an arm over her shoulders, pulling her closer. "A part of me is jealous that you were involved with him, that's all. I know what it's like to want you, you see. And from where I was, I could see that he wasn't over you yet. Not by a mile."

She sighed. "I hurt him. I told myself I'd make it up someday."

"The most important thing is that you stood in front of him and owned up to him. There's nothing harder than admitting you were wrong, especially in matters of the heart. I'm proud of you."

She studied Reed's profile for a second. She had come to understand this aloof man so well. He was thinking of his mother again. They stopped at the closet near the entrance, where everyone hung their winter jackets.

She pulled her jacket off its hanger, then turned to him, arching an eyebrow. "I can show you what I want, but we'll be late for Jazz's wedding."

"Are you trying to tempt me to choose between you and my commander's happiest day?"

She gave him an innocent look. "Would I do that?" She deliberately licked her lower lip, knowing that it turned him on when she did that.

He slipped both his hands under her jacket. "There are cameras everywhere in this building, you know," he remarked casually.

"Want to give COMCEN an eyeful?" she asked, grinning.

"Wretched wench," he said, pulling her toward him.

Epilogue

They flew to Louisiana for Lieutenant Jazz Zeringue and Vivi's big wedding, which was to take place the following morning. Reed wanted Lily to see his teammates out of uniform. He also wanted to introduce her to them in an informal setting. The wedding was the perfect time to let everyone know what Lily meant to him. She would be his date there, and his teammates would know that he wanted them to welcome her into their circle.

Vivi Verreau, Jazz's bride, had already met Lily several times. Reed was glad that the women had struck up a friendship because of their backgrounds. He had forgotten that Vivi was a runaway herself and was now a volunteer in an organization that helped runaways and orphans in Southeast Asia. Lily's interested questions had told him that her heart was still very much set on helping girls in similar situations. He filed that knowledge away for the future.

That night, when Lily lay quietly in his arms, he thought about all they'd shared since they met. From the moment he'd seen her up in the Macedonian mountain pass, he'd admired her strength and courage. She'd been a lone woman against insurmountable odds, and she'd survived. She'd been afraid to come back to the United States, but she had placed her trust in him and had gone through six weeks of intensive testing and "deprogramming," as T. had called it.

He wanted to take her away when the authorities finally okayed her papers. There was a beach in Florida he wanted to show her. He wanted to build a monster sand castle and walk her into it. And then he wanted to ask her to marry him. He smiled in the dark at the image of her sun-kissed face smiling back at him; drifting off to sleep, he thought he heard her say yes.

The Zeringue wedding the next day was as chaotic as a firefight. While the guests were arriving for the festivities, or being shown to the huge temporary structure in the back of the house where the nuptials would be held, an army of help in the main house was trying to make things go smoothly before the ceremony itself. There were men everywhere at the Zeringue household, and Reed grinned as he watched his commander's eight sisters act like field marshals, ordering them about on last-minute tasks. He left Lily for a bit when he had to give a helping hand to his teammates, who were trying to arrange the overflowing trays of food on a long table without spilling any of it on their suits.

"If you'd just move that plate with the meatballs

an inch, we can get this plate of wings in right here," Cucumber said.

"Why not just move the wings to the end of the table, man?" Dirk pointed to an empty place.

"Are you nuts, man? See this keg? We want the meatballs with the wings, right here, because we're going to be standing close to the target," Cucumber said. "Prime space, you know?"

"Oh, excellent strategy," Dirk said. "Let's move the beans down there then."

"But I like beans," Turner said.

"You're on crutches. Guys on crutches not helping with this difficult task don't get any top preference," Mink said.

"Come on, move that bird shit there. We have to get to the back soon, dudes, or we'll miss Jazz putting the ring on Vivi," Dirk said.

Mink slashed his throat with his forefinger. "Man's dead meat," he announced. "Wings clipped. Balls chained up. No longer able to think for himself."

"But on the plus side, he won't need to worry about his dick shriveling up."

The men laughed in agreement, adding their off-colored remarks.

"Are you going to say that about me?" Hawk interrupted as he walked past.

At the sight of their commander decked out in his best man's clothes, Cucumber, Mink, and Dirk, the "Stooges," whistled in unison and put on their Hollywood sunglasses. Reed grinned. It was good to see his teammates relaxed. He looked around, trying to see whether Lily was close by. They had to join the guests soon, too.

"You look good enough to eat, sir," Cucumber said.

"The shiny white's hurting my eyes, sir," Dirk chipped in.

"The best man always looks his best," Hawk told them, a corner of his lips lifting. "And I don't want any of you harassing Amber about her ring. Get it?"

"Ring? What ring? Did you guys see any ring on Amber?" Cucumber boomed out, pulling off his sunglasses to reveal wide, innocent eyes.

"No, I didn't see any diamond ring on Amber," Dirk replied, acting surprised.

"Nor I, have you, Zone?" Mink asked.

"You mean, the big shiny thing that has God knows how many carats on Miss Hutchens's finger? Nope, not me," Zone answered, nudging Reed.

"Nice finger," Reed said solemnly.

His teammates stared at him, some with their mouths open. Zone choked on his beer.

Cucumber thumped Zone's back. "Did Joker just make a joke?" he asked incredulously.

"Reed, we'll talk later," Hawk said, as he fidgeted with his boutonniere. "See you all outside in a few."

Reed didn't miss the slight edge in Hawk's voice. He nodded and watched as his commander made his way out toward the entrance. He had an idea what they were going to be discussing.

Someone tugged at his elbow. He turned and

smiled at Lily. "Guys, I want you to meet Lily Noretski." He gave his friends quick eye contact. Most of them knew her background already. "Lily, these are my teammates. The big guy is Luke. The other two with sunglasses are Dirk and Marcus. The one on a crutch is Jason. And that's Zodenko, but we all call him Zone because he won't talk to you if you call him anything else."

"Hi," Lily said, shaking hands. As they all followed the crowd out into the backyard, she whispered to Reed, "I hope I can remember their names. I'm not used to meeting so many people."

Reed slipped her hand into the crook of his arm. "You'll get to know my teammates," he said. "They are great people."

She eyed him solemnly. "I'm thinking they might not be comfortable around me because of what I've done."

He thought of Hawk's and Amber's injuries. His friends were a loyal group and fiercely protective. Because they didn't have all the facts, he knew his friends were going to be reserved for a while. He also knew they would be looking at Hawk, to see how he and Amber treated Lily.

"I'll take care of it," he said.

Lily pinched him. "Stop playing macho with me. I do know how to take care of hostile men, you know."

"Yes, and all of them have seen you in action, so I'm not going to worry about that," he said, a small smile playing on his lips. But he was still worried about Hawk. He gestured to two seats in the back. "Here all right with you?"

"Yes." Lily sat down, looking around. "Am I the only one around here not confused by all the Steves in this crowd?"

Reed laughed. "I was wondering when you'd get to that. All the McMillan men are named Steve or variations of that name."

"All of them?" Lily asked, a fascinated, horrified look on her face as she searched the crowd again. "All of them? Hawk too?"

"Yup, even Hawk. He's Steve too, and so is that man standing by him with the woman with the white leather jacket."

"They look alike from here, except Hawk's a bit shorter," Lily said, craning her neck. "Now that I think about it, those guys did all look kind of cute, like Hawk. Ow!"

"Wretched Wench," he whispered in her ear.

She rubbed her arm where he'd pinched her and made a face at him. "Well, at least I can't go too wrong if I start addressing every handsome man here as Steve, right? Except you, love, so stop pinching me."

Their lips met briefly. Reed loved these moments best of all, when they teased and shared a private moment, like lovers did. He wanted more moments like this.

The wedding march began and everyone stopped talking, looking back eagerly. Reed held Lily's hand as Vivi Verreau, in a simple white gown sewn with lace and pearls, walked past them down the aisle. Her lace veil was long, hiding her face, and she held a simple bouquet of lilies and roses. He suddenly had an image of Lily in a long white veil . . . and not much else.

Vincenzio, pay attention.

"Dearly beloved, we are gathered here today . . ."

But once that fantasy started, it was tough to get her out of his mind. He happily smiled at the image of Lily in a white bikini in a white veil on the beach. Now Arch would love that.

She would be tanned and her hair streaked from the sun. Her eyes would have that naughty sparkle that they always had when she was turned on. He would lift the veil away so he could nestle against her sun-kissed body. She would lift her face to him so he could taste the sea, and his hands would explore the soft skin, molding her smooth, almost bare, ass. Then he would slowly ease his way up her back. A string bikini . . . because that's the easiest to come off. . . .

He heard "I do," and blinked. He'd missed the exchange of nuptials. He smiled ruefully as he watched Jazz lift the veil from his bride's face. He'd never seen his commander look happier. The ladies around him sighed as the handsome groom bent his head and ravished his wife with a kiss. The men snickered as the kiss went on. And on.

"I have this fantasy of you wearing nothing but a long veil," Reed whispered in Lily's ear, knowing it would make her giggle. "And I slowly reveal each part of you and start kissing—"

She poked him in the ribs, her eyes still on the happy couple. "Shhh . . ." she ordered softly, a faint blush appearing on her cheeks.

"You know, like when I bathed you? Only this time I'll use my mouth. You know, where you go all crazy when I lick you—"

Lily quickly stood up, following the rest of the crowd as everyone clapped and cheered. Reed grinned as he joined her. Her eyes had that sparkle. He didn't see why he should be the only one turned on by his fantasy.

Eight sisters. Watching Jazz's family made Lily think of her own. She wondered where they were and what they were doing now. She watched Amber hugging Vivi.

Amber had been like a sister to her for four years. There was that painful pang in her gut every time she thought about what she'd done. She still couldn't believe that her friend had forgiven her, had, in fact, insisted that she wasn't killed right off the bat.

Everyone was hugging and shaking hands. She lost sight of Amber as Jazz's mother and sisters crowded around the couples near the front.

Lily sighed. It was good to see so many happy faces. She glanced up at Reed. Every time she looked at him in that suit, her heart went pitter-pat. The man was just too damn cute.

"That was a beautiful wedding," she said, smiling. "And no, I don't want to hear any more about your dirty little fantasy about a white veil."

He winked at her. "I have others."

"I bet."

They moved with the crowd slowly, heading back to the house for the reception. She could already hear Reed's teammates squabbling about beer and food.

"Yo, Zippy-do-da, shouldn't you be up on stage playing the guitar and directing the band so your brother and his bride can dance, man?"

"My brother is upstairs undressing his woman. Do you think he's going to be quick about it? Hand me a beer, dude."

"Zippy Zeringue! You get up on the stage and start the music, do you hear?" a woman's stern voice said.

"Yes, ma'am."

Lily laughed with the people around her. She had never seen or heard such chaos.

"Why don't you go join your team while I go freshen up?" she said to Reed. She didn't want to take him away from his buddies. "They sound really hungry."

Reed shrugged. "Okay, but I'll wait for you before we eat."

"Okay."

She made her way through the side door. The Zeringues had rented some portable toilets outside to accommodate the wedding guests. She bumped into someone coming in and froze at the sight of Hawk McMillan.

He was alone, and they hadn't talked since that night he and his men had stormed the building in which her girls had been captives. His eyes narrowed at the sight of her.

Lily took in a deep breath. "Hello, Hawk," she said.

"Lily," he said.

She waited a beat. When it was obvious he wasn't going to say anything else, she took a side step to walk around him. "Excuse me," she murmured.

His hand snaked out and stopped her. "While we have a private moment, I'd like to talk to you," he said.

She looked into his tawny eyes. There was no warmth in them. "I'm listening," she said quietly.

"If you put Amber in that kind of danger and hurt her again, I'll make damn sure you're locked up behind bars for a long time. I know all about your illegal dealings, and I'll use everything I know to put you away. Do you understand?" His voice was lethally soft and flat.

She didn't blink. "If I hurt Amber again," she said, "I'll give you the keys to lock me away."

Hawk nodded. "I just wanted to make that very clear. I don't care whether you had neuro-implants or you were under hypnosis. You gave her to Dilaver, and if she had been killed—"

She covered his hand, which was gripping her arm hard. She understood his nightmare that he could have lost Amber that night. She had had the same one too, except she would have been the one responsible for her friend's pain.

"Hawk, I know. I live with the guilt every time I look at her. I'll always live with the guilt. I love Amber, and I'll stay away from her if that's what you want."

The door behind her opened. She and Hawk let go of each other's hands.

"Is everything okay?" Reed asked, stepping into the cool night air. He studied them and slipped an arm around Lily. "Is there anything you'd like to say to me, sir?"

Hawk shook his head. "I've already said my piece to Lily."

There was tension as the men exchanged a long glance. Lily didn't want to be the cause of friction between Reed and his commander.

She moved closer to Reed. "It was nice seeing you again, Hawk. Please tell Amber I said hi."

Hawk didn't look away from Reed. "We won't be friends for a while, Lily," he said, "but that doesn't mean you can't talk to Amber. She loves you, in spite of what you've done. So she'll probably look for you inside." He finally returned his gaze to Lily, and his voice was a little warmer. "Friendships are important. Jazz and I are as close as brothers. Maybe in time, I'll see that between you and Amber again."

He nodded at them both and went inside.

"What did he say to you?" Reed asked as he walked her further away.

"Nothing I haven't said to myself," Lily said. "It's okay. He wasn't nasty or anything. Just wanted to make sure I know where I stand in his eyes."

Reed glanced back. "He had to spoil your mood, didn't he?" he asked angrily.

"No, love, really, it didn't spoil anything. It was good to have it out in the open. Now we're equals. I can look him in the eye and know that even though he's still angry at me, he's making an attempt to forgive me. So don't be mad. I wouldn't have liked him so much either if he had hurt you like I did Amber. You told me yourself it'll take time, right? I'm going to make it, don't worry."

He pulled her into his arms, and she hugged him back desperately. Did he know how much she needed him?

"We're going to make it, you mean," he said. "I'm going to take you away from here after GEM says you're okay, and we'll spend time together. I want to show you the beach where Arch lived. I'll even teach you how to swim and surf."

"That sounds nice," she said wistfully.

"Lily?"

"Yes?"

"I just heard Arch say one of his lines from our favorite author."

Lily smiled. She'd heard all about how Arch always talked to him at the most unexpected times. She'd even bought herself a copy of *The Little Prince* because Reed quoted from it so much.

"What did he say?"

" 'Love doesn't consist in gazing at each other but in looking outward together in the same direction.' "

She laid her cheek against the heat of his chest and listened to the steady beat of his heart.

"There's no one I want more in my future than you, Reed Vincenzio," she said. "If you'll have me . . ."

"Have you? I wanted you the first time I laid eyes on you, blond wig and all. And you know what?"

"What?"

"You were just about to go take a piss too. Providence, huh?"

Lily laughed. Her man had a way with words.

We know you expect the very best love stories written by utterly extraordinary writers, so we are presenting four amazing love stories—coming just in time for Valentine's Day!

Scandal of the Black Rose by Debra Mullins

An Avon Romantic Treasure

What is the secret behind the Black Rose Society? Anna Rosewood is determined to find out. Dashing Roman Devereaux has his own reasons for helping Anna—even though he *thinks* she's disreputable. Soon, their passion causes scandal, and what they discover could be even worse . . .

Guys & Dogs by Elaine Fox

An Avon Contemporary Romance

Small town vet Megan Rose only sleeps with a certain kind of male—the four legged, furry kind! But when she finds herself on the doorstep of millionaire Sutter Foley she starts changing her mind about that—and more! But how can she like a man who doesn't love dogs?

Pride and Petticoats by Shana Galen

An Avon Romance

Charlotte is desperate—driven to London to save her family's reputation, which is being assaulted by Lord Dewhurst. He's insufferable, but sinfully handsome, and soon she finds she must play the role of his bride, or face the consequences.

Kiss From a Rogue by Shirley Karr

An Avon Romance

Lady Sylvia Montgomery has no choice but to involve herself with a band of smugglers, but she needs help, which arrives in the irresistible form of Anthony Sinclair. A self-proclaimed rake, he knows he should seduce Sylvia and have done with it. But he can't resist her . . .

DISCOVER
CONTEMPORARY
ROMANCES *at their*
SIZZLING HOT BEST FROM AVON BOOKS